A Far

Kim Wiese

Contents

Chapter One
Vinland (East Coast of North America) 1087 A.D.

Alina crouched in the shadow of the trees just out of reach of the fire's light, waiting for her breathing to settle down, without much hope that it would. Ahead and to her left, the prow of the ship stood up on the water. Between the ship and the beach, about thirty men battled with spears and knives in the surf. To her left, not fifty paces from her hiding place, lay one of the women — *Kiah,* she thought — writhing and screaming under the weight of the man on top of her. To her right and farther down the beach lay Brega's body, forever still, her tunic soaked in blood. *Where is Agnes?* she wondered. *Did she also make it into the trees?* It was a dark night; only half a moon rode among the stars. And the one big fire on the beach had not been fed. The light from it was beginning to die. She stared to her left, searching the shadows, but soon realized what she was hearing. Agnes was screaming, too.

Alina's impulse was to cram her fingers into her ears to block out the screams. There were also screams from the water, both from her people and from the ones who had come to attack them. But she shook herself. If she was going to survive this night, she had to act quickly. Her attention turned to what lay just within arm's reach. A bow and a quiver full of arrows, abandoned by one of her people, one of the men who had been forced toward the water. If she got down on her belly, she could reach them and drag them into the trees with her. But did she dare? She glanced toward the water. The men who were still up and battling were being driven, step by step, back toward the ship. The fight would not last much longer. Now all the men's attention was on the fighting, or on the two captured women. These distractions wouldn't last long. *Be quick,* she told herself, and then with a glance skyward, *Help me.*

Carefully, quietly, she dropped to her belly, reached out, and snagged the quiver's strap, raised its mouth a little to avoid rattling the arrows on the stony ground, and dragged it into the shadows. She waited a few seconds, watching and listening. No one seemed to notice. But then, the man who had been raping Kiah stood up, and with a grin called out something. Another man came over to take his place, and Kiah, whose cries had turned to groans, started screaming again. The first man paused to watch, and Alina feared she would have to leave without the bow, but after a few seconds, he picked up a spear he had dropped and raced down to the water. Alina reached out and snatched the bow, but discovered that its length made it difficult for her to pull it in without hitting the trees behind her. After two pulls, angling the end of the long bow, she managed it.

She couldn't catch her breath, and the pulse of her blood shook her down to her fingertips. She also couldn't wait, so she backed up into a crouch again, slung the quiver over her right shoulder alongside the bag she already carried, picked up the bow in her left hand, and stood up, panting and a little dizzy. It had apparently rained recently. The leaves under her feet lay limp on the forest floor. She was glad for it. Wet leaves wouldn't make any sound underfoot.

She took one step away from the beach when she heard Agnes scream, "Alina! Help me! Please!" Alina's knees nearly buckled. She was powerless to do anything. She had no weapon beyond her knife and a hatchet tucked away in her bag. The bow did not have a string on, so it was useless. There were too many men there. Her own men were outnumbered, two or three to one. She could not fight them on thighs. Alina dropped to her knees, parted the fronds, and stuck one hand in. The ground underneath felt reasonably dry. She took the quiver and her pack off her back, then turned and crawled in feet first, maneuvering herself around the bases of the ferns, hoping she wouldn't find snakes or stinging insects. When she was sure she would fit and be hidden, she pulled everything in after her.

She wasn't nearly far enough away for her liking, but this place would have to do. She fumbled open her pack and pulled her cloak out. With some wiggling and grunting she managed to cover herself. She pulled her knife from its sheath at her belt, and gripped it in her right hand. *I won't be able to sleep,* she thought, *but it will be good to rest, and in the morning, I can use the sun to guide me. Maybe. If the sky is clear.*

She shifted a little under her feathery canopy. She was on the ground, but what caught her attention was the almost forgotten luxury of lying down. She had spent the last thirty-three days on a boat. She and the other women had sat on a built-in bench in the stern. There was no room to lie down, but even if they could have, the deck was always pitching this way and that, and awash with sprays of seawater. They had slept sitting up, hunched over the bundles they brought with them. After a few nights, they learned to sleep shoulder to shoulder. In this way they propped each other up. They even took turns being on the outside of the bunch, a sleeping position that felt colder and less secure. But now.... Alina stretched a little. This was all right. She could rest this way. Even though she was on land, she still felt the rocking and swaying water under her. That sensation would go away in time, she knew. She closed her eyes.

She had underestimated her fatigue. It was a stray shaft of sunlight poking its way through the trees and ferns and settling on her face that woke her. It took her a moment to remember where she was and why. She lay still for several minutes, listening. Bird song trilled high in the trees above her, but nothing else. Finally she stirred, turned on her belly and peeked out. Or she tried to. The thick fronds obscured everything. *Well, that's good,* she told herself. *If I can't see out, no one can see in.* But it was time to move. She pushed her things out first, shimmied out after them, and after another pause to look and listen, stood up. Then, turning east toward home, she whispered, "Our Father in heaven, hallowed is your name…." When she had finished the prayer, she added, "Please forgive me," hauled in a deep breath and turned westward.

Two things were necessary for the day – moving farther away from the beach and finding water. The morning was cool, so she left her cloak on. She dug in her pack until she found the bundle of dried meat stowed near the bottom of the bag, unwrapped it and broke off a piece. She re-wrapped the remainder and put it away. Then she slung the pack onto her back, hung the quiver on her shoulder, and picked up the bow. Now that it was daylight, she took a good look at the bow. It was too long for her, and she was pretty sure that none of her bowstrings would fit. She would have to cut the bow down, a little from each end.

The sun's position told her that it was almost mid-morning. Turning her back to it, she continued west into the forest, chewing on the meat as she went. It was dry and tough, and after a few swallows, she had to take a mouthful of water from the nearly empty bladder that hung from her belt. Alina grimaced. The water was brackish and stale. She needed to find a stream or a spring. *Does this place have springs?* she wondered. This new land might be different from her own. But it surely wasn't so different. There were pine trees here, and oaks, though they weren't quite the same as the ones at home.

She continued through the woods, stopping every so often to listen and to gauge the sun's position, finally halting when it was directly overhead. Now she would rest and wait until she was sure of the sun's course into the west. She sank to the ground at the base of a pine tree and took in a deep breath, gratified that the air no longer smelled of sea salt. This aroma, the pine needles, leaf mold, earth, growing plants, was familiar, well-loved. It smelled like home, like the hours she'd spent in the woods with her father and brother, and later, with her sons.

But this isn't home. She sat still as a stone, quieting her breath, listening. Plenty of birds called out overhead. She looked up once, searching for the source of a liquid song she didn't recognize — three long calls followed by four or five short ones. After a moment's search, she spotted it — a bird she had never seen before, scarlet as fire, singing its lovely call into the clear day. *Danger here,* she told herself, *but beauty, too. Just like at home.* Sparrows pecked at the ground some distance to her left. There was a faint rustle on the ground behind her and to her right. Some small animal, she supposed, until she realized that the rustling was continuous. Alina frowned. Animals usually stopped and started, so maybe not an animal. It wasn't a breeze, either. The air wasn't moving much. Her eyes widened. Could that be water? She stood and stepped that way, searching the ground, and after a minute, she found it, a tiny stream trickling off to the south.

She followed the water, seeking its source, and finally came upon a spring bubbling out of the ground near the base of a huge oak. She stopped one more time to look and listen before dropping to her knees and scooping up a handful of water to taste it. It was cold, and pure and sweet. A quiet laugh escaped her, and she clapped her hand over her mouth. *Quiet! Be quiet!* She waited and listened, searching the surrounding forest with her eyes before drinking another handful. She shrugged off her pack and dug around until she found her wooden cup. Alina filled the cup again and again. After such a long voyage, where she had to drink strictly rationed swallows of stale water, her body gratefully accepted. The cold liquid filled her, and it felt fine and right — until she'd had too much, and her stomach was sloshing. She untied the sheep's bladder at her belt, dumped the old water out, and filled it with fresh.

She glanced up at the sun's position again, noting exactly where it was in the branches overhead. Now she had to wait. Her thoughts turned to Bren, and to the others on the ship with him, the ship headed home. Headed home without fresh water. There had been so little left in the barrels when they arrived. How could they possibly make the long voyage? The wind would be with them, and the trip quicker, she supposed. And there were fewer men to use what little water remained. But still….

"I did warn him," she whispered. "Through great peril and hardship will you return." She had no way of knowing whether he would make it home, or whether the rest of what she had said would come to pass. Alina huffed out a breath and shook her head. No, it was true. She

be funny, but his humor was never at someone else's expense. It finally occurred to Alina that his character was exactly why Bren wanted him gone. Dirk was younger, a rising star. Bren had no room for rivals.

She was saying, "He told me he was pleased to be paired with me. He had been watching me, he said, and he thought I was a woman of good sense."

"And so you are," Alina answered, nodding. She half listened to Brega chatting away about Dirk, and smiled inwardly. They were a good match. Brega would be happy with him.

A couple of hours later, Brega got the food out for the evening meal. This was stored in a hold in the stern of the ship, just behind the women's bench. The food was packets of dried meat mixed with berries, and she broke pieces off and passed them out to the men at the oars, and then to Bren and to Rolf, the navigator. Finally, she gave pieces to the women. When her chore was done, she sat down again and leaned close to Alina. "On your left behind you. Wait until we begin to land, and then put it in your bag."

It turned out to be another whole packet of food, which she would need to survive the first few days. *The men won't miss it,* she thought. *I have already warned Bren. Not many will make the trip home.* She was going to find out what that meant, and the thought made her shudder and pull her hood closer around her face.

Late that afternoon they anchored the ship in a tiny bay — more of a cove, really. There was a spit of beach, maybe fifty paces wide, sandy near the water, and rocky as it climbed up toward the encompassing forest. A tumble of boulders edged in on the south side, and to the south of those was a longer stretch of graveled beach. The men decided to camp on the cove's beach, rather than on the long stretch. They gathered wood for a fire, and Bren directed the women to one side of the fire, and the men to the other. "Just for tonight," he added with a smile. "After tomorrow you can make your own sleeping arrangements." He laughed heartily, and the men joined in.

Yes, Alina thought, turning away. *That is a funny joke.* If she was going to avoid being paired with a man who was a rapist and a murderer, she was going to have to get away tonight.

"Alina, over here!" Brega called out. She had dropped her pack near the tree line. """It's not so rocky here," she added in a loud voice.

It was just as rocky, but Alina understood. The spot Brega had chosen was two, maybe three steps away from the forest's cover. Evening was on them. It would be dark soon. The men built a fire in the center of the beach, and everyone gathered around it for the evening meal. "Tomorrow," Bren announced, "I want Huus, Marik and Dirk to go and look for water. The rest of you can pair off and hunt, but we need to keep a couple of men here to guard the women. Then, tomorrow night, I will pair the women with their men. We will stay a few more days to build shelters — three at most, I think. After that, we will be off home."

Home. The bite Alina had just taken stuck in her throat and refused to budge. She swallowed one sparing sip of water to try to wash it down, but it took several gulps before the bit of food moved. When it did, it hurt all the way down. Her appetite gone, she stared into the fire. If she was successful that night, the only vestiges of home she would have left would be what she carried on her back.

There was talk, and even some singing after they ate, but she didn't hear much of it. The only thing she could do was steel herself and gather her courage for what lay ahead. Finally, the women left the fire. Kiah went off by herself about ten paces from the spot Brega had chosen. Kiah, for some inexplicable reason, didn't like Brega. Alina felt some relief that she had separated herself. She would certainly raise the alarm if she thought Alina was trying to get away.

She did notice that Huus, though he was on the opposite side of the fire, was up near the tree line as they were. *He knows,* she thought. *He will be watching me, probably plans to watch me all night. But he has been at the oars most of the day, and he has to be tired. He will have to sleep. He thinks he is watching me, but I will be watching him.*

She settled down, wrapped in her cloak, with her bag at her back, and her head pillowed on her arm. She could just make out Huus' shape, probably thirty paces away. *Just wait*, she encouraged herself. *Your moment will come.*

She started when Brega reached over and took her hand. "I will miss you," she said again in a low whisper. Alina squeezed her hand in reply. Brega was the one reason she might have had to stay. But even she was not reason enough. "When you go," she went on, "I will put my bag where you are now. It may fool them for a little while."

"I'll put mine there, too," Agnes murmured. "I can't wait to see Bren's face in the morning when he finds out you are gone."

"I am waiting for Huus to fall asleep," Alina began, realizing there was no way she could know when he did. But to her surprise, as if he'd heard her, he got up and went down to the water's edge. Was this her chance?

In answer, Brega also stood up. "You go. I will distract him."

Alina whispered her thanks, rolled over, grabbed her bag, and crept on her hands and knees into the trees. Behind her, she was aware of

Agnes moving the bags into the spot where she had lain. Once she was out of sight, she stood and allowed herself just a moment to think. She had originally intended to go around to the beach that led away south, but that way was closed to her now. Besides, there was no cover on the beach, and despite Brega's attempts to direct his attention elsewhere, Huus would be hunting for her soon. *West,* she thought. *I will have to strike out west.* However, just inside the tree line another tumble of boulders stood in her way, forcing her to circle behind part of the beach. She had just passed the stony barrier, when a shout, followed by a scream split the night. She crouched down, fearing that they already discovered she was gone. What she saw when she peered out though the undergrowth horrified her.

Men were leaping over the boulders on the beach's southern side, yelling as they came, brandishing spears and knives. They had dark skin and black hair. They were naked to the waist, and had black streaks painted on their faces. One of them grabbed Brega and held her against him with a blade to her throat, shouting at Bren and Huus with unintelligible words. Bren shook a fist and yelled back at him. "Let her go!" At this, as if in defiance, the brown man yanked his arm back, slicing Brega's throat. A gush of blood, red as rubies in the firelight, spilled down the front of her tunic. He released her body, and it landed in the sand with a soft thud.

Alina screamed, high and hoarse, and then clapped her hands over her mouth. But she needn't have worried anyone would hear. By then everyone was screaming or shouting. The strangers outnumbered her own people by at least two to one, and several were already rushing at Agnes and Kiah. As frightened as she was, she was distracted by the quiver and the bow that lay just within reach. *Probably Huus'*, she told herself, but she didn't care whose they were. Her men would not make it so high up on the beach again, and this weapon would help her survive. So she took it. She had a promise to keep.

Alina traveled on westward, now following the sun. She stopped only a couple of times more to catch her breath and take a few swallows of water. When the shadows lengthened, she started looking for a place to spend the night. These woods were not the woods she knew, but she guessed that some of the animals would be the same, just as some of the trees were. Were there wolves here? Bears? Lynx? *I had better assume that there are,* she told herself, as she rejected yet another possible campsite.

Finally, near dusk, she found a fallen tree bridging a dip in the ground. Ferns grew thick on one side of the trunk, but the side that faced more or less south was bare, and there was room for her to tunnel in. She first broke off one of the tree's dead branches and dragged it over toward the opening. She stashed the bow and quiver under the trunk first, then she put the bag down at the end where her feet would be. Finally, she backed in herself, pulling the dead branch toward her. Now both sides of the trunk were shielded from view. If anyone was hunting her, unlikely as that seemed, they wouldn't be fooled for long, but it would have to do. Clutching her knife, she watched the dark descend for a while before reciting her prayer again. She was thankful. She had found fresh water, and now shelter for the night. And she was alive.

The next morning she decided that ten day's walk should be enough. Going that far should get her away from the people who had attacked her people on the beach. Added to that, spring was now waning toward summer. She needed to find a place to make a shelter and gather food for winter. She hoped that eventually she could find other people — people of peace who would accept a stranger among them. There might be a village somewhere that would feel familiar. On the other hand, there might be more people like the ones who had attacked. Alina sighed. No way of knowing. But for this first season, she needed a place to hole up and store food and supplies.

She was glad now — so very glad — that she had ignored Bren's instructions to the women to take only the domestic things that he thought they should concern themselves with. He told them to take things to cook with, and things to make clothing with. Alina had been amused that he didn't even know what those things were. But he had insisted that the men would bring everything they needed for hunting and building. So, while a length of rope might arguably be in a woman's purview (she could hang laundry from it) a hatchet definitely was not.

She silently blessed old Holgur for not arguing with her about the hatchet when she asked him for one. He had stared at her for a long moment with his one good eye before growling, "I don't have a spare, so I will make you one."

I would never have dared leave if I had obeyed my husband, she thought grimly.

She had just turned fourteen when Bren came to her village with a few of his men. He was on his way east to trade with the Rus for horses. Alina's village straddled a river, and her father made his living by charging travelers to cross on his ferry. The trading eastward had grown so much in his lifetime that her father had become a wealthy man, and their village was growing and prosperous.

Her father had met the travelers, and being sufficiently charmed by Bren's flattery, invited them to dinner. Alina didn't know about this. She had been out riding and hunting, and brought back a pair of rabbits to give to the cook. She spotted Bren as she led her horse to the stable. He was lingering there with a couple of his men. She was used to seeing strangers in the village, so with nothing more than a courteous nod, she passed them and went inside. She was dirty and tired, and wanted to get home.

Bren followed her in. "Nice animal," he said as she led Hona into her paddock.

"Thanks." She continued to ignore him as she removed Hona's bridle and began wiping her down with handfuls of hay.

"Do you happen to know the master of this village?" he asked.

Her father. "I am acquainted with him."

"I only ask because he has invited me to dinner." He didn't quite manage to keep the boasting from his voice.

Alina turned her back so that she could roll her eyes. "Mmmm. Lucky you."

"It is not luck," he answered with a chuckle. "I know how to make men like me."

Alina sighed and turned back. "Was there something you wanted?"

"Yes. I was wondering about his family. Is he married? Does he have children?"

You didn't ask him that yourself? Young as she was, she understood that he was trying to make conversation with her, but this conversation wasn't much to her liking. She checked Hona's food and water, then stepped out of the paddock and shut it. She met Bren's eyes, which were a startling shade of blue. They were pale, like distant ice in winter. "He is widowed these three years," she told him, "and he has seven sons and one daughter." Alina had only one brother.

"Ah," Bren answered. "He keeps his daughter shut away, I expect. And she's probably spoiled."

Alina coughed to mask a snort. "No doubt." She drew in a deep breath and added, "Please excuse me. I have other duties."

Bren held up a hand to stop her, and he gave her what she would come to recognize as his most winning smile. "I am Bren. Will you tell me your name?"

"I am Hona," The horse nickered quietly behind her. She ducked her head to hide a smile.

Only then did he notice that she carried a bow and arrows and a pair of dead rabbits. "Did you hunt those yourself?"

"No," she told him. "The Rabbit King sent them to me as tribute."

Bren's face flushed, and his eyes darkened. Apparently, he wasn't used to being sassed. But he quickly recovered and grinned at her. "I guess I will have to ask the master about you, Hona."

"You do that," she said as she passed him.

"I hope we meet again," he called after her retreating back.

She didn't bother to reply. But a few hours later, when she had cleaned up and was standing between her father and brother to receive their dinner guests, she found it hard to suppress a smile at Bren's surprise and consternation.

Bren bowed and said, "Thank you for inviting me, sir." He straightened and his eyes met Alina's. "Good to see you again, Hona."

Alina's father shot her a confused look, and her brother snickered. After a moment, her father said, "This is my son, Ebbe, and my daughter, Alina." Then he turned to her. "You sit next to Bren at table, daughter." Alina kept the smile on her face, but groaned inwardly. Father must have figured out what she did, and now he was punishing her.

Once the welcome cup was passed around, and while the food was being brought to the table, Bren cleared his throat and asked quietly, "Where are your other six brothers?"

There was no point now keeping up the lie. It would get back to her father, and he would be exasperated with her. So she just smiled and said nothing.

"I have to ask you to forgive me," he added, "for earlier. I was...." Here he faltered.

"An ass?" Alina suggested.

A silence followed, then he chuckled. "If you wish. Yes, I was an ass. Please forgive me."

With some reluctance, Alina realized she had to give him credit, at least for keeping his feet on slippery ice. "You are forgiven," she murmured.

The rest of the dinner went better. Bren was a natural storyteller, and he regaled them with tales of hunting, and sea travel, and his life at the edge of the world. Time passed quickly, with Alina trying to imagine her own lake, grown a thousand times bigger, and with water that tasted of salt. By the time dinner was over, she decided that she had probably misjudged Bren. He was bold, yes, but was that so bad a thing? A man had to be bold to live as he said he did. And he did apologize for his earlier encounter with her. Maybe he was all right. Maybe.

CHAPTER TWO

The only place Alina could find that night was a hollow in another tumble of rock. She decided to risk a fire for the first time. She would need it, because earlier that day, she had spotted a large, dark shape among the trees, and recognized it. The bear was only a couple hundred paces away, but fortunately, the wind was brisk and out of the west, and the animal didn't smell her. She hid herself behind a trunk and waited, peering out at the bear. *That's a big one,* she thought, and hardened her grip on the useless bow. She needed to size it down. She needed a weapon besides her knife and the hatchet. At last, the animal moved off eastward, and Alina hurried away.

At the campsite, she built a screen for the fire out of fallen branches before laying wood for the fire itself. Then she took out the piece of flint she had brought, and striking it against the head of her hatchet, started a fire. She picked up the bow and examined it carefully, standing and hefting it in her hand. As she expected, it was too long. She could probably learn to use it with some practice, but it would be better if she cut it down. *The bowstrings,* she told herself. *I am sure they aren't long enough.* She sat down again and pulled out the wooden box that contained the strings. After playing with the strings against the bow, it looked like one hand's breadth off each end would be right. She took a stick and broke it off to the length she wanted, then with a bit of charred wood, marked each end of the bow, using the stick to measure.

After checking and double-checking her work, she gritted her teeth and cut the ends of the bow off with the hatchet. *Holgur did his job,* Alina thought with relief when the blade of the hatchet proved to be sharp and keen. She then tested the grip of the bow. It was made for a bigger hand, and was going to need to be pared down, but one thing at a time. Taking a deep breath, she got out her knife and carefully began whittling the ends, stopping between each stroke of the knife to consider the next. When she finally had the ends pared down, she cut new notches in each end for the string. Then she sat back, took a deep breath, and decided this was a good time to eat and rest before tackling the grip.

Alina broke off a piece of meat, noting that the block was nearly half gone now. She was going to have to start hunting soon. At least water was plentiful. She had found another spring that morning. Finding the water reminded her of her boys, of the hours she had spent with them in the woods near the village, teaching them about hunting and foraging. Gunnar had been so excited when he found his first spring. He had forgotten himself, and was jumping up and down. Suppressing a smile, Alina had simply laid one hand on his shoulder, and he immediately calmed his body.

Calming his excitement was another thing. "Water!" he gasped in a near whisper. "I found it!"

"You did," she nodded. "Very good work, son. Now, what will you do?"

He chewed his lip, considering. "Drink? And then fill my water skin?"

Alina shook her head. "The first thing is to study the forest around you. Are there other animals coming up on you that also want a drink?"

Now he began a slow turn. He studied every tree and bush around them. "I think we are alone."

"I think so, too," she murmured. "Now you may drink."

This was another way she was disobedient toward her husband. She had expected Bren to bring Gunnar out into the forest to teach him, but he had said the boy was too young.

"He's five years old," she had shot back. "Most of the other boys his age are going out with their fathers."

Bren shook his head. "He may be five, but he is not as mature as the other boys. I will wait another year."

Alina had walked away from that conversation chewing her tongue. The truth was, Bren couldn't be bothered. He did what he wanted, and what he didn't want was to shoulder the responsibility of teaching his son. That was when she decided she would have to do it. She refused to leave it to another man. Gunnar was her boy.

Now, on the other side of the world, Alina sat back and picked the bow up again. *He did learn,* she thought. *He knew that bit of forest from one end to the other.* She looked close at the grip. It was wrapped in a strip of leather, which would have to come off first, and she hoped she could save it and re-use it. She picked at it with a fingernail, but the leather was tucked in tight. *What else do I have in my bag?* She rummaged around until she found an awl. She used the tip to carefully, carefully pull at the tucked end of the leather, and little by little, managed to coax it out. The end was ragged from being pulled, but that was a tiny loss. She unwrapped the rest of the leather and studied the bare grip.

With the same care that she had used on the ends, Alina whittled some of the bulk from the grip, tested it in her hand, and whittled some more. The smoke from the fire was beginning to make her eyes water, but she pressed on. She wanted to have the bow ready to use as soon as she broke camp in the morning. After her fourth pass with her knife, the grip felt right in her hand. She stood up and hefted it, held it up as if she were taking aim. *Yes*, she thought, with satisfaction and relief. *That will do*. She sat down again and re-wrapped the leather strip.

Now she took the bowstring and tried to fasten it to the bow, but the bow seemed to have a mind of its own. It fought her as she bent it. Alina took a deep breath, steadied the bow between her knees and kept a firm and steady pull. A little more.... More.... Her muscles quaked by the time the loop of string finally settled in its groove, but the fitting looked and felt right. "You and I are going to have to be friends," she murmured to the bow, wiping beads of sweat that had appeared on her brow. "We will have to take care of each other." Deciding she would wait till morning to practice, she added wood to her fire, laid the bow and her bag behind her so that no stray spark would reach them. Then, rubbing her stinging eyes with her aching hands, she stretched out and stared at the fire until sleep took her.

It was on the afternoon of the sixth day that she heard it — the unmistakable sound of rushing water. Alina hurried toward the noise, a little north of where she was. She crested a small hill and found herself looking down on a river. It wasn't very wide, maybe thirty or so paces across, but it looked deep. She smiled. Here was a continuous source of fresh water. It might be a source of food. Even better, it appeared to be running west to east, so that if she followed the river's course, she would still be going west, more or less. It might also bring her to people, but that was a problem for another day.

She hunted around for a likely place to camp, but there was nothing at the water's edge, so she went back into the woods until she found a tree (some kind she did not recognize) that was surrounded by thick undergrowth. She burrowed in and slept. The next morning, she went back to the water. She had been crusted with salt from the voyage, and now was also crusted with dirt from sleeping on the ground every night. Her nails were black with it, and her hair felt grimy. Alina sniffed at herself and grimaced. She smelled like a chicken pen. She stowed her gear beneath some brush near the river's edge, then unlacing the leather straps on her boots, took them off.

It was the first time she had seen her feet since she left home. They looked small and pale in the sun, but they were whole and strong, with no blisters or cuts. They would carry her where she needed to go. Next, she untied the leather thong that was wrapped around the end of her long braid. This took a while. Her hair had become so tangled in the sea wind that she couldn't loosen the leather without breaking the snarls that had grown around it. But she finally got it off and began pulling the plait apart. Many more snarls and tangles later, her hair hung limp down her back. Only then did she step into the water, still wearing her tunic because it also needed a wash.

She sucked in a breath through her teeth. *Cold! Cold! Cold!* She forced herself to step in further. The rocks were slippery under her feet, but smooth, and she continued in until the water came up to her waist. Then she knelt down, squeezed her eyes shut, took a deep breath, and put her head under. She came up seconds later, gasping and blowing. She caught her breath, squatted down and felt around on the bottom until she found a generous deposit of sand. Pulling up handfuls of this, she rubbed it into her scalp and all over her skin before ducking under the water again.

When she was satisfied that she was as clean as the river could make her, she climbed back onto the bank, wringing water from her hair and her tunic. She retrieved her bag and found the bone comb she had brought, sat down on a flat rock and began untangling her wet hair, her skin scoured and stinging, her teeth chattering. *I could just stay here today,* she mused. *This isn't a bad place, and maybe I could catch a fish and find some greens to eat.* For a few minutes she imagined herself doing that, and finally decided against it. *No, I need to keep moving.* A breeze sailed down the riverbank, sending a shiver bolting through her. *I have half the rabbit I shot yesterday, so I will eat that and walk.*

"Four more days," she murmured, "and then I can stop walking and start figuring out how to make a home here, at least for this winter." When she had finished combing her hair, she started to stow the comb back in her bag when something inside stabbed her hand. Carefully, she grasped it and pulled it out. Her spoon. She had packed one wooden spoon, and it had snapped, most likely sometime during the voyage. She dropped the jagged piece back into her bag. It was unlikely that anyone was following, but she still wasn't going to be careless and leave a trail. She stood and wrung out the hem of her tunic again. The wet cloth against her skin was unpleasant, but the day was warming, and she would soon be dry enough. Alina packed everything back into her bag, stepped into her leather boots and laced them. Then she slung her bag and the quiver over one shoulder, picked up the bow, and followed the river west.

Bren returned to her village only a few weeks after that first visit, and he came several times over the next year —many more times than he needed to for trade. He courted her assiduously, brought her small gifts, including the bone comb. There was a figure of a bird in flight on the handle. "I made this for you," he said. It was the first of many half-truths. And, as always, he charmed her father, and persuaded him that he could make Alina happy.

Alina's father, who perhaps wanted to be persuaded, called Alina to him one afternoon during what turned out to be Bren's final visit. She met him in the chamber where he listened to the squabbles among the people and passed judgement. When she came in, he was sitting in his chair, and Alina's heart sank. Whatever this was, he meant business. Had she done something to anger him?

He smiled at her. "Come here, daughter." And there was something about that smile, sad but resolute, that made Alina's heart sink even further.

"Father? Is something wrong?"

"No, no. Not at all." It was then that she saw he held a cup — and it was nearly empty. He didn't usually drink early in the day. "What are you up to today? You're in a dress, so you're not hunting."

“No, Marna has taken ill, and I am going to sit with her until mid-day when her daughter comes.”

“Ah, that is good.” He sighed. “I suppose this is Marna’s final illness. She is old.” He allowed himself a small chuckle. “She seemed old to me when I was a boy.”

Alina nodded. “I will miss her.” Then she took a deep breath and plunged in. “Father, you asked to speak with me?”

“Yes.” The crease between his brows deepened. “I have been talking to Bren, or rather, he has been talking to me.”

Alina’s hands clenched. Now she knew what was happening. She should have seen it coming.

“He has asked for you to be his wife, and I have consented.”

Alina stared at him for a long moment, then lowered her head and chewed her lip. She loved her father, and obeying him was usually easy. But this….

“Father,” she began, “I don’t think I want to….”

He didn’t let her finish. “You must obey me in this, Daughter.” His countenance was stern, but there was something merry in his eyes. “You are still a child in many ways. I know a good man when I see one, and Bren is a good man.” After a moment, he added, “You will be happy with him.”

Even as he said it, Alina wondered if he was predicting her future, or issuing a command.

“Now, come here. I have something for you.” Alina stepped closer to the chair, biting her lip. Her father smelled of mead and, faintly, of wood smoke. He held out his hand to her saying, “Your mother would have wanted you to have this.”

He didn't let her finish. "I am sorry, Lady, but I have been ordered to keep you here this afternoon until we gather to eat."

Alina knew better than to waste her breath asking questions. Bren had something up his sleeve. She would have to wait to find out what it was. She peeled off her shoes and lay down on the bed. *Why am I so tired?*

Sometime later, she was startled awake by a knock at her door, and a woman bustled in without waiting for her to answer. Her wiry gray hair fizzed out from under a brown kerchief. She was nearly as round as she was tall, and her hands were red and chafed, as if they spent most of their time in wash water. She had a large clay pitcher balanced on one hip. "Hello, Lady," she squeaked.

Alina rubbed her eyes and sat up. "Hello."

"My name is Gerda. I am your maid. I am here to help you get ready for the dinner tonight."

If she hadn't seen Gerda, if she had only heard the voice, Alina would have guessed it belonged to a child, not to this substantial woman. "I see." She swung her feet to the ground. "I need to change, I suppose."

Gerda eyed her travel-stained dress. "Yes, Lady. Are your clothes in the trunk?" Alina nodded, and Gerda chirped, "Here is warm water for you to wash." She poured the water into the basin near the hearth and handed Alina a cloth.

This whole situation felt so strange. Alina was used to living in a big house with family, and servants and villagers running in and out. Here she felt penned in, and what was worse, she didn't understand why. After scrubbing her face, she turned to the maid. "Gerda," she began cautiously, "I am not sure what is expected of me this evening. Can you help me?"

Gerda's expression, which till now had been brisk and businesslike, softened. "If I were you, Lady, I would take care not to drink much tonight. You are going to meet a lot of people, and you will need to remember their names, at least." She pulled a green gown from the trunk and shook it out. "Ah, this is lovely. It will do very well." She turned and added, "Other than that, I cannot advise you. You will have to find your own way."

Gerda was holding up Alina's wedding dress. It was a beautiful garment, woven from wool so fine that the fabric draped and flowed when she moved. Alina hesitated. Did she want to wear this dress tonight? Memories of the wedding surfaced unbidden — Bren rushing through the vows as though he didn't care about them, the drunken minstrel who forgot his song, the resigned expression on her bother Ebbe's face when the ceremony was over. Not the kind of wedding she had hoped for. A long sigh escaped without her permission, and she thought, *Why not? I can't change what has happened, and I need to make the best impression I can.*

Gerda helped Alina change, and then combed out her hair. "You've nice hair. Just the color of honey." Alina fingered the embroidery at the edge of her sleeves — white flowers nestled in dark green leaves. Gerda braided a slender plait down each side of Alina's face, letting the rest of her hair hang like a curtain. Then she stepped back and studied her, fingering the amber pendant on its ribbon. "Pinch your cheeks. You look a little pale." She frowned. "Are you well?"

Alina sighed and did as she was told. "I think so. I must still be tired from the journey."

Gerda grunted and started to say something else, when a loud rap sounded at the door and Bren came in. "There's my bride," he smiled, holding out his hands. "Let's go. Our dinner awaits." He led her out of the little house toward a much larger structure. Alina noted that this main hall was ringed with small houses, each one similar to hers. Bren pulled at the heavy oak door of the hall and led her inside.

Alina intended to walk for ten days, thinking that distance might put her out of reach of the people who attacked her people on the beach. She didn't make it ten days. Late in the morning on the ninth day, she passed another massive rock formation. There had been many of these, some high as the hills at home, rising up from the ground like the half-buried bones of a behemoth. This particular formation was situated nearest to the river so far, hardly more than fifty paces away. There was a natural hollow in the rock that faced the river, and a scrubby tree filled part of the hollow.

Maybe something like that? Alina was thinking about what kind of shelter she would have to make for the winter. This hollow was closed in on two sides, and there was an overhang that could work as part of a roof. Something like this would give her some solid shelter; she would only have to add a side to enclose it, and figure out a way to extend a roof. She walked toward the tree, frowning. It didn't look right, but she didn't understand why until she came close and discovered an opening in the rock behind the tree, tall and narrow, but wide enough for her to slide in if she took off her pack. The oddest thing was that the opening wasn't completely dark. Alina took the bag and quiver from her shoulder, pulled out an arrow, and nocking it on the bow, quietly slid through the opening.

The cave was empty. There was a crack in the ceiling, more than arm's length above her head, that allowed a shaft of sunlight to pour through the crack. She went in deeper. The main part of the chamber curved on the right to a smaller space. The whole cave was dry, and the only signs of animals were one mummified creature – a rabbit, maybe, or a large squirrel – that had crept in and died. There was no smell. A tiny movement caught the corner of her eye, and she turned to see a beetle trundling across the sunny spot on the floor. The ray of light made the insect's black armor glimmer with blue.

Alina turned a full circle. The chamber was big enough to house four or five people. "This could be perfect," she murmured. She hurried back outside, picked up her things, and brought them in. "Well, it will be perfect until it rains." She stopped directly under the crack and looked up, then down at the floor. There seemed to be a kind of natural channel in the floor, and a depression where water had pooled along one side. Maybe she could cut that channel deeper and direct it out the cave's opening? She squatted down and scratched at the floor with the tip of her knife. It was packed earth, and not stone.

I am not even nine full days away, though. Is this far enough? Did I get away from them? There was no way to know. *Well, at least I can sleep here tonight.* She spent the rest of the morning gathering firewood and springy branches to sleep on, not bothering to hide from herself the fact that she was gathering far more firewood than she needed for one night. In the afternoon, she went down to the river. The water was broader and shallower here, racing over a bed of stones, so the fishing would not be very good, but there were deeper places. She went upriver a way and found another deeper spot.

One of the forbidden "man" things tucked away in her bag was a wooden box containing three fishing hooks and three lengths of line. It occurred to her that she should make a spear at some point. Those lines wouldn't last long, and a spear would be another useful weapon. She was just about to go back to the cave when something across the river caught her eye — a shadowed movement. Alina crouched down, sat still as the stones around her and waited. Presently, the shadow moved again, and she caught the profile of the animal. *Wolf*, she thought. *But is there only one?* Still she waited, but the shadow moved on. Either the wolf hadn't seen her, or it was onto something else.

She let out a long breath. So, yes. There were bears and wolves here. The cave would give her some security against wild animals, and there were ways to make it more secure, but she hadn't had anything to eat yet that morning, and her hands were starting to shake. She had no meat for her dinner, but there were plenty of cattails at the edge of the widest part of the river, and she gathered two of them before heading back.

She lit a fire on the same side of the chamber as the crack, but didn't put it directly under the opening in case it rained. Her wood was nice and dry, and soon she had a nearly smokeless flame going. She cut up the cattail and laid the pieces in the little iron pot, setting it right next to the fire. *I need to build a hob,* she told herself, *if I can find a nice piece of flat stone, that is.* She pictured it in her mind, and shook her head. Getting a large stone from wherever she found it to the cave would be a massive undertaking. *I could do a small one, maybe more round than long?*

Her thoughts went back to the wolf. The river would not be much of a barrier to him. She glanced at the opening. It was narrow enough that she could probably figure out a door to put up, but tonight it would have to be something simpler. A few of the branches of firewood had small twigs and dry, dead leaves. Before she went to sleep, she would scatter these near the opening and a pace or two inside. They would make noise if something tried to come in, and hopefully wake her. Alina got up and went just outside the opening. There were lots of little stones scattered around. She picked up several handfuls of these and stacked them in the opening, making a short wall. She could step over it, but anything else coming in would probably knock some of them down, making another noise. It would have to do.

She went back to the fire and plucked one of the pieces of cattail out of the pot. When it was cool, she bit into it, grimaced and dropped it back in. Not quite done. *A spoon*, she thought. I *need to replace the broken one, and I could get that done tonight.* Most of her firewood was too dried out, but there was one limb she had cut up that had fallen recently. Those cuts were stacked to one side so they could begin to dry. She examined the fresh wood, and found a piece to her liking, nice and straight, no knots on it. She wasn't sure what kind of tree it had come from, but the wood seemed sound enough. She knocked the bark off with her hatchet, then started whittling the handle of the spoon. When it was about half done, she laid the wood down and checked the cattail again. It was cooked.

Alina ate, not with any enthusiasm, but strictly to nourish her body. It would be better with salt, of course, but she had only brought a small box, and would need it to prepare meat for the winter. *If I get a fish tomorrow, I might use just a little.* She picked up her carving again.

What else should I make? Some kind of barrier for the opening. Maybe I could find grasses and weave a screen? That would at least let air though. And I need to deepen that channel for a drain, but I'll have to wait until it rains so I know exactly what the water does.

She sighed. The light outside was completely gone now, but she still had firelight to work by. Bit by bit the handle took shape. Once it looked mostly how she wanted, she turned her attention to the bowl of the spoon. This part would be harder to get right. She dipped her finger into the ashes at the fire's edge and smudged the wood. Her mark showed up pretty well, and in several passes, she drew the round shape. By the time the fire began to die, Alina had the bowl of the spoon done. It was rough, but she would get some sand from the river the next day and smooth it out.

She got up, and taking the spoon with her, crossed to the opening. Gazing out, she recited her evening prayer, adding, "And thank you for this cave. I could not have asked for a better shelter." Then she checked on her belongings, making sure everything was far enough away from the fire not to catch a stray spark. There wasn't much danger of that, since the fire was so low, but she wasn't taking chances. She sank down onto the pallet of branches, and all of a sudden found it hard to draw a breath.

Until this moment, she had been occupied with the task of surviving, of looking for food and for shelter at night. Tonight she had both, and this shelter might be hers for a long time. It might even be her new home. So, with the twin burdens of food and shelter satisfied for the moment, everyone she had lost, all the people she had been forced to leave behind crowded into the cave with her. Her sons, her brother and father, Brega, Marav, Gerda, Holgur. Even Kiah and

Agnes were there. Tears slid down her face unheeded. Full of a misery she hadn't asked for, she wrapped her cloak around her and lay down on the pallet of branches, letting her tears water the earth beneath. *I'm sorry. I wish I could have made things right.* The branches that made her pallet were mostly pine, with lots of fragrant needles. The fresh scent of them comforted her, and after a while, fatigue dried her eyes.

This was the most comfortable sleeping place she had found so far, but it was hard to relax with the shadow of the wolf in her head. As always, she had her knife ready in her hand, but now doubt overtook her. *I should probably have gathered more firewood,* she thought, unable to credit her warning system of the rock barrier and dried leaves, and hating that she had left herself unprepared. Her final coherent thought before she finally fell into uneasy sleep was the memory of sitting with Bren at that first dinner.

The hall was warm — almost too warm, and though Alina was accustomed to sitting next to the host at dinner, till now that host had been her father, and there had rarely been more than a dozen people at the table. But this was room was easily four times the size of her father's, with one long table on a dais, and the other tables arranged on three sides, so that the tables together, including the elevated table, formed a square. The people at the tables sat on the outside facing in, so that Alina's first impression was the feeling of dozens of eyes watching her. Bren escorted her to the raised table, took his seat in the center, and had her sit on his right. Another woman about Alina's age was already seated on his left, and an older woman sat on Alina's right.

Alina noted that the younger woman shot her one curious look, then dropped her eyes and stared at the table. Alina turned to the older woman. "Good evening," she said.

This woman, thin almost to the point of emaciation, nodded and replied, "Good evening." But she didn't so much as glance in Alina's direction.

Bren was busy talking to one of his men who had come up and was standing behind his shoulder. His voice and manner were almost boisterous, in sharp contrast with the manner of the women at the table. Something was terribly wrong. A thin film of sweat prickled her upper lip. What had she walked into? Trying again with the woman on her right, she said, "I am Alina."

"Yes." The woman picked up her cup and took a long drink. She set it down and seemed to think a moment before she finally turned her eyes to Alina. They were the exact same blue as Bren's. "I am Freda, your husband's mother."

"I am pleased to finally meet you," Alina answered. "Bren has told me much about you."

"Has he, now?" One corner of Freda's mouth toyed with a smile.

Bren had warned her that his mother might be difficult, but Alina was determined to be friends with her if she could. Freda was wearing a light gray dress of wool, and a blue scarf draped over her shoulders. "Your scarf is lovely," she said. "Is it silk?"

Freda's answering sigh made no sound, but Alina saw the rise and fall of her scant chest. "Thank you. Yes, Bren tells me that it is silk."

Alina nodded. "My father's village is on one of the trade routes. We see many kinds of goods passing back and forth."

"Including brides, it would seem." She turned her eyes fully to Alina, challenging and direct.

That stung. She had wanted to appear friendly, but maybe she was better off letting this woman know she would stand up for herself. After all, caution only worked up to a point. Alina answered, "Your son would not have been my first choice."

Freda stared at her a long moment, then, to Alina's shock, she chuckled.

She glanced at Bren. How was her new husband taking this conversation? But he was turned away from her, talking to the woman on his left. Alina glanced around the room. Everyone had been served by this time, so no one appeared to be paying attention to the high table. She asked Freda, "Who is the woman next to Bren? Is she his sister?" She had noticed that their coloring — dark hair and light eyes — was similar, but Bren had never mentioned a sister.

Freda picked up her cup and drank. When she set the cup down again, it was the gesture of a woman about to wade into battle. "That is his wife, Brega."

If Freda had shouted, she could not have created more of a seismic shift in the room, or in Alina. Apparently, everyone was still watching the high table, and they had been waiting for this moment. Conversation stopped. The only sound was the occasional clink of a dish. Alina had sometimes heard people say that they felt their blood drain from their heads when they were shocked. She had thought it an overstatement, but now she understood that it was not. *I will not pass out*, she told herself furiously.

She started to reach for her cup, but her hands were shaking, so she stuffed them in her lap instead. From the corner of her eye, she could see Bren watching her. He was her husband now, and she had to be careful. When she had got hold of herself, she raised her eyes to his. "You couldn't have told me?"

His mouth quirked. "Would you have accepted me, if I had?"

He already knew the answer to his question, so she asked another. "Did my father know?" It wasn't unheard of for men, especially men of means, to have more than one wife, but Alina couldn't stand the thought that her father had consented to her being anyone's second.

Bren shook his head. "I doubt it, but I also doubt he would have done differently if he had known."

So you deceived him, she thought. *You deceived us both.* Somehow, for the moment, this realization made her feel better. She reached for her cup again, gratified that her hand only shook a little. She didn't want to talk to him, or to anyone else now, so she turned her attention to the food. Her stomach roiled, but the food gave her something to occupy her hands, to make herself look busy and give her time to think.

I could leave here and go back home. She picked up a piece of fowl, a strip of meat from the breast, and nibbled at it. *But I wouldn't be welcomed. Father has sent me away to what he assumes will be a good life for me. He has done his duty, and he will not be happy if I show up again on his doorstep. I have nowhere else to go. I don't want this man now. I didn't really want him to begin with. I am stuck.* She swallowed the bitter truth, and found that it strengthened her. *I will have to figure out how to make the best of this.*

Alina forced herself to eat and drink as if nothing was amiss. Gradually, the conversations in the hall picked up again. *Now they know I am not going to fly out of my chair and scratch his eyes out,* she thought bitterly. After several eternal minutes, she remarked to Freda, "The mead is very good."

Freda nodded. "I make it myself."

Alina had not expected this. "Do you? I have tried my hand at making mead a few times, but the balance is always wrong. Perhaps someday you could teach me your secrets."

The smile that Freda gave her was full and genuine. "Perhaps so."

When the dinner was over, Bren stood and pulled Alina to her feet. To the rest of the room, he announced, "As you may have guessed, this is Alina, my new bride. She comes from a village far to the east from here. I expect you to make her welcome and show her the same respect and honor that you show Brega."

A general murmur of assent passed through the hall, and Bren tucked her hand under his arm to escort her out. As she turned to go, she heard Freda remark under her breath, "Well done, girl."

CHAPTER THREE

No wolf came in the night. No bear, either. Alina sat up and stretched. *This is a good place. I can winter here. I can make this my home, at least for a season.* She finished the two of pieces cattail stalk left in the pot, and went out. Today she would try to catch a fish. She unpacked the wooden box that contained her hooks and lines, attached a hook to one of the lines and took it outside. Finding a rod was easy. There were plenty of trees with straight branches. She cut off one that was the right thickness and stripped it clean of smaller branches and leaves. Then she notched one end and tied her line on. Now for bait. The river swarmed with minnows, but catching them without a net would be difficult. She decided to try digging for worms instead. She had to use her hatchet to dig, and hated doing that, but reasoned she could sharpen it later.

She found a likely spot near the water where the soil was soft, and a few inches down she found her worm, a nice fat one. She baited the hook and walked down to the deeper section of river, sat down on a flat rock at the shore, and put her line in the water. She raised her eyes and noted that there was a stand of willow trees on the opposite bank. *Those will be useful if I can get to them.*

After a couple of hours with no bites, Alina began to think that fishing this way was not the best use of her daylight time. *I could make a fish trap. I remember how to do it. There are lots of reeds at the water's edge.* She sighed. *I need to be patient and wait. If all else fails, I have the cattails.* She studied the willows again, trying to remember.

Their bark was good for medicine, and.... She sat up straighter. It was also useful to make cords. She could make a line with hooks that would sit in the water, which would allow her to do other things while she waited for fish. But for now, she counseled herself to patience. It was maybe an hour later when something tugged on her line. She waited, hardly daring to move. Another tug, stronger this time, and Alina tugged back on the pole, hoping to set the hook. It worked. A sharper tug nearly tore the pole from her hands. Now she was in a battle with the creature on the other end. Little by little, she wound the line around her hand to pull the fish in.

"That's a nice one!" Alina exclaimed aloud as she pulled the fish up, flopping and gaping, onto the bank. It was fully as long as her forearm, from elbow to fingertip. She grasped the animal behind its head and slit it with her knife. All at once, the image of Brega's dying rushed on her. Her fingers went still, and she closed her eyes against a sudden flood of unwanted tears. *No reason. That man killed her for no reason.* She opened her eyes again, wiped her face, and told the fish what she had often heard her father say when he had made a kill in the forest. "I am sorry, cousin, but I need your meat to survive." She had hardly spoken in days, and her voice sounded strange and rough in her own ears.

This catch would provide at least three meals. *I need to hunt,* she thought as she cleaned the fish. *I need to find deer, or something like deer.* She had heard a buck bellowing off to the south the day before. *I need the hides, and I could use the bones and hooves.* She took the fish back to the cave, along with another stalk of cattail, built a spit out of forked branches, and stuck them in the ground on either side of the fire. She ran another branch through the fish and set it into the forked branches. Since most of her day was gone, she decided to go out for a while and see what there was to forage nearby while her fish was cooking.

She found several mounds of brambles that had little green berries on them. Not ready to eat yet, of course, but she would try them when they were ripe. A patch of mint, deep green and fragrant, grew in a sunny spot not thirty paces from the cave, and wild garlic clustered a short stone's throw beyond the mint. Alina took several shoots of each. The garlic would go nicely with the fish, and she could make a tea with the mint. On her way back, she spotted some fungi. Its frills covered most of a dead log, and to her surprise and relief, looked exactly like the kind that grew at home. She cut a sliver and sniffed at it. It looked right and smelled right. After breaking off the tiniest bite and tasting it, Alina cut a generous piece to take with her. When she got back to the cave, the fish was done. She cut up a little of the garlic and some of the fungus to eat with the fish. It would have been better cooked with the meat, but it was all right, and she was so hungry it hardly mattered.

"I will try hunting tomorrow," she murmured. "I can go south where I heard the deer and start there." Daylight, softer now, but still generous, filled the cave's opening. Alina got up and went down to the river, where there were other reeds growing that were not cattails. She cut and gathered an armful and brought them back. She sat just outside the opening, and laid the reeds out to start a basket. If she did manage to bring down a deer, she would need containers for the meat once it was dry. Her fingers flew, and the base of the basket was done when the light faded and she had to go back inside. Alina continued to work on the basket by firelight, and before the flames died, she finished, and held it up to inspect it. The basket was lopsided, but sturdy. It would do.

Her plans for the next day had to be abandoned. She woke to rain pattering outside, and dripping inside. Alina sighed. Well, here was her chance to see what happened in her cave when it rained. She ate another piece of the fish and went and stood looking out the opening. It wasn't raining hard. Not yet, anyway, but the lowering clouds were black.

If I am able to bring in a deer, I will need more baskets. I will also need a drying rack for the meat. And a piece of flint that I can use as a scraper. There's plenty of flint near the river, and I can easily gather the other things before it starts pouring. Taking her bow and arrows and her hatchet, she stepped out into the rain. She first went upriver to where she had seen the flint the day before when she was fishing. She stood for a moment eyeing the willows across the water before deciding, *No. I won't risk that today.* Alina selected a half dozen stones and hurried back to the cave, dropping them just inside the opening before trotting back out again.

Now she went into the trees and cut four long, straight saplings for the drying rack, but she also needed something to bind them together. A tough looking, woody vine clambered up a nearby tree. Alina cut the vine at the ground, and then yelped. The rain in her face had blinded her to the thorns on the vine, and she had been stabbed. Irritated, she sucked at the tiny wound. Then, despite the thorns, she gathered several more long vines.

By the time she got back, the rain was pelting down. There was no point now trying to gather grass for another basket. It would be sodden, and impossible to use. *Well, I think I have enough to keep me busy,* she thought as she brought everything inside, *and maybe it won't rain all day.*

A shiver shook her as she sat down near the fire. It would probably take most of the day for her hair and her tunic to dry out, but she had gathered far more than one day's worth of firewood the afternoon before, and now had a nice stack in the back curve of the cave. She had been keeping water in her iron pot by the fire, so she tore up a few mint leaves and put them in her cup and poured hot water over them. The fragrance of the mint, clean and sweet reminded her of Freda, because after that horrible first dinner, Freda had taken it upon herself to teach Alina everything she knew about herbs and their uses. "When you have mastered this," the older woman told her, "I will show you my bees and teach you how to make good mead."

Alina learned so much from her, but nowhere near everything she wanted before Freda took ill and died. Now she wiped water from her face, not caring whether it was rain or tears. Freda had been good to her. There were many things about living in Bren's village that were good. Alina's father had told her that she would be happy, and she could have been perfectly happy — except for Bren.

She had been in the village at the edge of the sea for about a month when Gerda looked her up and down and said, "You're not far along yet. Another six or seven months, I think. End of winter, I would guess, or very early spring."

Alina's head was swimming. She had hardly eaten that day, and she wanted to lie down and be left in peace. "What are you talking about?"

Ignoring her mistress' peevish tone, Gerda chirped, "You are carrying a child."

Alina groped for the edge of the bed and sat down. "Oh." It was the only thing she could think of to say.

"I thought you might be when you first came," Gerda went on. "You complained of being tired, and with you so young, I thought something was up. And now I can hardly get you to go to breakfast of a morning."

Alina nodded slowly. "I can't stomach food early in the day, and the smell of cooked meat…." She didn't finish, but shook her head and sighed. "I don't know why I'm surprised. I guess I should tell Bren. He'll be pleased."

"Don't tell him yet." Gerda picked up an empty pitcher and went to the door. "It's still early. Better to wait."

"Yes." Her brother, Ebbe, had married the year before Bren showed up, and his wife had miscarried their first child, to everyone's grief and disappointment. Alina understood the wisdom of waiting, and so she said nothing to Bren. It was the first of many things she hid from her husband.

A few days later, there was a knock at her door, and Alina was startled to see Brega standing there. They had not exchanged more than a dozen words since Alina's arrival, though Alina could hardly blame Brega for avoiding her. "May I come in?" she asked.

"Of course." Alina stood aside for her. Brega was carrying a basket with a cloth laid over it. She set it on the table. "I came to ask you if you are comfortable here, and if there's anything you need that I can do for you."

This sounded rehearsed, but Alina smiled. "I have everything I need, thank you."

Brega faced her. "I know Gerda takes good care of you." She glanced around the room before adding, "I actually came to say that I see no reason why we can't at least try to be friends."

"I would like that," Alina said. She didn't know this woman, but she would be courteous. "Please sit down with me."

They both sat, and after a moment, Brega said, "This…situation is not something I would have chosen, and I think you feel the same, do you not?"

Alina considered saying that she wouldn't have chosen Bren at all, but checked herself. Maybe Brega loved him. "You are right."

Brega nodded. "Well, then. We can either be unhappy and suspicious of each other, or we can be friends and enjoy what we can."

This was possibly the most sensible thing anyone had said to her since her arrival. She smiled. "What's in the basket?"

Brega returned the smile and pulled back the cloth. Little flat cakes, pale, but perfectly formed.

"Is that anise?" she asked, sniffing at them.

"Yes, with a little pepper. They are spicier than they look."

"You are bribing me with sweets?"

Brega laughed. "Is it working?"

"When Gerda comes back, I'll get her to bring us something to drink." She took a deep breath. "How did you meet Bren?"

Brega lowered her eyes and studied her hands. "I grew up here. My father is a fisherman — well, he was. He had three boats, and Bren convinced him to use the boats for trade instead of fishing." She pulled in a breath. "And he met you on one of his trading trips?"

"He did." She met Brega's gaze. "To be completely honest, I tried to put him off."

Just then, Gerda came in. If she was surprised to see Brega there she didn't show it. She looked into the basket. "Cakes? Do you two want something to drink with them?" When they said they did, she disappeared again.

Casting about for something else to say, Alina offered, "I understand you have children. Tell me about them."

"I have two daughters," Brega told her. "Ava is four, and Inge just turned two." She thought for a moment before adding, "They are sweet girls. Ava has recently fallen in love with the goats that old Kari keeps."

"And Inge?" Alina asked.

Brega laughed lightly, "Inge is afraid of them. A goat tried to eat one of her braids, and now she won't go near them."

Alina grinned. "I find them a little terrifying myself."

Gerda came back a few minutes later carrying a steaming pitcher. "This will be nice with your cakes," she announced.

Alina stood and took two cups from the shelf. After a moment's hesitation, she took down a third. "Will you join us, Gerda?"

Gerda started to shake her head, but Brega was smiling at her. "Yes, please sit with us."

"Well, all right." She lifted the basin from its stool, and pulled the stool to the table. "This is a mix of herbs that I steeped for you." She picked up the pitcher and poured amber liquid into the cups. "There's also just a touch of honey in it."

Alina took a cautious sip. The tea was hot and bittersweet. She licked her lips. "Delicious."

Brega passed her a cake. "Have this with it."

Alina took the cake and bit off a tiny piece. The anise seed was fragrant, the cake lightly sweet, and then there was a hint of heat. *Pepper,* she thought. *Nice.* "Did you make these?" she asked Brega.

She nodded. "I make them for the girls often, but without the pepper."

"What other spices has Bren brought home?" Alina asked.

"Let me think…." Brega took a sip from her cup.

"Cardamom," Gerda said. "Pepper, of course, and there's a new one. I don't remember what it's called."

"Mace," Brega said.

"Yes, that's it. Mace." Gerda drank from her cup.

The three women chatted about nothing and everything, and they were laughing at something Gerda said when the door swung open. In strode Bren, and when he saw them, he put his hands on his hips. Alina noted the calculating look in his eyes just before he grinned. "Talking about me?"

"No, husband," Brega answered. Her mouth still smiled, but that smile didn't touch her eyes. To Alina she said, "I should be going. It's time for me to feed the girls." With that she stood, and taking the now-empty basket, slid past Bren and out the door.

Gerda said nothing, but she gathered the cups and the pitcher, and also went out.

When they were alone, Bren said, "It seems I have broken up your little party." He crossed the room and put his arms around her. "Now we can have a party of our own."

It rained the rest of that day, and Alina was glad to have enough to keep her busy. First, she stripped the small limbs off the saplings, then turned her attention to the vines. It wasn't difficult to remove the thorns; her knife made swift work of them. The problem with the vines was that they were woody and stiff at the base, so she had to use just the more slender ends that had been newer growth. But that was all right. She had probably gathered enough to make it work, but if not she could split the woody parts and soak them to make them more pliable

Alina cut the saplings to the same length, and tied the tops together. When this was done, she stood them up and spread the feet out in a square, which gave her a pyramid frame about her own height. Starting at the top end, she tied branches to each of the four sides about a hand's length down, then repeated the process another hand's length down from that, and continued until there were four levels of these. She set this construction very briefly over her fire, and was satisfied that the rack was both big enough and tall enough. Finally, Alina cut small branches to lay across each layer. These were the branches that she would drape strips of meat on — if she was able to bring down something big enough.

After she had stopped to eat the last of the fish and a chunk of the fungus, she set the drying rack in the back of the cave and turned her attention to the puddle that was now forming in the depression of the main chamber. Water wasn't just dripping from the crack now, it was falling in a steady stream. One of the flint pieces from outside had had a natural edge and some length on it, but still fit nicely in her hand. She picked it up and stood at the puddle, glancing from it to the opening and back again. Kneeling a little way from the edge of the depression, Alina began scoring a trench in the dirt leading away from the depression toward the opening. This trench would act as a drain. She kept digging with the stone, moving backward as she went, until the trench reached the opening, where she dug on one side until it was out in the rain.

She stood up and went back in, surveying her work, deciding that the trench needed to be deeper. She went over her digging again. When the trench was finished, she dug the short length to the depression until the trench reached the puddle. Immediately, water flowed out. She watched and waited. Water soon began to puddle in a place where the trench wasn't deep enough. Alina had expected something like this would happen. Instead of trying to dig while the water was flowing, she jammed a stick upright into the ground at the place where the water puddled to mark where she would dig deeper when the water was gone. That part of the chamber was something of a mess now, but the mess was unavoidable.

Now what? The cave was still bare except for the few things she had managed to make. Living here the past couple of days had convinced her that this was going to be her home for the winter. What else could she do now to make it better? The first thing would have to be finding a way to store her food off the floor. Her people always put food up on shelves, or hanging from beams, to keep it away from mice and other small animals. She stared at the ceiling, then shook her head. She couldn't think of any way to hang something up from there. *Maybe I could make some kind of shelf?* A free-standing shelf would require a lot of wood, and she had no way to plane it, so the boards would be rough. She stared at the wall, and an idea came to her. She gripped the trenching rock in her hand, and stood up. Would it be possible?

Alina went into the back curve of the cave and scratched at the wall with the stone she had used to dig the trench. The wall's rock was softer than the rock in her hand. She stood back and considered. *If I cut round holes in this wall, I could drive wood pegs in and lay boards on those. That might work, if I can make them level enough.* She decided to try cutting one hole, just to see how it went. She marked the spot with ashes and began to dig into the wall. After about an hour, during which she dug with her right hand, and then switched to her left, and back again, she had a hole maybe half the depth it would have to be. At that point she stopped, her back and arms aching, and sat down with the stones she had collected.

One of these was smooth and round. It would be her hammer. She picked up the flint, considered its size and weight. She hadn't made a stone tool in a long time, not since leaving her father's village. "Well," she murmured, "I won't get a perfect result, but there are plenty of rocks out there. I will have the chance to practice." With that, she set the flint against her knee to steady it, and struck it with the other stone.

She was nearly done with the first pass when the rain slacked off. The only food Alina had left was a piece of fungus and a handful of greens. Picking up her bow and quiver, she went out. By this time, the light was failing. She allowed herself to go into the trees briefly, but found nothing to shoot. So she went back to the river's edge for more cattail. She bent over to dig one up when she heard a rustle and a plop as a turtle launched itself in and started swimming off. Shucking her boots as quickly as she could, Alina waded in and gave chase, but the turtle submerged and disappeared.

"What were you thinking?" she scolded herself. "You could have caught him on land, but never in the water." Grumbling under her breath, she climbed up onto the bank, harvested a couple of cattails, and went back to the cave.

That evening, after her meager meal, Alina decided to finish unpacking her bag. She hauled it over to her pallet and removed everything, laying each item on her cloak. First came the coil of rope. Then there was the little box of hooks and line, followed by another box, slightly larger, that contained two more bowstrings and ten iron arrowheads. Then, her winter tunic and leggings, a pair of felted wool booties to wear inside her boots in cold weather, a handful of rags for her monthly bleeding. Under that was a leather pouch that held a ball of wool thread and a single, precious needle. Next came the tiny box of salt and then the awl, its pointed tip embedded in a block of wood. Finally, down at the bottom was a roll of leather, tied with a rawhide strap. Tears started in her eyes, and she wiped them away with an impatient hand.

Gunnar, her older son, had given her this. It was his parting gift. There was something rolled up in the leather that he had made for her. He would not tell her what it was. She could see him exactly as he had been in that moment, staring at her, his blue eyes wide and solemn. He made her promise two things, that she would live, and that she wouldn't open this roll until she had made a home for herself. She promised both, knowing her promises might be empty. But here she was, and now she had a place to consider her home, at least for a while.

She caressed the leather with the tips of her fingers. "My boys." She had sent them away a few days before the ship that brought her here set off. She wondered where they were now. Then, shaking herself, she untied the strap and began to unroll the leather.

CHAPTER FOUR

Another moon waxed and waned. Summer was fully on the land. Alina had managed to bring down two deer in the past month. The meat was dried and stored in baskets, the skins cleaned and laid out on her bed. She had put up two long shelves in the rear part of the chamber, and the top shelf was nearly full of the stored meat. If she could get another couple of deer before winter, that should be enough food to get her through.

The main thing that she was now uncertain about was whether winter in this place would be anything like winter at home. The summer was young, but was already warmer than any summer she'd ever known. Did it even snow here? Surely it did, though she had heard traders telling stories of places that were so warm it never snowed. She had dismissed such talk as fanciful tales. How could there not be snow?

She had hunted to the south and west of her cave. On this day she decided to cross the river and see what was there. It might turn out to be a long walk, so she packed food in her bag (a couple of pieces of a goose she had shot the day before) belted on her knife, and picked up the bow and arrows. She wanted to look for branches to make new arrows. So far, she had been able to recover all but one of the arrow heads, but the shafts had been broken. And she would collect willow bark on her way home.

Alina took off her boots at the water's edge, and tucking their tops into her belt, stepped gingerly in. The water was swift here, but not deep. The current was over her knees when she reached the middle. There she stopped a moment to accustom herself to the force of the flow and to scan the opposite shore. She had not forgotten the wolf. But this morning, nothing appeared to be moving in the trees except squirrels and birds. Her steps were slow and deliberate, each step a new task that had to be accomplished before she took another. She didn't want to fall in the water and get everything wet.

She counted her steps under her breath, and when her foot touched the opposite bank, she had gone sixty-two paces. So, the river was wider than more than she guessed, or her steps were shorter than usual. Alina sat down and pulled her boots back on. *Now which way? West? If I follow the river on this side, it will be easier to find my way back.*

But there was a rise to the north, and she was curious to find out what was on the other side. It meant walking away from the river, but as long as she could hear the water, it would be easy to find her way back. The trees were sparser here than on her side. She walked through wide clearings before coming upon a meadow just where the land began to rise. The meadow was covered with wildflowers. Little purple lupines brushed her boots. Tiny blooms like miniature white daisies clustered in clumps between them, alongside pink wild onions. There was a yellow flower she didn't know that had a green tip pointing out of the middle of each blossom. And standing tall and proud among them were wild carrots with their white domes of blooms. She stopped in the meadow a moment to breathe and enjoy it.

At the top of the rise, she found herself looking down on more forest, thicker here, but there was another meadow at the bottom. It was nearly mid-day now, so she decided to go down this side to rest and eat. Alina found a rocky spot where the meadow met the rise, and skirting it, sat down in the grass, opened her water skin, and took a long drink.

She stayed there for about an hour, eating and watching a parade of puffy clouds sail overhead, and reveling in the beauty of the day. She was just about to stand up when a rustle in the grass caught her attention. The sound was on her left, and coming closer. She drew her knife and sat still as the stones and waited. A few heartbeats later, a red fox stuck its nose out of the grass and sniffed the air. Alina didn't move, and the animal came another few steps closer. Then it saw her and froze for a moment, its amber eyes studying her before turning tail and scurrying back the way it had come.

Alina stood up. Hunting the fox didn't interest her, and it was time to start back. She wanted to collect some willow bark and get across the water before sunset. She gathered her things and took a few steps toward the rise when the fox darted out in front of her. Maybe the animal thought Alina was a threat. It sprinted off a few yards to her left — and disappeared. That wasn't surprising, but she heard a squeal and then a thud, faint but clear. Frowning, she went toward the place where the fox had vanished.

Alina nearly vanished herself. The front half of her right foot found the empty space before her eyes saw it. She jumped back, her heart pounding. There was a hole in the ground that hadn't even been visible from the rise. The opening, rimed on the inside with white stone, was obscured by tangles of vines and brush. Alina approached again and peered into the hole. The top to the bottom of the hole was at least twice her height. The sides were streaked with veins of white stone. And on the ground lay the fox, its head turned against its back. Its neck was broken. "I'm sorry, little cousin," Alina whispered. "I never meant for this to happen to you."

She didn't want to just leave him in the hole, but there was no way to get down there — not and get out again. She sighed and looked around. She could use the vines, maybe bring his body up. She cut a handful of the vines, stripped their leaves, knotted them together, and tied one end around the shaft of an arrow. It was difficult to find her footing to shoot down, but when she figured out the place to stand, she put the loose end of the vines under one foot, took aim, and shot.

She missed on the first try, hauled her arrow back up, nocked it and tried again. This time the arrow caught the fox's body in the neck. Alina carefully pulled him back into the light, which was beginning to mellow toward evening. It was time to go. She started to turn away, but when her shadow moved and the sun fell fully on the hole again, the white stone sparkled in the sunlight. Curious, Alina knelt at the edge of the hole and with her fingertips, managed to dislodge a small piece of the stone. It glittered in her palm as she rolled it back and forth. She sniffed at it. No smell. Gingerly she touched it with the tip of her tongue.

Salt!

When she was a child, a trader passing through her father's village had mentioned a salt mine he claimed he had seen. Salt underground. She could hardly imagine it then, but here it was. Her people had always gotten their salt from those who made it from seawater, and that was a laborious process. Easing herself onto her stomach, Alina tapped at the white mineral with the butt of her knife until she had a good handful, which she stowed in the bottom of her bag. Now it was really time to go. She climbed back up the rise, stopping for a moment at the top to look down again where the hole was, to the right of a cluster of three stones.

By the time she reached the river it was mid-afternoon. Turning west, she followed the water to the stand of willows. She spent the next hour stripping bark, a little from each tree. When she had as much as she could safely carry, she went back to the shallow stretch of river across from her cave and started across. She stepped up onto the bank and then remembered that the willow bark had to be soaked before it could be turned into cord. She turned back to the river. There was a sort of a shallow pool just to her left. She curled most of the bark and submerged it, using nearby stones to hold the bark down. It would be ready to use in the morning.

She still had a couple of hours of daylight left when she got back to the cave. Now her mind was on the salt. If she found other people (or if other people found her) salt would be valuable to trade. But in order to do that, she had to find a way to get down into the hole and back out again. Those streaks of white inside the hole were probably also salt. Alina puzzled over the idea of how to safely get more salt while she skinned the fox and put it on the spit to roast.

Her coil of rope was long enough, but it would have to be tied to something, and there were no trees near the hole. If she had a ladder, maybe? She picked up a stick and drew a sketch of a ladder in the dirt. Alina closed her eyes, trying to visualize the ladders she had seen at home. It wouldn't be that difficult to make one, especially if she was successful turning the willow bark into cord. Imagining herself crossing the river with her gear and a ladder made her understand what the difficulty would be. It had taken every bit of the care she possessed to make it back and forth with her bag and her bow and quiver. Adding a cumbersome ladder to the mix would be dangerous. Could she just go across and construct a ladder over there? There were plenty of trees, but the problem with this idea was that making a ladder would take hours, and she wouldn't have the protection of the cave.

After more thought, she decided to make the ladder on her side, and take one trip across the water carrying only the ladder. She could leave it there and come back across to get her other things. It was still risky — two trips over instead of just one — but the salt was worth it. *I need a container,* she told herself.

Alina had found a generous deposit of clay near the fishing spot. She had already made a bowl and a couple of pots. She hurried upriver, dug some clay and brought it back to the cave. Using spoons full of water from her pot, she rubbed bits of clay between her palms to make coils, stacking the coils atop each other until they had formed the shape she wanted. Then she added more clay to the outside to make it smooth. By the time darkness fell, a small pot for the salt, along with its lid, were sitting near the fire to dry and harden.

Alina banked her fire and lay down on her pallet. "One of these days," she murmured with a yawn, "I should think about raising my bed off the floor." She stared up toward the ceiling where feathers of different sizes and colors shifted and twirled above her head in the dying firelight — her sons' gift. When she had unrolled the leather, she had found three wooden rods, each about as long as her forearm. They were attached to each other in the center with lengths of cord, so that there were three horizontal rods — a top one, a middle, and a bottom. The construction now hung from a straight limb she had found, its end driven into a hole she carved in the wall above her pallet, as high as she could reach. On each side of each rod dangled three feathers — eighteen in all. The feathers were tied to the rods with the same kind of cord. There was a long, white feather that must have come from a sea bird. Another long feather was striped rusty brown. That one was probably from a hawk's tail. A white one with black spots was from a snowy owl. Then there were smaller feathers — a couple of yellow ones, one scarlet that had to be from a woodpecker, and one blue one. The rest were white, or brown.

These feathers had been Gunnar's collection. He had kept them in a box under his bed, and when he found an interesting one, he showed it to her and asked what bird it had come from. Tears started in her eyes all over again. Her son had given her the most precious thing he could think of. He had spent hours in the woods and along the shore to find them.

Alina let out a long sigh and closed her eyes. *I miss you.*

There were two things Alina remembered vividly about Gunnar's birth. One was that Bren left her alone when she finally told him she was pregnant. Freda had warned her this would happen. During one noon meal when Bren was absent and the two women sat together, Alina told her about the coming baby, and asked, "Bren will be pleased, won't he?"

Freda gave her a sympathetic look, and Alina realized that a doubt about Bren's reaction had been nagging at her. "Here is what will happen," Freda said after a moment's consideration. "Your husband will greet the news well enough, I think, but he will quit your bed. He will tell you that he's concerned for the baby's safety. He will find a woman in the village." Her eyes, steady and unflinching, met Alina's. "Do you understand me?" Wordlessly, Alina nodded, and Freda went on. "He will leave the village before your baby is born. He'll go off on one of his trips. He won't come back until he judges that you've given birth."

"He did this with Brega?" Alina asked, feeling a surge of anger for Brega's sake.

Freda grimaced. "Both times."

The other thing she remembered most clearly about Gunnar's birth was the ice. Winter slapped them hard, and in her little house, a rime of ice had formed on the inside walls, even with the fire roaring in the hearth. Alina was bundled under so many layers of blanket that she could hardly move.

Her pains had started in the morning, but she didn't tell anyone. Every time a pain came upon her, she did her best to relax, having quickly learned that tensing up made the pain worse. Bren was off on a trading trip, as Freda had predicted. It didn't seem to matter to him that it was midwinter and that he was risking his own life and the lives of the men who went with him. Gerda was doing her usual bustling in and out, though Alina did notice that the older woman was watching her as a hawk watches a rabbit.

She had just managed to make it through the morning's routine, and was leaning on Gerda as they came back to the house from the noon meal when a particularly hard pain seized her, and she groaned. Once they were inside, Gerda said, "Get yourself in that bed and let me have a look." Alina quickly found out what she meant by having a look. She examined her with icy fingers that made Alina gasp and shiver, and said, "You have a long way to go yet. Perhaps by tomorrow morning your baby will be here. Now, lift your hips and let me slide this under you." Alina obeyed, and Gerda placed a thick fold of blanket under her.

Tomorrow morning. How was she going to be able to endure this pain that long? "Tired," she muttered.

"Yes, I imagine so. You rest as much as you are able. See if you can get a little nap." Gerda covered her up to her chin. "Don't worry about anything."

Alina did doze off a few times that afternoon, but the pains were too close together to allow her much rest. Time passed in a blur of drowse and pain. Once, Alina woke and asked, "Is it still today?"

Gerda chuckled. "It is always today, child. But yes, it is about dinner time now."

"You should go eat," Alina murmured.

"Brega will bring me dinner."

"Brega knows?"

"Child, the whole village knows. Are you thirsty?"

She was, and Gerda gave her a cup of hot mead, supporting her shoulders while she sat up to drink. She lay back again and dozed, but moments later she started awake and realized the bed was wet. She tried to struggle up.

"What is it, child? What's the matter?"

"I… the bed is wet." Alina wanted to weep. "I didn't mean to."

Gerda gently pushed her back down. "You're having a baby. This is what happens. Stay where you are. You'll be warmer." She went to a pile of bedclothes near the fire and picked up a folded blanket. She pulled back Alina's covers, took out the first blanket that she had put under her and replaced it with the warm, dry one, saying, "Let's have another look." Apparently, there wasn't much to see, because Gerda said nothing, but laid the wet blanket beside the door.

People came and went. A burly man who turned out to be Gerda's brother brought armloads of firewood. Brega came and sat with them a while. She and Gerda talked in low voices, but Alina paid no attention. Her pains were coming on much stronger now, and along with them, the urge to bear down. Alina pushed with each pain, but it didn't feel like she was getting anywhere. The wind howled outside, and as the hours passed, Alina felt like howling herself.

Sometime later, a woman came in whom Alina didn't know, though she had seen her a few times around the village, and knew she was the midwife. This woman was a workhorse, compared to Gerda, broad in the shoulders, her arms as muscled as a man's. "How are things going here?" she asked, setting down a substantial bag and crossing to the bed.

Gerda said, "Her waters broke a few hours ago, and she's been pushing. I was just about to look at her again."

"Well, let's both look," the stranger said.

She bent over Alina, and Gerda said, "This is Willa. She is here to help you."

When they had examined Alina, Willa added, "I want to find out what this baby is doing." With that, she pulled Alina's dress up further and laid broad, warm hands on her swollen belly. She felt around, pressing and nudging. Then she said, "The baby is sideways."

Even in the near dark of the candlelight and firelight, Alina saw Gerda turn pale. Panting and swallowing hard, she asked, "Am I going to die?"

"We need to turn this baby," Willa answered, laying a hand gently on her forehead. "It will hurt. But if we don't do it, you and the baby will both certainly die."

Alina choked back a sob. Pain and fear were nearly all she had — pain, and fear, and the tiniest sliver of hope. "Do it," she moaned.

"How can I help?" Gerda asked.

"Get behind her in the bed and hold her while I do this," she answered. Then she dug around her bag and pulled out a clay pot. She removed its lid and dipped her fingers in. They came up shining with some kind of fat which she rubbed into the palms of both hands.

Alina broke down and wept while Gerda climbed in behind her. "It's all right, child," Gerda crooned. She stroked Alina's hair. "Lay your head against me. I have you."

Another pain flooded in, and Alina groaned. Willa waited until it passed, then placed her oiled hands on Alina's belly and started pushing at the baby inside. Alina heard a scream. It sounded like it came from far away. She thought maybe the scream was her own. Then everything went black.

When she came to, Gerda was still behind her, and Willa stood over her, pulling the blankets back up. "The baby has turned," she said.

But Alina still had to push, and after a couple more hours, she thought she might die anyway. She had no energy left. Willa told her, "Your baby is nearly here. I can see its head. Just a few more pushes.

"I can't…." Alina whimpered.

"Of course you can," Willa insisted.

Alina gathered what was left of herself. With the next pain, the baby's head was born, and minutes later, the rest of him followed. He wailed, his tiny fists waving, furious at being forced out into the cold.

"Ah, look at you, little baldy," Gerda laughed. She got out of the bed and took the baby from Willa. "Let's wrap you up."

"Boy or girl?" Alina asked.

"It's a lovely boy." Willa smiled. She continued to tend to Alina until the afterbirth came. "I will go now," she told them.

When she was gone, Gerda handed the baby to Alina, saying, "He's perfect."

And he was. Alina thought her heart might burst out of her chest as she held the little bundle close. He had stopped crying, and was staring at her with bright, blue eyes. "You are perfect," she whispered, stroking his cheek with the tip of one finger.

Gerda pulled a chair to the bed and sat down with a sigh. "Well, that was a night to remember."

It was, but though Alina would never forget the pain, the joy of holding her firstborn in her arms eclipsed it. He was a beautiful boy. She picked up one of his tiny hands, astounded at the miniature perfection of it. His little ears, like pink, translucent shells lay against the sides of his head – just as they should. Her body had done this. She had made a tiny new person.

Alina woke in the middle of the night from a dream she could not remember. Tears streamed down her face. Above her the feathers shifted and swayed in invisible currents of air.

The next morning, she got up and was just about to eat when an unwelcome sound at the cave entrance caught her attention — snuffling and grunting. *Bear!* she thought, and snatched up her bow. She slung her quiver over her shoulder and quietly moved to where she could see out. Nothing for a few seconds, but then a vast bulk appeared, blocking the light. Another snuffle. *He smells my food,* Alina thought. *But he's too big to get in.*

That is, she hoped he was too big. He was trying. One huge forearm reached through and clawed at the rock inside the opening. Alina had an arrow nocked on her string, but there was no point in shooting. It would only infuriate the animal. Her heart hammered in her chest, but she took a deep breath and forced herself to think.

He can't get in here. Even a bear can't tear down this much rock. So, for the moment I am safe. Another long breath. *I can't do anything but wait for him to go. But how will I know he is gone? And if he thinks he can get to my food, will he ever go away?* Another handful of breaths, and her thoughts shifted. *He has enough meat on him to last me through the winter — meat with fat in it. And that pelt would be warm.* The shift in thinking from prey to hunter calmed her.

Then, all at once, he disappeared. Alina slowly lowered her bow. She took a cautious step toward the entrance and stopped to listen. Nothing. Was the bear standing to one side, waiting to pounce on her? Another step. Now she heard his footfalls. He was still there, just not in her line of sight. She waited, tense and still. A grunt, and the footfalls were going away. She stepped into the entrance and peered out. There he was, a great hulking beast, moving down toward the river.

Can I kill him with just arrows? she wondered. *Well, I could, if the arrows struck him in the right place.* Just now, his back was toward her, and there was no place to aim for. If she had any chance of killing him, he would have to be facing her. *I could certainly make him turn around.* She almost laughed at the madness of the thought. Bears were fast and powerful. And smart. Not for the first time, she wished there were other people with her, but this was useless thinking. If she was going to bring down a bear, she would have to do it alone.

Without a sound, Alina stepped outside. The animal was almost to the water's edge now. *Whatever I do,* she reasoned, taking a few more paces, I *cannot let him get between me and the cave.* She had come several more steps when the bear caught her scent and turned his head. His eyes met hers, and she froze and felt her stomach drop. *What have I done?* Its huge head swung back toward the river, as if considering. Then it turned, and with terrible grace began a lumbering run back up the slope toward her.

In panic, Alina took a shot, but the arrow only hit the bear in the shoulder. It stuttered one step, roared, and came on. Alina turned to flee to the cave, but her ankle twisted under her, and she went down hard on her left knee. That knee hit rock, and afterward she was never able to understand how she got up again. The pain was immediate and intense, but she ran. It was only about a dozen steps to safety, but it felt like a hundred. The bear's hot breath chuffed behind her just as she squeezed through the opening. She wasn't fast enough, though. It swiped at her, opening gashes in her right calf. The impact of the blow made her fall. Her right foot was still outside, and the bear bent its head to take her foot in its mouth. She screamed and kicked its nose as hard as she could with her other foot.

The bear bellowed and shook its head, buying her the few heartbeats she needed to get her feet inside. She scooted back like a crab, and after a couple of heaving breaths, stood up. All this time, the bear roared and swatted at the cave opening. Ignoring the pain in both her legs, gasping and sobbing, Alina nocked another arrow, and when the bear stuck its face in the opening and roared again, she sent her shot into its open mouth. The noise of the beast's rage was cut off. It coughed and pawed at its mouth, trying to dislodge the arrow. Alina took aim again and put another arrow into its chest. The bear backed up a step, moaned, and sat down so hard that Alina felt the impact shake the ground. After a few more seconds, the animal fell over on its side, twitching.

Alina leaned against the wall of the cave, shivering with pain and fear. She closed her eyes and taking great gulps of air, set her bow down, pulled off the quiver and let it fall to the ground. Blood trickled warm down the back of her right leg. She had to do something about that before she did anything else. She took a quick look at her left knee. It was turning blue, but the skin wasn't broken. And she could put weight on it. She limped to the fire and took her iron pot away from the coals to let the water cool. Then she gathered her four menstrual rags from the shelf. They would have to be enough. Next to them lay the leather pouch that contained the ball of thread and needle. Alina closed her eyes, trying to imagine doing what she needed to do.

I need medicine for these wounds. Honey would be ideal, but I haven't found any yet. I do have the wild garlic. She picked up a bunch of that and took everything to the fire.

Bracing herself against the wall with both hands and lifting her right leg, Alina looked back at it over her shoulder. It was hard to tell with all the blood, but it looked like there were two gashes, maybe three. Then she took the smallest deer skin from her pallet and spread it out to sit on. Getting down on the floor hurt, and blood stained the deer skin. She sat cross-legged so that she could reach the wounds. Alina tested the water in the pot. It was warm, but not hot because she hadn't built up the fire yet that morning. Dipping one of the rags in the water, she washed the wounds, hissing with each touch. There was one gash about as long as her hand. The second was shorter and not as deep. As she washed off the blood, she found a third gash, shorter and shallower still.

The deepest gash was still bleeding, and Alina understood that binding that wound was not going to be enough. She glanced at the needle and thread — which she had intended to use to stitch the rags together — and her heart quailed. Sometimes her people sewed wounds shut, but could she really do that to herself? She groaned as she sat up straighter and gritted her teeth. I *am very lucky. That bear could have killed me, and all I have are a bruised knee and these scratches. I need to get out there and start working on the meat.* She hauled in a deep breath and whispered, "Help me."

Alina threaded the needle. It took some doing because her hands were shaking and slick with her own blood. She looked at the gashes again. Only that one wound probably needed to be stitched. She grabbed a stick that was lying close by and clenched it between her teeth. Then she began. She squealed and bit down hard on the stick with the first stitch. Once the thread was through, she tied it off, let her head fall back a moment, took another breath, and began the second. Tears scalded her eyes, and she had to stop and sleeve them off. Another moment's rest, another deep breath, and again....

Alina put five stitches in the wound. By the time she tied off the last one, she had to lie back and close her eyes for a little while. Waves of trembling shook her. She took the stick from her mouth, and looked at it before tossing it into the fire. She had nearly bitten it in two. *Enough*, she told herself. *It's over. Do what you have to do*. She sat up again and ground up garlic leaves and some of the bulbous root and made a paste before washing the wounds and applying the garlic paste to all three of them. Then she wrapped everything in one of the menstrual rags and stitched the ends of the rag together so that it would stay on her leg. After that, she ate a little and drank as much water as she could. The bleeding had just about stopped, so she stood up, shaky, but feeling better now that the wounds were tended to and covered. She picked up her hatchet and went outside.

Stopping often to rest and catch her breath, she skinned the bear, dragged the pelt inside, and laid it out, fur side down. She went back out and started on the meat. The flies were horrible, but she laid the meat on the inside of the skin and folded the skin over it while she sliced thin pieces and hung them on the drying rack. While she was at it, she cut a nice steak, spitted it, and put it over the fire to roast for her dinner.

I have to get this done, she told herself every time her energy lagged. *I have to do as much today as I can.* In the back of her mind were awful images of a wound gone bad. She had only seen it once, when she was a girl, and one of her father's men had been beset by robbers on the road to her village. The man had a horrible gash across his chest and shoulder that would have killed him then and there if it had gone any deeper. He had been carried to her father's house, and the women had treated him as well as they could, but the wound went sick, and he died after a few days.

Alina was not supposed to go into the room where he lay, but she sneaked in a couple of times, and though the wound was mostly covered up with cloth and poultices, she did get a glimpse. Worse still, she got the smell. The same thing could happen to her now. *If I die, I die*, she finally reasoned. *But if I live, I need this meat and pelt for the winter.* So she plowed ahead, trying to ignore the pain in her legs.

It was close to nightfall when she trudged back out for the last large piece, a foreleg and shoulder. But Alina stepped outside just in time to see a wolf dragging that very piece away. She backed into the entrance, watching. It might be the same wolf she had seen that one time on the other side of the river. The wolf was alone, not part of a pack, but this did not reassure her.

It half-carried, half-dragged its prize down to the water. There it stopped and looked back. Alina didn't know if it could see her, but it stood still for one long moment, testing the wind with its nose, before it picked up the piece again and stepped into the river. She could barely see it by the time the wolf made it across. "Oh, well," she muttered, going back inside, "It's a small loss."

It wasn't good for her to stay up all that night, but she pushed herself, and when gray light appeared again in the opening, Alina had started most of the meat drying, and had scraped the skin. Her head was swimming by the time she reached a point where she could stop.

She changed her bandage, applied more garlic to the wounds and wrapped them up again before adding wood onto the fire -- just enough to keep it going another few hours. That finished, she fell onto her pallet, and sleep overcame her.

When she woke, it was late in the afternoon, and she knew she was in trouble.

Gunnar was two months old before Bren came back from his journey. He saw the boy, and said he was proud to have a son, but he still would not come near Alina, and he would not touch his child. Freda told Alina that this, too, was his usual way. "I would have been surprised if he had done otherwise," she remarked, frowning.

He finally came back to Alina's bed when Gunnar was four years old. One afternoon that summer, Bren said, "I have someone for you."

"Someone for me?" she repeated, confused.

He gave a light laugh. "I suppose I should say that I have something of a job for you." He sat down at her table. "There is a village south of here — about a day's ride. The chief of that village and I have known each other a long time. He has a daughter." Now Bren rubbed his hands together as if he were washing them. "There are no women of any standing there, only peasants, and he's worried that the girl's ways are becoming rough. So he asked if I could bring her here and let you and Brega take charge of her."

Alina had many questions, but would only get to ask a few. So she said, "How old is this girl?"

"Oh, I think she's only about twelve," Bren answered. "You and Brega can just treat her like a daughter."

"And when are we to take charge of her?" Gunnar had been napping, but now he was awake and wanted something to eat. Alina handed him a piece of bread and a cup of goat's milk that Gerda had brought in for him.

"She is supposed to be here within the month," he replied, glancing at his son, and then away.

"I see." She did see. This girl would end up being someone's wife — most Bren's. And it would be up to her and Brega to prepare the girl for that role. "And will she have her own place?"

Bren started, as if he hadn't considered the practicalities of having another woman there. "Yes, I need to get the men started on that." So, Bren did intend to marry her.

When he was gone, Alina sat down and pulled Gunnar into her lap. Twelve years old was young for a girl to marry, but not unheard of. *Has he told Brega?* she wondered, *or is that my job, too?* The more she thought about it, the more she wanted to laugh at the sheer audacity of Bren asking his second wife to babysit his third. He thought he'd made himself sound reasonable. "Treat her like a daughter," Alina muttered. "Who does he think he is fooling?"

The new girl, a brunette named Agnes, arrived a couple of weeks later. Alina saw at once why Bren wanted her. She was slim as a reed except for her breasts, which were large and heavy looking. *And she's only twelve?*

Two men escorted the girl. One of them (Alina never learned his name) went back the very next day. The other, a skinny giant named Huus, stayed. Alina disliked him almost immediately. There was something about the way he watched the women in the village — following them with hungry eyes — that made the hairs on the nape of her neck stand up.

Alina didn't like Agnes much, either. She tried to be friendly to the girl. Brega tried, too. Agnes, however, had other ideas. She avoided the women — all the women — as much as she could, and flirted with every man who glanced her way. "This isn't going to end well," Alina remarked to Brega one afternoon when Agnes went missing. "I am not going looking for her again."

Brega sighed. "Nor am I. But we should tell Bren because if anything happens to her, it will land on us."

"Would you mind telling him?" Alina asked. "He listens to you better than he does to me."

"Does he?" Brega laughed, but she agreed, and went off in search of their husband.

The men found Agnes about an hour later, wandering in the woods near the village. She was not the least bit contrite for making them search. She seemed to take it as her due that men would look for her. In her own eyes, she was so successful with that disappearance that she began to slip away on a daily basis, either to the forest, or to some lonely place at the shore, or down past the bend of the river where she couldn't be easily seen.

At first, Bren was amused. "She's a little wild cat," he said happily. But as the weeks wore on, his amusement turned to exasperation. He had put his head in Alina's door one afternoon, asking if Agnes was there. When she told him the girl had disappeared after lunch, he growled, "She's gone again?" He eyed her up and down. "And what have you been doing all day?"

"Tending to your mother," she answered mildly. "Raising your son." Freda had fallen ill, and Alina and Brega took it in turns sitting with her. "And I should tell you, Husband, that I am carrying another child." She wasn't going to bother to keep the news to herself this time. She had already heard this story, and knew how it ended.

Bren huffed and left.

The following week, the hammer fell. Agnes was gone again, and no one, not even Bren's most loyal men, wanted to go looking for her. The day waned, and when the sun started to go down, Alina found she was worried about the girl in spite of herself, but not so worried that she bothered to go looking. Dinner that night was a quiet affair in the hall, with only the lowest murmur of conversation. Bren was sulking and didn't speak a word to anyone.

When the meal was over, Alina walked with Gunnar back to her house. She pulled the door open, and there was Agnes, wrapped in a blanket, huddled next to the hearth. Her face was a mass of purple bruises. "What in the world!" Alina exclaimed. "What happened to you?"

Agnes sniffed. "I went down to the river." She ran one hand over her face as if to erase the ugliness. "I didn't do anything wrong."

Alina put Gunnar in his bed and told him to lie quiet. To Agnes, she said, "The river didn't do that to you."

Agnes shook her head, and a single tear slid down her face. "No. Huus did."

A chill shook Alina. She held out a hand. "Can you stand?" Agnes nodded, and she helped her up. "Let me see the rest." Gently, she pulled at the edge of the blanket. After a moment's resistance, Agnes released her grip on it. Alina sucked in a hiss. Bite marks covered Agnes's neck and chest and breasts. Many had broken the skin. A few still oozed blood. She tried to keep her voice calm. "Huus did this?"

Just then, Gerda swung the door open and came in. "I need to take that dress you said was torn," she began, but stopped. "Oh." She shut the door. "What can I do?"

"Do you know where Brega is?"

"Yes, I will go fetch her."

"Agnes will also need something to eat," Alina told her. "And do you have something for these wounds?"

"I'll get some honey," Gerda nodded. "And I'll bring some clean cloths, and maybe a change of clothes?"

Agnes's dress had been ripped right down the front. "Yes, thank you, Gerda."

When she was gone, Alina said, "Sit down here at the table. Are you cold?"

"A little," Agnes answered, drawing the blanket close again.

Alina fed the fire in the hearth. The blaze had just caught the new wood when Brega came hurrying in. "I have the honey and cloths from Gerda," she said as she moved toward the fire. "We'll need to heat some water."

She set water over the fire, and Bren burst in. "What is this?" he demanded. "What is going on?" He stopped in his tracks when he saw Agnes's face. "Who did this to you?"

"Huus did it. He hurt me," Agnes answered. Her voice trembled. Alina turned to look, and saw the faintest suggestion of a simpering smile.

Bren approached the girl. "Let me see."

She didn't grip the blanket this time. Instead, she stood and let it fall from her shoulders, giving Bren a full view of her bruises and her breasts.

Alina saw the hungry expression in Bren's eyes as he looked Agnes over, and she thought she might be sick. The girl was young, but she knew what she was doing, and Bren was on her hook.

"Well," he said after a moment, then cleared his throat. "Well, this is bad. I will go and take care of this." With that, he turned on his heel and went out the door.

Bren "took care of this" by marrying Agnes before her bruises healed. Alina stood next to Brega during the short ceremony, watching her face register dismay and resignation in turns. Later Brega said, "Bren felt he had to marry her, you know. He and Agnes's father have been friends a long time. And Bren failed to protect her, so…." Her voice trailed off. Alina didn't answer, only took Brega's hand and squeezed it. "Yes," Brega murmured, as is she had read Alina's thoughts. "You are right. The truth is not in him — at least, never the whole truth."

Alina nodded. Bren had a knack for taking bits and pieces of truth, stitching them to bits and pieces of lies, and constructing stories from these to suit himself. She and Brega started for the hall. They were expected to attend the banquet that evening. She said only, "We have nothing to be ashamed of, Brega. We will hold our heads high."

Brega's smile was wan, unconvinced, but she said, "You are right. Thank you."

A month or so later, Brega was saying, "Poor Agnes. I wish, for her sake that she would listen to us."

Agnes fell pregnant almost immediately, as Alina had, but unlike Alina, she did not believe that it was wise to wait to announce her condition. "You want me to keep it to myself? Why? Do you think you will somehow win him back?" She looked Brega and Alina up

building up the flame again and checking the strips of meat. They were nearly dry. She would need more baskets soon to store her food. That wasn't a hard chore, was it? Surely she could gather grass and make a basket or two. But first things first. Taking another handful of garlic, a clean rag, and the needle and thread, she sat down on the blood-stained deer hide and went to work.

She cut the threads that held the ends of the bandage together, and went to lift the cloth, only to find that dried blood had stuck the rag onto the wounds. She carefully trickled warm water from her pot onto the stuck places until they gave way. The result was not encouraging. Her whole lower leg looked red and swollen — angry, Freda would have said. Just looking at it made her head swim. But the stitches held. That was one good thing. She had the garlic, and some of the willow bark. She could make a tea with the bark. It was supposed to help with pain. Alina pounded more of the garlic and applied it to the wounds, wrapped her leg, and stitched the cloth together. She pulled up her skirt. Her left leg was nearly a solid mass of bruise from just over her ankle to halfway up her thigh. It looked awful, and ached when she put her weight on it, but she thought that leg would heal in time if she lived long enough.

I should eat, she thought, though she didn't feel the least bit hungry. She took a chunk of meat and chopped it up. This she dropped into the water in the pot before adding some of the garlic, a pinch of salt and a handful of greens. It would make enough stew to feed her for several meals. She brewed and drank a cup of willow bark tea, wincing at the bitterness. Then she went out — remembering her bow and arrows this time — and gathered grass for baskets. By the time she got back, those small chores had exhausted her, and she had to lie down again.

The next time she woke, it was dark, and her fire was low, but the stew smelled like it was done. She spooned some into a clay bowl, but her hands were shaking, and she kept slopping it onto the deerskin. Finally, she raised the bowl to her lips and drank. It tasted nice enough, but after a few swallows nausea hit her like a wave, and she had to give up. Dumping what was left back into the pot, Alina lay down again.

Am I dying? she wondered, staring up at the feathers. She closed her eyes, not for sleep this time, but because she was trying to remember, and it was hard to remember. It was hard to think. Was there anything else she could do now that she hadn't already done to heal herself? Freda had encouraged sick people to eat if they could, and to drink as much as they could stand. She had told Alina that drinking a tea, or water, or warm mead flushed sickness from the body. Groaning, she got up again, filled her wooden cup, and sat on the pallet, watching the fire and taking small sips of water. Her stomach was still unhappy, but she thought now that she might be able to keep the stew down.

Sleep overtook her, along with images – not dreams so much as moments in time, Gunnar falling and skinning his knee, Bren fingering the torque at his neck, Brega bouncing Dag in her lap, the pitching deck of the ship awash with spray, a shower of sparks from Holgur's hammer, a gray shadow gliding through the trees....

Agnes had fallen in love with Bren, and it was terrible for her when he abandoned her. Lacking the sense to realize that Brega and Alina had tried to help her, she blamed his neglect on them." You don't respect him," she shouted once at Alina. "That is why he goes away."

Alina didn't bother to answer. It was true that she didn't respect Bren, but her lack of respect had nothing to do with his being gone, had nothing to do with how he treated Agnes, had nothing to do with much of anything. Bren would do what Bren wanted to do, and nothing anyone said would change his mind. Nothing any woman said would, and that was certain.

Bren had chosen his new girl for when he was home. Her name was Leda, and she was the daughter of one of the poorer fishermen in town who was eager to ingratiate himself with Bren. She was very young, a sweet little sparrow of a girl. When Bren was away, she became a sort of pet to Alina and Brega. Leda loved children, and she played with Gunnar and with Brega's girls every chance she got.

"Do you think he will marry her?" Alina asked Brega one evening.

Brega shook her head. "Not if he holds true to his form. He will give her to someone else in marriage as soon as she falls pregnant. Probably a good outcome for her. Her husband will treat her well and provide for her and her child." Then she shrugged. "I am assuming that's what will happen. Bren might take her for himself. Who can say?"

Alina nodded. "I actually wouldn't mind Bren marrying this one. I like having her around."

Brega smiled wanly and nodded, but didn't say anything.

About a month later, Bren came back home, three days after that, Leda went missing. They were having the first snowfall of the season, and Alina became worried about her. She and Brega and Gerda went to every house in the village, searching. Finally, she spoke to Holgur, the blacksmith. He was crouched over a length of metal when she approached him and asked if he'd seen Leda. He looked up. Years before, a spark or a sliver of metal had flown into his right eye. Now it was white as winter. His other eye met hers as he said, "I saw her just after the noon meal. She was walking toward your house, Lady." He hesitated a moment, staring at the ground and added, "I noticed a man following her."

"Which man?" Alina's heart was thudding hard and slow in her chest.

"The tall one that came with the new wife. What's his name?" Holgur now squinted at the ceiling of his shop.

"Huus?" Alina asked.

"That's the one," he nodded. "I only noticed him because he had that look in his eyes." He glanced at Alina and added, "You know it. The look of a hunter going after prey."

A shard of ice seemed to rip down Alina's spine. She wanted to ask Holgur why he hadn't told someone, but instead asked, "Do you know where Bren is?"

"Yes, I saw him going back into the hall just before you came."

"Thank you, Holgur." Alina ran to the hall. She explained everything to Bren, who hadn't realized Leda was gone. The time she had to spend persuading him was fatal. Bren finally made some joke about shouldering the burden of women's worries, and reluctantly took his men went into the forest. It was nearly dusk when they returned with Bren in the lead, carrying a limp form wrapped in his cloak. His face was grim and set. He went into the hall. Everyone followed him in; the only sound was Gerda and Brega weeping.

was about to be sick. She hurried out of the hall, ran around to the side of the building and vomited.

A single shaft of light shone through the clouds of that day. Just before dinner that evening, there was a knock at Alina's door. She opened it, and was surprised to find Holgur standing there, wringing his shapeless felt hat in his blocky hands. "What is it, Holgur?" she asked, her arms crossed over her stomach because it was roiling again.

"Sorry to disturb you, Lady," he answered. "I just wanted to say that you were right. Huus was after that little girl. I saw it, and I did nothing." His good eye was red-rimmed and wet. "Please forgive me."

Part of Alina wanted to scream at him, but the part of her that was still holding on to her sanity answered gently, "I am not the one who was hurt. It isn't my place to forgive you. Perhaps you could speak to her father?"

He shook his head. "I know that one. He's useless, and probably sleeping off his drink somewhere. It's too late for the little girl, but I will never let it happen again. If I ever see Huus, or any other good-for-nothing going after a woman, I will do whatever I can to stop him."

"I see." Alina hadn't been able to protect Leda. She had also failed her. Whatever anger she felt toward the blacksmith faded away. "At the least, come and tell me, or Brega, or Bren, or some man you know you can trust."

"Pardon, Lady, but it won't be Bren," he answered. "I heard him. He believed the liars over you and me." He ran one hand down the side of his face. His white eye gleamed like a pearl in the near dark. "I won't let it happen again."

She laid a hand on his arm. "You see better with your one good eye than most men see with two." He nodded once and went away.

The next time Alina woke, it was to the sound of pieces of her drying rack hitting the ground. Her eyes flew open, and she was alarmed to discover that she wasn't alone. The lowest level of the rack was scattered on the floor. A few pieces of dried meat lay on the floor as well, and there were two gray-furred animals in the cave. They were larger than cats, with ears like a cat's, but with ringed tails. They had black fur around their eyes that made them look like thieves. As she watched, one of the animals stood on its hind legs to reach with paws—clever little paws like tiny hands — for the next level of the rack and the meat hanging on it. "No!" Alina shouted, and sat up. The animals froze, staring at her through their black-ringed eyes. The one that had been standing hissed at her before dropping back to all fours. Then they both scuttled for the opening and were gone. Every bit of the meat that had been drying on that lower level — close to half of it — was gone with them.

Were those creatures *vittra* — the spirits that her mother had sometimes warned her about? She had never seen an animal like these, so maybe they were spirits? Had she offended them by claiming this cave as her home? If so, she had paid dearly for it. All that meat….

Alina moaned and got to her feet. *How long have I been asleep?* she wondered, staring around the chamber. She thought she had probably slept more than one night. For one thing, she was dreadfully thirsty. Her eyes were gummy, and her tongue stuck to the roof of her mouth. She had her cup filled with water sitting near the bed, so she took several swallows before doing anything else. It was then that she noticed other signs that she had been out for a long time. Her fire hadn't just died down, it was completely cold, not one ember left. And something stank of rot.

Her heart fell. The meat that had not made it onto the drying rack was going bad, and she had just lost a lot of the meat that was dry. She ran one hand over the top of her head. *Think, Alina!* she ordered herself. *Check your legs first.* The bruises on her left leg looked as bad as ever, but maybe she could make out some yellowing at the edges. She grabbed her knife and cut the threads from her bandage on her right leg. When everything was peeled away, she sighed with relief. The swelling had gone down a little, and the gashes didn't appear to be as red at their edges as they had the last time. The smallest gash was fully scabbed over, and the next largest was forming scabs at each end.

Her stitches still held, and that wound, while still mostly open, showed no sign of sickening. She needed to eat, but couldn't stomach it with the stench of the meat. So Alina began picking up the pieces that were rotting. It was so much meat. She had forgotten how much. She carried it outside, depositing it on the pile of bones. She would gather firewood and burn it along with the rest of the carcass when the sun went down so that darkness would hide the smoke. The stew by the fire had gone cold and smelled rancid. Knowing it would probably make her sick, Alina dumped it into the river, and scrubbed the pot with handfuls of sand.

Now though, she had to eat. Since landing on this side of the sea, her body had become thinner than it had ever been, but now it felt hollowed out. She washed her hands in the river and filled her pot. It was hard going just walking back up to the cave. She was out of breath by the time she slipped inside. *Fire first*, she told herself. Gathering kindling and dried leaves, Alina went and rummaged on the shelf for her flint. When she found it, she sat down and struck the flint against her iron hatchet head. It took several tries, but finally a spark kindled on the leaves. Gently fanning and then blowing, she coaxed the infant flame and fed it more kindling, and then larger pieces of wood.

She sat back and let out a breath. *Next I will have to wash the rags, and go find more garlic.* But first she took another long drink of water and ate a couple of pieces of meat and a few berries she had found before the bear showed up. She surveyed the damage the black-eyed animals had done, and rubbed her forehead with both hands. By the time she had recovered enough to hunt again, Alina would have eaten all, or nearly all of what was left of the bear meat. She had been counting on that meat for the winter. *Well,* she thought, letting out a long sigh, *at least I have the pelt.*

It was after midday before she was able to dress her wounds again. She had washed the rags and hung them on the drying rack near the fire. The rack was still in good shape. It was just the little cross branches on the bottom level that were knocked off. Alina pounded out some of the new garlic and made a fresh poultice. As she re-dressed the two bigger wounds, she wondered how long she would have to keep them covered. She sniffed and grimaced. And how long it would be before she could bathe.

She decided to give herself a partial bath. She had one nice, tight basket, so she took it out and filled it with water, then gathered a half dozen smooth rocks from the river. She dropped the rocks into the edge of the fire to heat. While she waited she thought about what she might be able to do that day. She still wanted to try to make a ladder

"They have." She sat in the chair by the bed. "This one's pretty enough, I guess."

"Until she falls pregnant," Freda growled. She shifted in her bed and said, "Do you know what irks me the most about all this?" Without waiting for an answer, she said, "People assume Bren is the way he is because that is how I raised him."

"I didn't assume that," Alina smiled. "At least, not after exchanging a dozen words with you."

Freda chuckled. "What an awful way for him to introduce you to us. You walked into that dinner blind." Her smile faded. "It was cruel of him."

Alina considered this before answering, "I don't think he meant to be cruel."

"Then he is a coward," Freda said, and she downed the rest of her drink. "What I have never told you is that Bren had a half-dozen siblings." She let out a huff of breath. "Four brothers and two sisters."

Alina kept her words carefully neutral. "I think I heard from someone that you'd had other children, but I didn't know it was so many."

Freda nodded. "Two died during birth. Three of various sicknesses when they were small, and one – he was named Gunnar, like your boy -- drowned in the river when he was seven. Bren was ten."

Alina shook her head. "I am so sorry, Freda. I can't imagine…."

"Bren's father," Freda interrupted her, "He was the one who took that drowning the hardest. Gunnar had been his favorite, but after he died, Bren was his boy. He could do no wrong. And when Bren was barely a man, his father died in a hunting accident. Bren became master. There was no one to say no to him." Her eyes, ringed with dark circles, met Alina's. "That is to say, there was no man anymore. He hadn't listened to me for years."

A small shiver ran up Alina's spine. She didn't know her husband. Not after all this time. He only let her see what he wanted her to see. *Well, most people do that*, she thought as she left Freda, *but he has become a master at hiding himself.*

Three days later, Alina was on her way to her house to check on Gerda and Gunnar. When she rounded a corner, there was a small crowd blocking her way. Beyond them, she heard laughing, and Gunnar's giggling. She pushed through to see what was going on, and found her son playing sword fight with sticks against a man whose back was turned to her. Not Bren. Bren didn't play with his son. Gerda was looking on with her arms crossed over ample bosom, and a wide grin on her face.

"Take that!" Gunnar yelled, lunging forward and jabbing his stick at the man's arm. The man fell with a cry of mock pain. When Gunnar turned in triumph toward Gerda, the man swatted his behind with his stick. "Hey!" Gunnar yelled. "Not fair!"

"Never turn your back on your enemy," the man replied, laughing. Alina knew that laugh.

"Ebbe!" she cried. He stood and turned, and she ran to him and threw her arms around his neck. He lifted her off her feet and swung her around as he had done since they were children.

"So good to see you, little sister!" He set her down and stepped back. "And look at you — a picture of health."

"You look well yourself," she laughed. "What are you doing here?"

"Father sent me." A line between his brows deepened. "He's been having disturbing dreams, and wanted to reassure himself that you were all right."

She laid a hand on his arm, and put her other arm around her son, who had just squeezed in. "I am all right. How is Father? He's not ill, is he?"

Ebbe shook his head. "I think he's just getting a little old and a little anxious."

"Have you seen Bren yet?" she asked.

"No." His eyes narrowed. "Is something amiss?"

Alina looked around. She was going to have to explain this. She raised her voice and announced, "People, this is my brother, Ebbe. He has come on a long journey to us. Please welcome him as you welcomed me six years ago." Smiles and nods followed this, and a few people began to disperse. To Ebbe, she said, "Let's go inside, but leave the door open."

"Ah, yes." He turned to see curious eyes still watching them. "The less gossip the better."

Gerda went off in search of refreshments. Ebbe sat down and pulled Gunnar close, saying, "I have something for you, Nephew." From a pack of his things that had been lying on the floor, he pulled a leather-wrapped bundle about as long as Alina's arm. When Gunnar untied the strings, he pulled out a short bow and quiver of arrows. "Now listen," he told the boy as he admired his gift, "This is not a toy. This is serious business, understand?" When Gunnar gave him a solemn nod, he went on. "Never, ever aim an arrow at anything or anyone that you do not mean to shoot."

The arrows were blunt at the tips, and Alina remembered how she had gotten a set like this from her father when she was Gunnar's age. To her son, she said, "Why don't you go over and visit with Inge and Ava for a while. I want to talk to your uncle. You can start practicing with these when you get back."

Gunnar left them, but he dragged his feet and kept looking back at his bow until he was out the door. Ebbe leaned toward Alina and fingered the amber pendant, murmuring, "I remember this."

Alina asked, "How did you know I had a son?"

"Bren told us. I think it was two years ago."

Alina felt a sudden stab of hurt. "Bren came to see you?"

"He did. Another trading trip. We were disappointed that he didn't bring you with him."

Alina was disappointed, too, but not surprised. "Did he give a reason for my not coming?"

"He said you didn't want to leave your son while he was so small."

Another half-truth to add to Bren's hoard. "I would have come." She dropped down into the chair opposite her brother. "But he didn't tell me he was going to see you, and he would never have brought me."

Ebbe frowned. "Why not?"

Just then, Gerda came in with a pitcher and a basket. Alina glanced at her, then back at Ebbe. "Because I would have told you the truth."

Summer was on the wane by the time Alina took the stitches out of the largest wound. It hurt to pull the threads out, but there was something satisfying about watching them come loose from her flesh one by one. Several of the places bled little beads of scarlet, but she knew they would heal quickly. The wound itself was now one long, jagged scar running alongside the two smaller scars. She was going to carry the scars for the rest of her life, and this one wound still hurt inside, a burning ache that made her wonder if the pain would ever go away.

In the past weeks, while her legs were recovering, she had made a ladder, a fish trap and a wooden barrier that served as a door. When she slept, Alina propped the door shut with a pair of large rocks. It was enough to keep small animals out, but that was all. The ladder was made from a couple of young trees. She had tested it out, both inside the cave and outside. It was sturdy enough to hold her weight, and after some adjustments, steady enough on the ground.

She intended to cross the river with it that day. The weather was still warm, but wouldn't be for long. So, packing some food and taking her bag and her bow, she hefted the ladder over her left shoulder and went down to the water, where she stopped to take her boots off. She watched the current for a moment, gathering her courage, then stepped in. She had decided, after more deliberation, to attempt the crossing carrying everything, instead of making two trips. With great care, one step after another, Alina settled her feet with each step before taking the next. When she was about halfway across, her right foot slid sideways on a mossy stone. She gasped and planted the front end of the ladder on the riverbed, which gave her a moment to regain her balance. *This was a terrible idea,* she thought, but she was already committed to it, so she pulled the ladder back onto her shoulder. Gritting her teeth she took another step. And another. After what seemed like a lifetime, she was at the far bank. Once there, she sat, panting and waiting for her heart to calm down.

She closed her eyes. Somewhere off to her right sounded the rattle of a woodpecker. She focused on that, and after a bit her breathing slowed. Alina put her boots back on, got to her feet, hefted the ladder, and set off. A flock of little birds was feeding in the meadow, tumbling over each other and chattering. When they saw her coming, they flew up in a mass, circled the meadow once, and took off. The day was mellow, but when she stood atop the rise, a bank of clouds, black like a sooty smudge stretched across the sky to the north and west. She didn't waste time studying the oncoming clouds, but started down the hill as quickly as she dared. She found the set of three stones, looked to her right, and saw the white of the hole's rim.

Putting her gear down first, she carefully lowered the ladder into the hole. She had been afraid that it might not be tall enough, but the end jutted out of the hole about a hand's length. She rocked the ladder a bit to make sure it was steady on the ground below. Her heart started racing again as she contemplated climbing down. *I can't sit here all day,* she reminded herself after a minute. *There's a storm coming.*

Alina got on her belly, turned her feet to the ladder, and set them on the second rung down. She pushed herself back until her toes touched the next rung. Now she put her hands on the ladder, and slowly descended into the hole. The bottom was dry and firm, and after a little bit, her eyes adjusted to the dim light. She appeared to be at the very end of an underground cave that opened up to her left. How big it was she couldn't tell, and would never be able to tell unless she brought light down with her. She took a few steps away from the ladder, and felt something give underfoot. She stepped back and stared, bending down to see in the gloom. It was a desiccated animal, some unfortunate creature that had fallen in so long ago there was no telling what it had been. She turned back toward the ladder. She had gone far enough.

Next time I will bring a torch, Alina thought, blinking at the dark. She set her gear down and got out her hatchet. With the dull end, she pounded at one of the white veins running across the rock surface. She had brought another clay pot with her. She filled it with the salt, tied the lid on the pot, and stowed it away in her bag. It was time to go. She gathered everything and climbed back up into the light.

By the time she reached the river again, the wind had picked up, and it had a chill in it. Alina shucked off her boots and started across. She had left the ladder in the hole. There were no signs that anyone else used the salt hole, and she didn't want to have to carry the ladder back and forth across the water every time she went there. The wind was out of the north, and it pushed at her back as she maneuvered over the slippery stones. She checked the fish trap before climbing the bank on her side. To her surprise, there was a fish inside. Not a big one, but enough for her dinner.

She was hunting and gathering every day again, trying to lay in food for the winter. The cold was coming, and she wasn't quite ready. She did have a good stack of firewood – enough to last about a week, and there were baskets of dried deer meat, and what little was left of the bear meat. In one corner of the back curve of the cave sat two good-sized baskets full of some kind of nut that Alina had discovered on the forest floor several days before. *One more deer,* she told herself. *I need the meat and the skin. If I get one more, that might be enough.*

The next day, she went out with her bow and arrows to hunt. She was wearing her winter tunic, but not the leggings. The day was cool and bright. It had rained the night before, and now the sky had that scrubbed look, pale blue, that she associated with autumn. She followed game trails for several hours before finding fresh deer droppings. She dropped to a crouch and studied the ground. There were tracks – lots of them – in the soft earth, and she thought they had to be close. A few minutes later came the distinct bellow of a buck. They were downwind of her, so she circled around where the noise had come from, and topping a small ridge, she spotted them. There were maybe a dozen or so animals in the herd. The buck was on the far side, but there were plenty of females. She came in closer, quiet as a cat, and when one of the females turned, took her shot.

For a second, she thought she had missed. The rest of the herd took off, and it looked like her deer was with them, but only for a second. The doe dropped in mid-step. Alina hurried over to inspect her kill. "I am sorry, cousin," she whispered. "I need your meat and hide." The arrow had gone into the animal's lungs. Its death was nearly instant. That was good. She hated when she missed a lethal shot, and the animal suffered.

"You're a big girl," she murmured, tugging at the doe's front legs. The doe probably outweighed her. How was she going to get it home? She started by pointing the doe's head downhill and slitting her throat. While the blood ran out, she gutted the carcass and put aside the parts she didn't want, keeping the liver and small intestine, and the bladder. Then she cut off the head. That lightened the load some, but was it enough? She stood back, assessing. *No, I am going to have to drag this home.*

She cut down two sturdy saplings, stripped the branches, and laid the trunks side by side. Then she took the coil of rope out of her bag, and working quickly, laced the deer to the poles. When the carcass was secure, she stepped to the ends of the poles and picked them up. Turning her back, she tucked the poles under her arms and started moving. She was about an hour's walk from the cave. She took a deep breath, leaned into the pull, and hauled the poles downhill before turning toward home.

Every so often she looked back over her shoulder to make sure nothing was stalking her. About halfway through her trek, she paused to take a drink. When she looked behind her, a familiar shadow went sliding between the trees, probably more than a hundred paces back. Turning again, she picked the poles up and hurried forward. Now, every time she looked back, it seemed that the shadow was nearer than it had been the time before.

Finally, she made a decision. There was no way she was going to make it home before the wolf caught up with her. So she dropped the poles, turned, and put an arrow to her bow. The wolf skidded to a stop about fifty paces away and stared at her. "A wolf is not a dog," her father had said many times. "Do not expect it to act like one."

But in that moment, Alina was struck by this animal's similarities to dogs. The very canine way it held its head, the tilt of its ears, the snuffing nose. "I don't want to kill you," she called out, and raised the bow to aim. It could not have possibly understood her, but maybe her stance scared it, because it trotted off and disappeared into the trees.

Alina did note that it didn't go back the way it came. It had gone off to her left. She waited a minute before putting her bow and arrow away and taking up the poles again. After what seemed like a lot more than an hour, the rock formation that was home loomed above the trees. She was nearly there. She thought she was going as fast as she could move, but with home in sight, she picked up her pace, even though the long scar on her leg screamed with burning pain. She kept looking behind her. Nothing.

Finally, she was at the opening, and realized that here was another problem. Getting this carcass inside was going to be difficult. She could drag it on the ground, but that would risk damaging the hide. She thought for a moment, then ran inside and got the deer hide she had been using for a rug. She brought it out, untied the deer from the poles, laid the carcass on the hide, and inch by inch, dragged it in. She sat down for a second to catch her breath, and saw a gray shadow moving across the opening. Alina jumped to her feet and nocked an arrow to her bow, shouting. "Go away!"

The bear had been too big to squeeze through the opening, but this wolf was not too big. She didn't want to shoot it, but thought she might have to. The wolf stared at her for a long moment, then turned and disappeared. Alina let out a breath. Then she put her weapon down and slid her door into place and anchored it with the rocks.

That night she dreamed she was in the salt hole, standing at the ladder, looking up. She needed to climb the ladder, needed to get out, but the bear was there, pacing back and forth, snuffing at the hole. And then it wasn't the bear anymore. It was Huus. He stood at the lip of the hole, watching her with a sly smile on his face, and a knife in his hand. In the way of dreams, Huus became Bren, who didn't threaten her in any way. He wouldn't even look at her, but he wouldn't let her come up, either. And finally, Bren was gone, and *she* was standing there, smiling down at Alina, clearly satisfied by Alina's distress. Finally, she said, “Let me take care of this,” and she pulled the ladder out of the hole, leaving Alina alone in the dark

CHAPTER SIX

Freda died about a month after Bren brought Kiah to the village. Alina and Brega stood, hand-in-hand at the opening of the burial mound. The rest of the villagers were ranged behind them watching the men carrying the bier through the village and down the hill. Alina heard sobs from the crowd. Freda had been a stern woman, but she had loved her people, and they had loved her. Their sorrow tore at her own heart.

She was the best mother-in-law anyone could ever have," Brega murmured with a sniff.

"She was," Alina agreed, her vision blurry with tears. "She has gone too soon."

When the bier came close, she saw that Bren was one of the men carrying it. And the man just behind him was Marav, the gray-eyed man she had spoken to on the day Kiah came. He looked up as he passed, met her eyes for a moment, and lowered his gaze again.

After the funeral was over, Alina asked Brega, "Why was Marav one of the bearers? Is he kin?"

Brega nodded. "He's a cousin, the son of one of Freda's brothers, I believe."

"I would never have guessed," Alina answered. "He and Bren look nothing alike."

"No, Bren takes after his father."

"Did you know Bren's father?" Alina asked.

"Only a little," Brega said. "He died before Bren and I were married.

"Was Bren like him? I mean…." Here she faltered.

Brega gave her a knowing look. "I don't know for sure, but I don't think he behaved as Bren does. Can you imagine any man doing to Freda what Bren does to us?"

Alina felt a smile tug at her lips. It was the first in many days. "She'd have had his head in a basket."

Now Brega looked troubled. "You and I are not Freda, but we are making our way through this, aren't we?"

Alina put her arms around her and hugged her hard. "We are doing what we must, Sister. I am so glad I have you. I don't know what I would have done if you had been like Agnes." After a moment, she added, "Or Kiah."

Brega returned the embrace, but when she pulled back, she said, "We should try to help Kiah. She does not understand what is happening with Bren."

"She isn't pregnant yet, is she?" Alina asked.

"If she is, I haven't heard," Brega answered. "But that day is coming, and we should try to prepare her for it."

"I don't know, Brega. There is something about her that makes me think she would not welcome anything from us."

Brega raised her eyebrows. "Not even the truth?"

"Especially not the truth," Alina said. "I don't think the fourth wife will appreciate the first wife telling her about her husband. She won't want to hear what's waiting for her."

Brega sighed. "Well, maybe so."

But Alina learned that this conversation was not the end of the matter when Kiah took a sudden dislike to Brega. The following week, on an afternoon when the four women were sitting together spinning thread, Kiah sighed and shifted in her seat again and again. Every time she looked toward Brega, her eyes shot darts at her. Finally, Brega spoke up. "Is something bothering you, Kiah?"

Kiah's cornflower blue eyes teared up, and she said, "You are no true wife to Bren." She glanced at Alina and Agnes, and added, "Not one of you is."

Agnes scoffed and rolled her eyes, but it was Alina who answered. "Can you tell us what you mean by that?"

"You don't welcome him into your beds anymore, do you?" Kiah's eyes swam with tears, but her expression was triumphant. "He only comes to me."

Biting off each word, one by one, Agnes asked, "Are you pregnant yet, Kiah?"

"Agnes…." Brega reprimanded her softly.

"Why do you keep asking me that?" Kiah cried. "You and her." She pointed to Brega and Agnes. Then she looked at Alina. "But not you."

"I only asked because I am trying to prepare you…." Brega began.

"You are lying." Kiah threw her spindle down and stormed out.

At the river's edge lay a dead tree that had been ripped from its moorings long ago, maybe by a flood, maybe a windstorm. Alina had, over the months, harvested its dead branches for firewood, but she left the trunk where it was. It made a nice place to sit and watch the water.

On this day, she had a fish she had roasted, along with some greens and fungus. She knew the weather would turn soon, and wanted to spend as much time outside as she could before that happened.

She was about halfway through her meal, thinking about how she might construct a hob to cook on, when a fluttering noise startled her. A crow had landed on the other end of the tree trunk. From her earliest childhood Alina had been told stories of heroes receiving messages from crows. "Well hello, Crow," she said. "Do you have a message for me?"

The crow didn't answer, but stared at her with his black eyes, bright as polished obsidian. He flapped his wings, and that was when she saw it. His left wing – the one away from her – was injured. He was holding it out a little from his body. She had started to put a piece of fish in her mouth when she remembered another story, one the priest had told her. Something about a holy man living in a cave in a wilderness, and crows bringing him food. She glanced at the piece of fish in her hand. The crow was looking at it, too.

"Are you hungry?" she asked, holding the piece a little higher. Sure enough, his head cocked to see the bit of fish she held aloft. Slowly, slowly, she reached out toward him with the fish. He bounced back a couple of steps, but didn't try to fly off. When her hand was about halfway across the trunk, she laid the piece down. "There you go." She turned her face away to be less threatening, and waited. After a few seconds, she heard a scuttling noise. When she turned back, the crow was back on his end of the trunk with the fish in his beak.

Alina knew it wasn't usually a good idea to feed wild animals. Her father had instilled this into her from the very beginning of her training in the woods. Feeding something like a wolf could be a very bad idea.

But this crow? What could it hurt? When he had finished the fish, she laid a piece of roasted fungus down to see what he would do with it. After considering her offer, he took it and ate it, too. Alina continued to share her dinner with the crow until the food was gone. She held up both hands to show that they were empty. "That's all there is."

Still, he didn't fly off. Alina turned her attention back to the river. The shadows had grown long. The sun skimmed the tops of the trees. It would be dark soon. "I should go in," she told the bird. "Thank you for your company." Moving slowly, and keeping her face turned away from him, she stood up. She stooped to retrieve her bow and arrows, and that's when she heard the fluttering that told her he had flown from the trunk. But as she turned to go back to the cave, she spotted him perched on the branch of a nearby oak, and he was still watching her with his bright eyes. For some reason, this made her smile. That night, when she said her prayers, she added, "Thank you for the crow."

The third time Alina took Gunnar into the woods for his training, Marav spotted them leaving and called out, "Where are you going, Lady?"

She hesitated, wondering if he would be the kind of man to tell Bren what she was doing. Gunnar decided for her. He answered, "We're going hunting."

Marav grinned. "Are you, now? Would you like some company?"

She hesitated again, but he gave her a pointed look, and she understood. There had been a rash of attacks from outlaws in the forest over the spring. The attacks had been to the south, but Marav was probably right to be concerned about a woman and child alone in the forest – even if that woman was armed and capable. "All right," she said, "You can come."

"That's great, thank you." He directed his comment to Gunnar, as if it was the boy who had given permission. "Let me go get my bow. I'll be right back." And he ran off.

"Who is he?" Gunnar asked her.

"He's a cousin of your father's," she answered.

Moments later, he trotted back into view, slinging his quiver over one shoulder. "So, where are we going today?"

"No place in particular," Alina answered. "Gunnar needs practice with his bow," here she shrugged, "and I need practice with mine. We will give whatever we kill to the cook."

They chatted about nothing much until they were well into the trees, when, as if by unspoken agreement, they fell silent. Marav was a good hunter. He took down two geese, and he gave Gunnar some tips to correct his shooting stance. Alina decided it had been a good afternoon when she finally put Gunnar to bed that night. She liked Marav. He had complimented her on her shot when she got a fat rabbit, he was kind to Gunnar, and acted like he felt easy in their company. He was protective and, unlike his cousin, not too busy to spend time with them.

A few days later, Kiah sought Alina out to reprimand her about her behavior at dinner the previous evening. She caught her arm just outside the great hall and said, "You won't even talk to him," referring to their husband.

Alina had to suppress an incredulous laugh as she wrenched her arm away. "Do you think he is bothered that I don't talk to him?"

“I’m sure he is,” she said, drawing herself up. “Men need women to talk to them.”

Alina’s experience had taught her something quite different. “Who told you that?” From the corner of her eye, she noted that a handful of people had stopped to watch and listen.

“Well,” Kiah’s blue eyes rolled heavenward, trying to remember. “My mother,” she spluttered, “or maybe it was my aunt.” She stopped, thinking before she finished, “You cannot be so stupid that you don’t know this. Every woman knows this.” It sounded like something she had recited to herself to make sure she got it right. Or maybe it was something that had frequently been said to her

Alina rubbed at the place between her eyebrows where she could feel the beginnings of a headache. What she wanted at the moment was to get away from this woman. She swallowed her pride and managed to keep her tone mild as she answered, “I am sure you are right. Please excuse me.” With that, she walked away, pushing past a spectator without bothering to see who it was.

An hour later, with Gunnar happily ensconced at Brega’s house, she got her bow and arrows and went into the woods by herself. She just needed to breathe.

She thought she was alone, but after a few minutes, she heard the sound of someone clearing his throat behind her. She turned, half raising her bow, but it was only Marav. When he saw the expression on her face he asked, “Are you all right?”

She let out a long sigh. “Are you following me?”

He held up both hands. “I don’t have to be following you. I can go back over there and hide behind those trees. You’ll never know I am here.”

This made Alina laugh, despite her mood.

He took a few steps toward her, his expression more sober. "I noticed you talking to the new wife a while ago. Or rather, I noticed her talking to you. Is she the reason you're here?"

Alina nodded. "She is the reason today." She gestured to the trees around them. "I didn't come out into the woods for a long time after I came to this village, but lately…." She trailed off, thinking, then said, "I guess I need to get away from people sometimes."

Marav narrowed his eyes. "Your home village is a long way from here?"

"Yes, about four days' journey east. Why do you ask?"

He lifted a shoulder. "You are far from your own people. That must be difficult."

"There are people I miss," she admitted, "but I've been here long enough now that the people here are mine."

He gave her a slow smile that lit up those gray-green eyes. Alina felt the pull of them and had to look away. He gestured to her bow and arrows. "Are you hunting today, or are those for show?"

She laughed again, and said, "That's one of the nice things about hunting. If you don't come back with anything, everyone shrugs and wishes you better luck the next time."

"Then may I join you on your unlucky hunting trip?"

Since they weren't hunting, they talked as they went deeper into the trees. He told her about his home village and family. "I am the third of five sons," he said. "I think my father was relieved when I decided to go off and seek my living elsewhere."

"And your mother?" Alina asked.

"My mother cried and cried," he answered solemnly. "She's probably still crying."

This struck Alina as so funny that she burst out laughing, and had to hang on to the trunk of a nearby tree. When she wiped her eyes, Marav said, "See? You're crying, too."

"Stop it," she told him. He just grinned in reply.

After a few minutes more of walking, he asked, "Would you like to see my favorite place?"

She was surprised. "You haven't been here that long. You already have a favorite place in these woods?"

"I do. And I think it might become your favorite place, too. I am happy to share."

"Is it far? They will expect me back for the evening meal."

It's not far, just a little bit of a challenge to find." When she nodded, he said. "Follow me."

They had only gone a few minutes more when they came to the bottom of a steep hill. Alina recognized it. She had been here several times, but the steepness of the rise always made her turn back or turn to the side. "Up there?" she asked doubtfully.

He smiled, "That's too much work. In here." He gestured toward a tumble of boulders at the foot of the hill. "Come behind those."

She followed. They had to climb up to get behind the boulders, but between them and the hill was a ravine that broadened into a tiny valley tucked behind a fold of rocky land. It was like the crusted end of bread that falls away and hangs off a loaf. "How did you find this?" Alina asked. "I would never have guessed from the outside that there was anything here but the hill."

He nodded. "It hides itself, doesn't it?"

The valley was dotted with tiny white flowers. "It's a perfect hiding place," she murmured.

"That's what I thought," he agreed. "Just enough sunlight comes in to keep it warm, and the rise of the land around it keeps out the wind." He plopped himself down in the grass and gestured to her to do the same.

Alina sat, just out of arm's length, facing him. "You are lucky to have found this place." She drew in a long breath and let it out. "It's peaceful here."

He nodded, and then shrugged. "It is, until a storm comes along."

She cast about for something else to say. "Why did you come to our village? I mean, you could have gone just about anywhere."

"That's true. I could have." He plucked a stem of grass and began toying with it. "I suppose I chose to come here because Bren is family. I hoped that connection would help me find my place in the world."

"And has it?"

His eyes met hers briefly before he looked away again. He had little of Bren's bravado, she decided. And that might be a good thing. Finally he said, "Far too early to tell, but I keep hoping."

Several minutes passed where the only sound was the breeze that lifted stray strands of her hair. Alina closed her eyes, enjoying the warmth of the sun on her neck and back. One by one, her muscles loosened and relaxed. Then there was a rustle in the grass. She opened her eyes. Marav was now lying on his back, knees bent, his hands folded on his chest, his eyes searching the sky. Alina glanced up, too. The sun's position told her that she still had plenty of time to make it back to the village for supper.

She plucked one of the little flowers and twirled its stem in her fingers. When a bee settled on a blossom near her knee, she sat still and watched it. She had no real fear that she would be stung, and the insect's dance on the face of the bloom entranced her. After another moment, it went buzzing away over her head, and something about its sudden flight made her mentally shake herself. What was she doing? If she and Marav were caught together, even though they had done nothing wrong, Bren could kill her or sell her into slavery, separate her from her children.

She was about to get up and go when Marav said, "Can I be honest with you?"

The question startled her, and she quieted. "Of course." Her hands were shaking now, so she stuffed them in her lap.

He sat up again. "I think you should know that I…" he coughed, then cleared his throat. "Well, from the first time I saw you, I knew you were special." He sighed. "In truth, you have become dear to me." He looked up and met her eyes. "And I believe that you feel something for me, too." When she started to protest, he held up one hand. "You don't need to say anything. I won't endanger you." Then he looked around him and added, "Well, maybe I already have." His eyes turned back to her. "You are dear to me, and for that reason, I want you to hold your head up when you're among the villagers and Bren's other wives. You are more than you give yourself credit for."

She started to argue, to tell him that she had a very firm sense of her own worth, thank you. But as she thought about it, she realized that lately she had stood in the background more often than not. She had let Kiah rail at her that morning and had not put her in her place. Throughout her childhood she had been loved, which should have sustained her inner strength, but then she came here. Bren did not love her. He never had, never pretended to. Brega loved her, of course, and Gerda, but that was different. And now Marav…. Finally, she said, "You have put us both in danger, Marav. But when is life ever safe?" She stood up. "We should go."

He stood, too, his expression chagrined. "I will take you to the edge of the woods and leave you. I'll enter the village at a different place." He sighed and added, "And don't worry, I won't bring it up again."

He looked so sad that she took three steps to him, put her hands on either side of his face, and kissed him. After a startled second, he circled one hand around the back of her neck, and returned her kiss, his mouth on hers tender, but hungry. Alina only allowed it for a moment before she pulled away. Tears stung her eyes. "I should not have done that. You and I…we cannot be." Leaving him where he stood, she climbed up and out of the valley and hurried home alone through the woods. Remorse flooded her. *Shouldn't have…shouldn't have….*

When she got back she was grateful to find that she was alone in her house. Gerda was far too perceptive, and Alina didn't want to have to make up a story to satisfy her. She also had some time to compose herself before the meal. She used it to change her dress – though there was nothing wrong with the one she had on – and wash her face. Then she sat on her bed and tried to calm her thundering heart. After several long minutes where she cleared her head by thinking of nothing but waves hitting the shore, she got up and went to Brega's to get Gunnar.

The crow became Alina's companion. It followed her, flitting from branch to branch as she hunted and gathered food and supplies for the coming winter. He never flew far, and Alina guessed that he could not because of the way he held his wing. She fed him every time she ate a meal. It was only a few scraps each time, so it didn't feel like she was wasting her food. She did worry about Crow. The weather had turned colder, and soon it would be dangerously cold, or so she assumed. Many birds flew away in the winter and came back in the spring, but she wasn't sure that crows did that. Even if they did, this one couldn't.

On the third evening that she fed him, Crow showed up to the tree trunk with something already in his beak. He came a few hops toward her and dropped what he was carrying. Then he hopped back to his place at the far end.

"What's this?" Alina reached out and picked it up. Crow had brought her a white pebble. When she turned it in her hand, its surface caught the sun and glittered. It wasn't salt. She had seen a lot of this kind of stone, but didn't know what to call it. To Crow, she said, "Thank you. This is pretty." She stripped off a bit of the rabbit she was eating and placed it where Crow had dropped the stone.

In her cave was an irregular bit of jutting rock that formed a tiny shelf. It was too small for practical use, and she had thought she might try to carve deeper into the wall above it to make the shelf wider, but had never done it. When she went to bed that night, she laid the pebble on the little shelf. In the following weeks, Crow brought a number of gifts. Once it was half a shell from a river mollusk. The outside of the shell was dull brown, but the inside had an iridescent sheen, white and pink, and blue. Another time he brought a leaf that had turned scarlet.

He even brought a feather – not one of his own, but a brown one with white stripes. All of these she placed on the shelf. It was interesting to her to see what Crow thought was valuable. Bright things. Pretty things.

She noticed over time that he seemed to be flying higher, and he was going longer distances. Either his wing was healing, or he had learned to compensate for his injury. One afternoon she came down to the river, and he was waiting for her on the trunk. And in the middle sat his gift. Alina's eyes widened as she picked it up. It was a leather bracelet with five round seeds strung on it. The seeds looked like they had been dyed yellow and green. "Where did you get this?" she whispered, trying it on her wrist. It was too big, so it had probably belonged to a man.

So, there were people close by, or close enough for Crow to find this bracelet and bring it to her. She sat very still for a minute lost in thought, until Crow cawed and flapped his good wing. "Thank you," she told him, and dropped a piece of meat on the trunk. *Maybe there aren't people that close*, she reasoned. *Maybe someone passed through a while back.* "Or maybe not," she muttered. The bracelet had obviously been worn, but it wasn't weathered as if it had been lying on the ground for a long time. So that meant someone, at least one person, probably a man, had been close enough for Crow to bring her his bracelet, and recent enough that the bracelet was still in good condition.

She thought about the people who had attacked her people on the beach, and the hairs on the back of her neck stood up. "It could be people like that," she murmured. "Or it could be people of peace." Then she shrugged. "Or it could be people like mine – sometimes peaceful, and sometimes not." She knew she would run into others, maybe sooner than expected. They would find her, or she would find them. Finally, she put her questions aside and began eating her dinner. She had no power over the future. She could only try to prepare and take care of herself. With that, she dropped another piece of meat on the trunk for Crow.

One afternoon, Alina took her bow and disappeared into the woods again. Gerda was watching Gunnar, so she didn't have to be back till nearly sundown. "I am going hunting," she told Gerda. She told herself the same thing, but she knew it wasn't entirely true, and little by little, her feet carried her toward the hill and the hidden ravine. She had shot a goose, so she reasoned that she had something to show for the time she was gone. She kept looking back over her shoulder to see if Marav was lurking somewhere behind her, but saw no one. Finally, she climbed up behind the boulders and stepped into the ravine.

Marav was already there, sitting on the grass with his back to her. He didn't turn around, but said, "Hello, Lady."

"Please call me by my name," Alina answered. She dropped the goose and her bow and quiver to the ground before she sat to one side of him, but facing him.

He lifted his gray eyes and met hers. "I should go."

She laid a hand lightly on his sleeve. "Before you do, I wanted to talk to you."

He leaned a little away from her, his expression wary. "About what?"

She swallowed. This wasn't going to be easy. "First, I want to thank you for what you said to me the other day. You were right about a couple of things. I was beginning to allow other people to disrespect me." She smiled. "I had it out with Kiah yesterday. She tried to come at me again, and I put her in her place."

He nodded, but kept his gaze on his hands. "I am glad."

She took a deep breath. "You were also right in another matter." Now she was the one who had to look away. "You have become dear to me." She tried to take another breath, but the air didn't want to go all the way down into her lungs. "As I'm sure you can see, I am pregnant." When he didn't answer, she added, "And because I am pregnant, I can't get pregnant." There. It was out. Her heart was racing in her chest.

For a moment, Marav looked confused, but then understanding dawned and his face cleared. "Oh." He reached out and touched her face.

They made love for the first time in the little valley under the summer sun. Their lovemaking was gentle and slow, and when it was over, Alina felt almost happy. She allowed the feeling to wash over her for a while, but then murmured aloud, "What we are doing is risky and stupid."

Beside her, Marav nodded. "It is worth the risk to me, but the risk to you is far greater." He reached over and touched her amber pendant. "This is a pretty thing."

"It was my mother's." Alina had been lying on her back. Now she turned toward him. "You have to understand this, Marav." She stroked a stray blade of grass out of his beard. "As soon as I go into labor with this baby, you and I are done. I won't be able to see you again. Not ever."

She was ready for protests from him, for his ideas about how they could carry on. So she was surprised when he answered, "You say the word, Alina, and I am gone. I will leave the village, and I will not come back."

So he did understand. He understood that she could not leave her children and run off with him. He understood that she could not take the children with her and run off. Bren would come after them. He understood that to continue after the baby was born was impossible. She would get pregnant again, and she might not be able to lure Bren into her bed to cover it up.

"When you to expect your baby to come?" he asked her.

"Late in the fall," she answered.

"I would rather be with you for a few weeks and never again than not be with you at all."

Now tears sprang to Alina's eyes. She kissed him, then sat up and prepared to go. "It's not much of a choice, is it?" With that, she got up, picked up her things, and left the valley.

They agreed to meet no more than twice in one week, but it wasn't long before Alina found herself wishing she could be with him every day. He loved her – she was certain of it, and he was kind, and intelligent, and funny. She found herself lying alone in her bed at night, wondering if there really was a way they could be together. Surely she could figure something out. But she came up blank every time. Then a new problem rose. Alina thought they were being careful, but at the end of the second week, when she and Gerda were alone in the house, Gerda remarked, "You and Marav are going to have to hide yourselves better."

Alina didn't bother to feign innocence. "In what way?" she asked.

"I watch you," Gerda replied, "so I notice things before anyone else would. But in time, other people will notice. You cannot be seen talking to Marav, at least not without Bren standing there." She grimaced and went on, "And you are looking far too happy to be one of Bren's wives."

"Ah." Alina nodded. Too many smiles. Too much contentment in her eyes. She would have to train her face into more dismal lines. She could do that. She said, "The only time I speak to him is when we are arranging to meet."

Gerda stared off at nothing for a moment, then said, "Use the pot."

"The pot?" Alina echoed, mystified. "What pot?"

"The one that cracked last month," Gerda told her. "I never bothered to move it. It's sitting just outside the door. Lay it on its side, or turn it upside down. Figure out a signal and quit talking to him."

"That is a good idea." Alina then asked the question she had to ask, "Do you really think no one else has noticed?"

Gerda shrugged. "I can't be certain, but in my experience, people spend most of their time thinking about themselves. If you fix this now, you may be all right."

"Are you angry with me?" It was a child's question.

Gerda glanced at her, and her expression softened. "I am angry that you are in this situation. If Bren would behave like the man his father was…." She didn't finish.

Alina sat on the edge of the bed. "What we are doing is risky for you, too."

"I will take my lumps if they come," Gerda told her, "but I worry about you. Be careful."

The next time they met, Alina related her conversation with Gerda. Marav suggested that they should never have any kind of routine. They would vary the days they met. And they agreed to use the pot for their signal. If Marav could meet her in the woods, he would turn the pot upside down. If Alina could not meet him, she would turn the pot right side up again, so that he would know when he came back that she had seen his signal, but couldn't come. This only happened once in the fall, when Gunnar took ill.

The boy had a fever and a cough, and it took more than a week of anxious nursing before he began to recover. Soon after this, though, Alina knew her time with Marav was more limited than she had thought. Gerda and Brega both remarked that it was not a good idea for her to be traipsing in the woods when she was so heavy with child. What if she went into labor out in the wild and couldn't get back?

They were right. Nothing she could do to draw attention to herself would be worse now than wandering in the woods with a baby due any day. So one morning, she made sure to pass Marav as he was coming toward the hall. "We have to talk," she murmured.

That afternoon, she opened the door of her house, and was startled to see Marav there, sitting in one of the chairs. She shut the door quickly. "What are you doing here?"

"Gerda let me in," he answered.

Alina sat opposite him. Her throat was already thick with unshed tears. She stared at her hands, locked together in her lap. How was she going to say this?

"It is over, isn't it?" Marav said quietly.

Alina nodded. In the little time she spent with him, she had felt her heart opening to him like a flower in bloom, despite her warnings to herself not to. She loved him, and now she could never be with him again. The top of the table went blurry in her vision.

Marav said nothing for a long time. When Alina finally looked at him, tears were streaming from his closed eyes, and he was quietly sobbing. Alina stood up and went around to his chair. She laid a hand on his shoulder, and that seemed to stir him. He rose and gathered her in his arms. “I am sorry,” he whispered. “So sorry.”

Her own broken voice was muffled in his shirt. He smelled of mead and salt. “Don’t be sorry. You have given me such happiness, and I will never forget it.” She let him hold her another moment before she pulled away. “I hope you find someone you are free to love.”

He nodded, wiping his eyes on his sleeve. He could not wish the same for her, but he said, “You will always be my beloved. And don’t worry. I will do whatever I must to keep you safe.” He kissed her tenderly, then kissed her forehead, and he was gone.

Alina turned around to survey the now-empty room, and that was when she saw it. Sitting on the bed was a bag made of white wool. She opened the drawstring and pulled out a carved wooden cup. She knew Marav had done the carving, because on one side was a depiction of the hill where the ravine lay hidden, and on the opposite side were little flowers, just like the white flowers that grew there. She counted them, and saw that he had carved one flower for each time they had met in the ravine. She clutched the cup to her, dropped into the chair, and sobbed.

By the time the first winter storm came, Alina felt that she was ready for it, and was grateful that it had come later than she expected. She had enough food to last four months, enough firewood to last a couple of weeks, and several clay pots full of water in case she got snowed in. She also had supplies to make baskets, arrows, and cord – enough to keep her hands busy for several days.

The storm hit late in the afternoon. The sky was lead gray. Alina gathered as much firewood as she could. She checked her fish trap, and was not surprised to find it empty, so she pulled the trap from the river and brought it inside. She looked around for Crow. He had been perched in the nearby trees that morning, but he wasn't in any of his usual spots this afternoon. The wind started to kick up, and it had a real bite in it. She hurried inside and put the door up against the opening.

The door didn't reach to the top of the opening. There was a gap about two hands high above it, and wide enough for Crow to come through. She had spent some time in the past couple of weeks trying to show him that he could get inside if he needed to. She would stand inside and wave her hand out over the top of the door and call to him. She knew he had seen her, but didn't know if she had made him understand.

The cave was dim on this short, cloudy day. She wished, not for the first time, that she could do as the bears did and simply sleep through the winter. It was then that the first rain started drumming against the door. In minutes, a familiar rattle of sleet sounded in the rain. She sat next to the fire, her knees drawn up to her chest, and stared at the flames, listening to the fire's crackle and the rattle of sleet outside. Winter had started, and now she was going to have to be inside for the better part of three months, at least. She sighed and rested her forehead on her knees.

The sound of fluttering at the opening made her raise her head. There was Crow, perched in the crack above the door. "Hello, Crow," she said quietly. Would he come in, or was he afraid of fire, as so many wild animals were? She picked a piece of meat from the stew she had cooking, and took it to her bed, away from the fire. When she had sat down, she held the piece of meat up so Crow could see it, and laid it down an arm's length away.

She waited, and after several minutes, thought she could not entice him to come in, but finally, he fluttered to the floor and hopped over to take the meat.

Chapter Seven

The priest arrived in the village when Alina's second son, Dag, was about a year old. Alina had heard that a new religion had been introduced into villages to the south and east, and now it was here. The rumors were that the priests of this new god were dirty, ignorant men, worthless for any kind of real work, and that the stories they told were beyond ridiculous.

Brother James was not the kind of man the rumors suggested. He was clean in his habits, he knew how to read and write, and he seemed happy to wield a scythe, or haul in a fishing net with any of the best men of the village. Some of his stories, told in a thick accent that marked him from somewhere far away, were hard to swallow, but most of them fit in with the kinds of stories Alina had heard from childhood. The one story, however, that she could not stop thinking about once she had heard it was how the son of God was sacrificed on a cross (the priest had to explain this sort of execution) in order to save people from their sins.

"After three days, he rose from the grave, and now he lives to give life to everyone who believes." Brother James concluded.

His listeners – most of the village at that point – were largely silent. Alina glanced at Bren, who had folded his arms across his chest, and was regarding the priest with a cynical smile. A few of the men shook their heads and walked away. Kiah, who had given birth to twins a few months before, was standing beside Bren. One of the babies started fussing, and when she picked it up to nurse, Bren also turned and walked off. Most of the crowd dispersed quickly after that, but Alina sent the boys home with Gerda saying, "I want to ask the priest something." Alina hung back in the knot of people until Brother James had answered their questions and listened to their remarks. When the others were gone, she stepped forward. His eyes met hers. "Lady?"

"I am Alina," she told him. "I am Bren's second wife." He nodded, but did not reply, so she went on. "I want to ask you about sin. What I might think is wrong, someone else might think is acceptable. What does your religion say is sin?"

"We sin when we break God's law," he told her. "Many generations ago, God gave his law to a man named Moses." Here he paused.

"All right," Alina said. "And what are those laws?"

"The easiest way for me to explain is to tell you the first ten laws," he answered. "Every law that follows springs from these." He looked around him. A pair of tree stumps nearby were a favorite place for the people of the village to sit and talk. "Here, let's sit a moment." When they had settled themselves, he continued, "The first law says, 'I am the Lord your God. You shall have no other gods before me.'" He held up two fingers. "Second, 'You shall not make for yourself an image in the form of anything in heaven above or on the earth beneath, or in the waves below, nor shall you bow down to them.' Third, 'You shall not misuse the name of the Lord your God.' The fourth is, 'Remember the Sabbath day by keeping it holy.' Fifth, 'Honor your father and your mother.' The sixth is, 'You shall not commit murder.' He held up seven fingers. 'You shall not commit adultery.' The eighth is, 'You shall not steal.' Ninth, 'You shall not give false testimony against your neighbor.' And the tenth law is 'You shall not yearn to possess anything that belongs to your neighbor.'"

When he had finished, Alina said, "Most of those are simple. At least, they make sense to me. But what is Sabbath?" And what do you mean by false testimony?"

"God commanded his people to keep one day in seven as a day of rest," the priest replied. "One day to give over to prayer and communion with him. That is what Sabbath is." He shifted a little on his stump. "Giving false testimony is about lying. Lying is the sin."

Alina didn't answer. She was guilty of breaking several of the laws. There was her time with Marav, of course, but that was a hard thing to regret. She had wanted so badly to be loved. And there were the lies, too. She had over-flattered Bren, had withheld things from him. Aware that the priest was studying her, she pressed her lips together.

"At least one of these laws bothers you," Brother James finally said. "Are you willing to tell me which ones?"

Alina was certain she would never tell anyone about Marav. So she said, "I sometimes lie."

Brother James nodded, and Alina saw no judgement in his eyes. "And why do you do that?"

Alina frowned. What a question! As she thought about it, she realized that the only person she lied to was Bren. After a few minutes, she said, "I think because I am afraid. I am afraid of what….someone may do if they know the truth." It suddenly seemed that the stump she was sitting on was digging into her flesh. To divert her mind and the conversation, she asked, "Is this law the same for men and women?"

She saw a flash of consternation cross his face. He was aware of Bren's reputation, then. "The law is for those who believe."

She nearly laughed. He had neatly wiggled out of that snare. She understood and even respected how carefully he handled her question. She asked, "And those who believe are forgiven?"

"Those who believe are forgiven," he nodded.

"But just because someone believes, it doesn't mean they won't sin again."

"That is true. Believers confess their sins, and God forgives them," he said. "This is why he sacrificed his son."

"I see." Alina stood up. "Thank you for your time." She walked away, but not toward her house. Instead, she went into the woods. She didn't go far. She just wanted to be alone to think.

Marav was gone. Just as the time for her baby's birth approached, Bren went off on one of his trips, and took Marav with him. When he came back, he told everyone that Marav had decided to stay in the east to make his living. Alina secretly wondered if Bren had killed him. It was likely she would never know. Her heart was broken at losing him. She felt hollow and leaden at the same time, but she managed to hide it from everyone but Gerda.

"You are sad, Lady," Gerda told her one afternoon. "I have seen women become sad after the birth of a baby." She laid a hand on Alina's shoulder. "Do not worry. It will pass." Gerda wasn't fooled. She knew exactly why Alina was sad. She was giving her an excuse in case anyone else remarked on her mood.

But now she had the priest's story on her mind. Alina had grown up with the tale of how Odin tied himself to a tree for nine days in order to gain the wisdom of the runes. But this new story stunned her. What god sacrificed himself for people? This made no sense. She turned it over and over in her mind. The gods were just like people, selfish, vain, capricious, sometimes cruel. The idea that a god loved people was strange enough. The idea that a god would die on purpose for anyone else was absurd.

Or was it? "I would die for my sons," she murmured aloud. "But they are innocent, and I love them." Then she thought about the part where the priest said that his god had risen from the dead after three days. Alina didn't have a problem with this. Of course a god could rise from the dead. A god could pretty much do whatever he wanted. Then the thought came full circle. If he wanted, a god could die. For whatever reason he chose.

Would believing in such a god mean that she was betraying the gods she had always known? She would have to ask.

That night, Alina dreamed of Odin, the king of the gods. She was in a forest at night. The moonlight shone blue around her. She was seeking something, though she didn't know what it was. After a time, she came upon the tree where he was tied. In the dream she wasn't afraid of him, but she was curious. She approached the tree and said, "Father Odin?"

He did not answer her, but he looked up when she spoke. His eye sockets were pools of darkness ringed with bruised shadows. She knew Odin had only one eye, but the shadows were so black she couldn't tell which eye was still there. His hair hung lank and lifeless down the sides of his face. Alina had never seen a living being look so much like a corpse. He gazed around him, but he could not see her. "Father Odin?" she said again. "Can you help me?"

Now she knew he heard her because he answered, "No. Don't you see that I am doing something important? Go on about your business. I can't help you. I don't know you."

When she woke and remembered the dream, she was deeply disturbed, though she couldn't understand why. After all, why would any god know her? She lay still for a time, remembering each bit of the dream. Then Dag began to fuss, and she picked him up to nurse him. Alina sighed. She had to get on with her day.

But that afternoon, she went and found Brother James again. "I have a few more questions," she said. "But first I want to tell you about a dream I had last night." He listened with interest, and when she finished, she said, "I want to ask you, is it possible for a god to know me? I mean, I am not a mighty hero. The gods know who the heroes are, but I am just a second wife and the mother of two sons."

"The Lord knows his children," he answered. "I think that word, children, will probably make the most sense to you. You see, we are not just his people. We are not just his servants. He has called us his children. So, yes. If you are his child, he knows you."

She did understand a child's relationship with a parent. Something dangerous stirred in her, but she pushed it away. "My other question is, if I believe in your god, do I have to stop believing in mine?"

He leaned toward her, and in a half-whisper answered, "What has your god done for you?"

Alina shook her head. She had no idea. Probably nothing. "I will talk with you again." And she left him.

That first storm kept Alina inside for two days. Rain and sleet continued to pound outside, and the pool inside the cave was full, with water constantly running out the drain. Crow seemed to like the pool.

He bathed in the water several times, in spite of the cold. When he was done, he would fly to the drying rack and perch on the top.

Alina talked to him as if he could understand her. She told him stories and even sang the kinds of nursery songs that she had once sung to her boys. Part of her felt that she was being ridiculous, talking to a wild animal, but the bigger part of her was glad he was there. Besides, no one else would see her and judge her.

The third day dawned sunny and cold. Alina threw her cloak on and went out. Crow followed after a minute and perched in one of the trees near the river. The ground under Alina's feet was slick with ice, and she half-walked, half slipped down to the river's edge, where she paused, watching her breath steam the air. Her little piece of the world had transformed. Thin patches of ice lined the riverbank. The lingering leaves were gone from the trees, whose branches now stood out like black skeletons against the sky. The grasses were dead and brown. They bowed their heavy heads to the earth. Only the pines were still green, and their branches drooped toward the ground, laden with ice that sparkled in the sunlight

She had little else to do, so Alina decided to hunt for a flat stone to use as the top of a hob. First, she went upriver, thinking that the fishing spot might have something, but found only round stones there. They would make a good base, but she didn't bother to pick them up. She could always come back. She continued following the river for a while, but didn't find what she was looking for. Crow went after her, flying from tree top to tree top, sometimes squawking.

The day was nice enough, so she turned south into the woods. Maybe she would find a stone away from the river. When she was just about out of earshot of the river, she began blazing the trees with her knife, leaving a sideways 'v' in the bark so that she could find her way back. After about an hour, she came to a clearing that had a boulder squatting off to the right. She went to it, examining it and looking around its base. No flat stone there. Now it was about midday, so she sat on the rock and pulled a few bites of meat from her pack. Crow flew down and joined her.

"We should probably go back," Alina told him as she laid a scrap on the rock. She noticed that Crow no longer kept his distance from her. He was standing just a few inches away. She laid her hand down, palm up, next to him. He regarded her hand for a moment, but didn't seem bothered by it. She reached a little farther, and stroked the side of his neck with one finger. Still, he did not move away. They sat together like that for a long while, until the cold of the rock, which had been seeping through her clothes, began to make her shiver.

"Let's head home. The daylight won't last much longer." She had seen a lot of dead-fall between this clearing and the river, and decided to pick up as much as she could carry. She gave Crow one final stroke, saying, "Where are your own people? Did they leave you like my people left me?"

Alina asked to be baptized the following week. Brother James said, "I will, as long as you bring a couple of witnesses." She thought she knew, but she asked him why. "Baptism is a public declaration," he explained. "Choose people you trust."

She chose Gerda and Brega, neither of whom understood what she was doing or why. "If you are wanting to hear from Odin, I know someone who can read the runes for you," Gerda said.

Alina shook her head. "I have already heard from Odin. This is something I believe I must do."

"What do you think Bren will say?" Gerda asked.

"I don't think Bren cares one way or the other," Alina told her. "He is only interested in making his trades and bedding women."

Gerda let out a sigh. "You may be right."

"I think, if you and Brega come with me…." Here she stopped. "Do you think you will be in trouble as a witness?"

Gerda, who had been frowning, now chuckled. "Child, I will be in far less trouble with this than I would have been with your other adventure."

In the end, Brega and Alina left their children with Brega's maid, and the three women went to the river with Brother James. Holgur also went with them. Alina had made friends with the blacksmith, and when she told him what she planned to do, he insisted on coming along as their escort and guard. "You women have no business going into the woods on your own," he told Alina with a pointed look.

"Brother James will be with us," Alina said, smiling.

Holgur chuckled. "So he will, and he's not a bad sort, but you might need more than just a priest."

The day was fine, but turning chilly by the time they came to the water's edge. Apart from a knot of women about a hundred paces away who were out doing their wash, no one else was around. Alina shucked off her shoes and stepped into the water with Brother James.

When they were in about hip deep, he stopped and turned her to face the others.

"Alina, wife of Bren, mother of Gunnar and Dag, you have confessed your faith in Christ to me. Do you now confirm that faith to these who are here?"

"Yes, I confirm it," she answered through clenched teeth. She was trying to keep them from chattering with the cold, and with nerves.

"I now baptize you in the name of the Father, the Son, and the Holy Spirit." With that, he lowered her into the cold, cold water. Something bolted through Alina in that moment, whether the cold or something else, but when the priest raised her back up out of the water, she felt like a new person.

Gerda stepped forward as they came up out of the river. She handed a cloth to Alina so she could dry her face. Then she covered her with her cloak, and they headed back to the village. They hadn't been gone an hour. No one had missed them, and children were running in the lanes, women walked by them with baskets of vegetables from the village gardens, a man strode past them leading a horse. Alina marveled that everything seemed to carry on as it had when they left. She thanked Brother James and gave him two silver coins. "I know you will make good use of these," she said, and went into her house.

Gerda came with her, her expression tight-lipped. "What's the matter?" Alina asked with an inward sigh.

"You didn't need to give him that silver, you know," Gerda replied. "The village feeds him, and your husband supports him as his scribe."

Alina nodded. "True. But I am hoping the silver will help him in his work." When Gerda did not reply, she added, "I have done what I have done."

Gerda gave a short curtsy. "Yes, madam."

Alina almost laughed, but Gerda was far more than a maid to her. Swept up by the day and by her love for her, Alina crossed the room and pulled her into her arms, heedless that she was still wet from the river. "You are the best of friends," she murmured. "I know you don't agree with what I have done, but that's all right." She pulled back. Gerda's eyes were swimming with unshed tears. Wordlessly, Gerda reached up and patted Alina's cheek. Then she left, closing the door softly behind her.

Alina peeled off her wet dress and changed into dry clothes. She had tightly braided her hair that morning, and now decided to leave it as it was and dry it in front of the fire before she went to bed. When she was dressed, she went out to get her boys. She was about halfway to Brega's when she ran into Bren. He firmly grasped her arm and said, "I hear you had a dip in the river."

Alina didn't try to pull away. Any show of resistance would only feed his anger, if he was angry. His expression was hard to read. But she was determined now not to lie. She stepped toward him until her breasts pushed up against his chest. "I did." She tugged at the end of her braid and smiled. "I should have chosen a warmer day."

He actually smiled back. "I should have been there. Maybe I will come tonight and warm you up."

She kissed him at the corner of his mouth and gave him a sidelong look. "Later?" he grinned, but he did release her, and she went on her way, breathing a sigh of relief. Bren wasn't angry. She wasn't sure she wanted his favor, but at least this was a game she understood.

Brega's maid was gone, and Brega was there playing with the children. She looked up and wrinkled her nose when Alina came in. "I think Dag is dirty."

Alina picked him up and grimaced. "You're right. Thank you for watching him, Brega, and thank you for coming to the river."

Brega nodded. "You're welcome. I still don't understand the point, but it was important to you, and that's good enough for me. I am going to see my father tomorrow, and my maid is sick. Can you keep the girls?"

"Of course." Alina smiled at Inge. "We will find something fun to do."

Bren did come to her that evening well after the boys were asleep, but he didn't stay the night. Before he left her, he whispered, "I have been watching you. If you care for the people around you, you had better behave yourself."

A chill raced up her spine, and she lay very still, watching the door long after he was gone. "Help me," she whispered to the dark. It was her first prayer.

The next winter storm brought snow. When Alina woke and moved her door aside, she found a waist-high drift lodged against the opening. She kicked the snow out and stamped it down to make a path for herself. Snow was still coming down in fat, wet clumps. But when she got to the river's edge, she found a trail of fresh footprints. She squatted down to study them. "Wolf."

"No," he answered, "and this language is Latin. Not a language anyone speaks around here."

She glanced up at him. "But you know it."

He nodded. "I learned it as a boy."

Alina ran her fingertips over the page. "What does it say?

"I will translate for you." He drew in a breath and ran a finger across the words on the page as he spoke. "In the beginning was the Word, and the Word was with God, and the Word was God. He was with God in the beginning. Through him all things were made, and without him, nothing was made that has been made. In him was life, and that life was the light of men. The light shines in the darkness, and the darkness has not overcome it." He paused and looked up at the people gathered. "This is the start of an account of the life of the son of God, who was called Jesus," he explained. "There are four accounts. This one was written by one of Jesus' followers."

"How can a word be God?" The question came from Melo, one of Bren's chief men. "That makes no sense."

"The writer refers to Jesus in this way," the priest answered. "I am not sure why. It may be because everything Jesus said was true. Or it may be because He created the world with words."

Melo, who was standing with his arms across his chest laughed. "What? He said things and the whole world appeared?" When the priest nodded, Melo laughed again and pointed to an empty space. In a commanding voice, he said, "Chair!" When nothing happened, he grinned. "I don't think even a god could make anything with words." Brother James started to answer, but Melo waved a hand as if batting away a fly. He then walked off, and a couple of the other men went with him.

“Can you – that is, would you be willing to read this book to me?” Alina asked. Far from being intimidated by Melo’s mockery, she was captivated by the beauty and mystery of the words.

“It was my hope that you would want to hear it,” he answered.

They continued to meet, but now it was always with the book, and little by little he read the entire thing to her. By the time Bren returned from his trip, she had not only heard the book, she had memorized parts of it. Bren didn’t seem to be taking any notice of what she was doing, but she always made sure that they met when other people were present.

There was a long prayer that Jesus had prayed over his followers, and Alina worked hard to commit it to memory. She was planning to recite the whole thing to Father James one afternoon, but he never came into the hall. She waited, and watched people going in and out. After about an hour, Huus lumbered in. He looked over at Alina and guffawed. Two more men followed him in. One smirked at her, the other studiously avoided her eyes. A sudden chill ran up her spine. Something was terribly wrong. She stood up and started for the door, but ran into Gerda coming in with the boys. The maid handed Dag over to Alina and whispered, “Child….”

Alina’s stomach dropped. “It’s Brother James,” she said dully, not knowing how she knew.

Gerda’s eyes were swimming. “I am sorry.”

“Where is he?”

Alina tried to push past her, but Gerda grabbed her arm. “There is nothing you can do for him, and you must not take the boys there.”

“Where is he?” she repeated.

"Edge of the woods behind the stables," Gerda answered. "They nailed him to a tree."

Alina sank to the floor with Dag in her arms. Her breath was shallow and rapid, but she gritted her teeth. When Gerda knelt beside her, she asked, "Bren ordered it?" She ran a hand over her face. "Of course he did." *He warned me,* she thought. *I tried to be careful. I was careful, but he had already made up his mind, about Brother James and nothing I did would be enough to protect him.* So Bren had ordered his men to crucify Brother James, thinking it a fitting end for the man who followed a crucified god.

"You need to get up," Gerda broke in on her thoughts. "People are coming in, and you have to show yourself strong for your children's sake."

Alina didn't exactly understand this, but she let Gerda help her up. "Please bring dinner for me and the boys to my house," she said. "There is no reason for me to put up with everyone's gloating faces."

That night, after she had put the boys to bed, she tried to go to sleep herself, hoping for temporary oblivion, but sleep would not come. She would not be able to help Father James. She could not rescue him. Gerda had told her that Bren had posted a guard. *How long?* she wondered. *How long will it take him to die?* According to Brother James, Jesus' crucifixion had taken hours, not days, but he had been badly beaten first. Had Bren's men beaten Brother James? It wouldn't surprise her. She got up from the bed and paced the room. "Lord," she prayed, "If there is anything I can do for him, please tell me."

Finally, as she paced toward the door, her eyes fell on her bow and arrows. *No!* Her heart quailed, and she turned away from the weapon.

I can't kill him! Her pacing slowed as reason took shape. Brother James was already a dead man. Shooting him would ease his passing.

She checked on her boys. Both were sleeping soundly. It was now well past the middle of the night. If she was going to do anything, it had to be now. Alina threw on her cloak, took her bow and arrows, and went out, telling herself that she should at least see this, that she should remember what had been done to a good and kind man. The night was very dark with no moon. She wove through the village on silent feet, meeting no one, keeping to the deepest shadows as she went.

As she neared the forest's edge, she saw firelight. She crept behind the stable, careful to avoid the mound of manure that was piled there, and looked around its corner. There Brother James was, stretched out on a tree not a hundred paces from her. His head was bowed over his chest, but she thought she saw the slight movement of breathing. The scene reminded her of her dream of Odin, but this was no dream. Blood, deep crimson in the firelight, still dripped from one hand and the blood from his feet pooled in a dark stain on the ground. She turned away for a moment, leaned her back against the wall of the stable and blinked up at the black sky, gathering herself.

After a few moments, she turned back and looked again. One guard sat to Brother James's right. He was not a good guard. Bren probably figured that no one would dare hinder this execution. The man sat, his arms crossed, and his head bent forward, fast asleep.

She drew an arrow out of the quiver and inspected it. It was not one she had made herself, so it would not be traced back to her. Not that anyone would really doubt who had done this. *If Bren punishes me, he punishes me.* Alina straightened her stance, nocked the arrow and took aim. A scrap of the memorized prayer came to her then. "'Father,'" she whispered, "'I want those you have given me to be with me where I am, and to see my glory.'" She shouldered the tears from her eyes and took a deep breath. "Please forgive me." And she let fly.

Alina had been counting the days from the first winter storm by making scratches in the dirt in one corner. She figured there would be at least ninety days of winter in all. But even when spring came she would struggle to feed herself. It would take time for the plants she depended on to grow again, time for the animals to come out of their dens and holes, time for the water to warm up and set the fish moving. She squatted at the back of the cave, counting the marks. Almost eighty. She hoped winter would turn soon. She had only two baskets of dried meat and berries left, and the nuts were more than half gone.

A mix of snow and rain was falling from the sky today. It sent a constant stream dribbling down through the ceiling. She had spent part of the winter lining her drain with pebbles, which wasn't necessary, but it looked nicer. Now she got up and followed the drain, making sure, as she did each time it rained, that the water was going out. It was, and there was nothing left to do inside. If she wanted to keep herself busy, she would have to go out.

I could dig some clay, she thought. *The pool is full and running, so I have a good supply of water. I could make a few pots.* She stared at the fire a moment. *I wonder if I could make the cook top for a hob out of clay? It might just break, but maybe I could start with a small one and see what happens.*

So, with a plan in her head, Alina pulled on her cloak and went out. It wasn't raining hard, but it was cold, and it didn't take long for her to feel like she was wet through. She dug the clay and hauled as much as she could carry back inside. She shrugged off her wet cloak and hung it on the drying rack, then sat down between the pool and the fire and smoothed the floor there with her hands. After a moment's thought she decided to construct the flat piece the same way she did pots, but instead of working with the clay, started by laying out cattail leaves. She could construct her clay atop them, so that the clay could be moved, and if the leaves stuck to the clay, they would eventually burn off.

Next, Alina rolled out more than twenty clay ropes, each about as thick as her little finger and as long as her forearm and hand. She laid these out side by side and touching until the resulting rectangle was a little more than half as wide as the ropes were long. Using her knife, she cut the ends of the ropes so that they were uniform in length.

Alina was doing this when Crow came in. He had recently discovered the shelves at the back of the cave, and he flew there to continue his investigations. After a couple of minutes, Alina heard a thud and turned around. Over the winter she had made a lot of cord, reasoning that she would always have a need for it. She had wound the cord into a ball and left it on the shelf. Crow had found the ball and knocked it off onto the floor. He stood on the shelf, his head cocked in curiosity as the ball rolled away. After a moment, he hopped down and approached the ball. He pecked at it.

Alina laughed. "What are you doing, you crazy bird?"

As if in answer, he flapped his wings. One wing hit the ball and set it rolling a short way. Crow hopped after it. It didn't take him long to learn to roll the ball so that he could chase it. When the ball came within Alina's reach, she pushed it so that it rolled toward the back of the cave again. Crow squawked and went after it.

Alina shook her head in amusement and went back to the panel of clay rope she had made. She let this construction dry a bit while she prepared more clay, immersing it in the water, squeezing and working it in her hands to make it wetter and looser. She had to stop every so often to warm her numbing fingers over the fire. When the consistency was right, she began spreading this clay over the lines of rope, filling in the gaps and using a small flat stone to smooth out the surface. She sat back, surveying her work. It would need to dry for a long time, maybe several days, but she liked the size of it. She hoped it would be sturdy over fire.

By this time, the rain had either stopped, or it had slowed to a drizzle. She went to the opening and moved the door aside, and for the first time, Crow flew up and perched on her shoulder, and there they both stared out. "What do you think?" she asked him. "Go out and collect rocks for the sides of the hob?" It was drizzling, and Alina shivered. Her tunic was still damp from her earlier foray outside. "Maybe tomorrow," she told him. She turned away from the opening to get the door, but Crow flitted out and perched on the little tree near the opening. Alina put the door up. Crow could suit himself. He would come back in when he was ready.

She picked up the ball of cord and set it back on the shelf. She reached up for the basket of dried meat, took a handful out, and dropped the meat into the pot to stew. To this she added a handful of dried greens and a pinch of salt. Then she bent over the flat clay piece and touched the surface with the tip of one finger. She sat down on the deerskin rug and recited the prayer that she had learned. "'Father, the hour has come. Glorify your Son that your Son may glorify you...."

She was no longer sure that all the words were exactly right. She had learned them years ago, and the priest wasn't here to help and correct her. But, as he had told her, she was reciting in translation, so maybe the words could not be exact. She came toward the end of the prayer and recited that one sentence. "'Father, I want those you have given me to be with me where I am....'" This always brought back the image of Brother James, his arms and legs splayed out and nailed to the tree, and again, Alina bowed her head. "Forgive me."

At that moment, something thudded hard against her door, and Crow screamed. Alina leapt to her feet, grabbed her bow and arrows, and moved to the door. Silence. She set the door aside and peered out, but saw nothing amiss. It wasn't until she stepped outside that she noticed them — dozens of black feathers littering the snow. Finally, a movement at the river's edge caught her eye. The wolf was wading into the stream. It looked back once, and Alina could just make out something in its mouth – something black.

She let an arrow fly, but even as she did, she knew it would do no good. The wolf was halfway across the water now, moving fast, and her arrow landed uselessly in the water. Crow was gone. "No, no, no...." Alina turned back toward the opening, trying to read the signs of what had happened. It wasn't hard to piece it together. Crow had flown to the top of the opening to go in. The wolf had been waiting, maybe behind the one tree that stood there. It had jumped up as Crow tried to enter. That was the banging on the door.

Alina's shoulders slumped. She let the bow fall to the ground. Then she fell to her knees in the middle of the scattered feathers, put her face in her hands and wept.

Bren soon took off on another of his trading journeys, but Alina wasn't about to let him go peacefully. The morning of the day he left, she watched him and waited until he was alone. He had been in the stables and was on his way toward Holgur's smithy when she came up and took him by the arm.

"Bren. Wait a minute." He turned, and she released him and took a step back.

"What is it?" The expression in his eyes was impatient, unfriendly. "I am in a hurry."

"I know you are," she answered. "But I need to know why you ordered your men to kill Brother James."

He drew himself up. "I am master of this village. I don't have to explain myself to you."

She chose her next words carefully. "So you cannot tell me why?"

If she had said "will not" instead "cannot" he would have shaken her off and gone on his way. Instead, he put his hands on his hips and narrowed his eyes at her. "You were not sleeping with him, so you think I had no cause for complaint." Alina held herself still, waiting while he tried to stare her down. When she wouldn't avert her eyes, he repeated, "I don't have to explain myself to you."

He started to turn away, but Alina blurted out, “The miller’s daughter is not for you.”

He swung back toward her, his eyes dark with barely suppressed rage. “What did you say?”

Alina didn’t know where the words came from. They were not her own; she hardly knew what she was saying, and she was baffled by the knowledge. Where had it come from? “The miller’s daughter is not for you,” she repeated. “If you touch her, plague and sorrow will be your lot.”

“So the priest told you….” He began.

Alina shook her head. Her heart was beating wildly, but she still had her wits. “He told me nothing. But you have just told me everything.” Without waiting for a reply, she turned on her heel and fled, half expecting him to come after her. He would beat her, or maybe kill her. But at least now she knew.

She hurried away from him, her heart pounding, her mind racing. When her feet faltered, she stopped and blinked. She was behind the stables, in nearly the same spot where she had stood to shoot Brother James. The pile of manure gave off a sharp scent that brought her back to herself. She rested her back against the stable wall, arms crossed tight against her chest. No one was around. The horses had already been taken out for Bren's men. She whispered, "What was that, Lord?" She knew the words hadn't been hers. Did this make her a seer? She thought about the one seer she knew, an old man, toothless and bald. He was a cousin of Gerda's, or maybe an uncle. He wore a filthy leather pouch strung around his scrawny neck that contained flattened pieces of bones with runes inscribed on them. For a small fee, he would shake them out and see the future for you.

Alina shook her head. *I didn't see the future,* she reasoned. *I was only given words about the present — and a warning.* Apparently, Brother James had said something similar to Bren, and Bren had him killed. What was he going to do to her? Bren was leaving after the noon meal, but he could easily order his men to kill her. Alina bit her lip until it bled. *I don't want to die!*

How do you want to spend your life, my child?

The question came so clear to her mind that she stood up straight and pushed herself away from the wall. *How do I want to spend my life?* Brother James had spent his confronting Bren's wickedness and defending an innocent child. Stories ran through her mind, then. So many stories of heroes fighting impossible battles and dying glorious deaths. It came to her that this was another kind of battle. Defending the miller's daughter, who was barely ten years old — this was a worthy way to live. It was a worthy way to die, if it came to that. Alina's heart slowed. She swallowed, took in a long breath and raised her eyes toward the sky. "Is there something else I should do with this knowing?" As soon as she asked, she knew there was.

The miller, and his family, including the little girl, had become believers in the priest's god. *Which is probably why the Lord wants her protected,* Alina thought as she hurried toward their home.

"I had no idea," Farn the miller said when Alina finished her story to him. He ran a hand across his mouth. "I thank you, Lady, and I thank God that He sent you."

At that moment his wife, Meli, came in, trailed by her three children. "Farn?" She looked from him to Alina. "What is the matter?"

"Send the children out so we can talk," he told her.

The little girl, whom the parents had named Alina (they had liked the sound of it, they told her) went out last, throwing one look of nearly grown-up concern over her shoulder as she went. In her mind's eye she saw Bren hulking over this tiny girl, and her stomach clenched. She explained the situation to the miller's wife, who sank into a chair and held her hands fisted in her lap. When Alina finished, she shook her head. "He cannot have her." A sob came from her throat. "May Christ help us. He cannot!"

Alina pulled a chair up opposite the woman and took her hands in her own. "Bren has just left. You know that, yes?" Meli nodded, and Alina went on. "He will be gone a long time, and until he comes back, your child is safe from him."

Alina was gratified to see the expression of sorrow leave her face to be replaced by one of angry determination. Between clenched teeth Meli said, "Before he does come back, we will send her to my sister. She will be safe enough there."

Farn said, "So you believe that they killed Brother James because he knew of Bren's interest in our girl?"

"They murdered him because Bren wanted him out of his way," Alina answered, "but yes, it had to do with your daughter."

Farn grunted. "Well, when it comes to it, I will take her away myself." He let out a long breath. "I suppose we should pray for a new priest to come to us."

Alina was glad, when she left them, that they had a plan to keep their child safe, but in the end, their plan proved unnecessary.

The last couple of weeks of winter seemed longer than the months that had gone before. Winter's dying gasp came in the form of a light snow, followed by rain that washed it away. The next morning dawned chilly but bright, and the wind was blowing from the south. Spring was coming. Alina hardly cared.

She had picked up every one of Crow's feathers. One she added to the feathers that hung over her bed. Another she laid on the little rock shelf where she kept Crow's gifts. The rest she had put into one of the now-empty food baskets on the shelf.

Now, looking around her, Alina thought, *I need to get out. I need to try hunting.* But she did not stir. If she hunted, if she fed herself – what then? She'd have to do it again. And again. Just the thought of living this way for however many years she might have left exhausted her. She recited her prayer for the morning, but the words left her mouth and fell to the floor. She seriously considered lying down again and sleeping the day away. But when she imagined doing that, something shook loose in her.

She stood up, gathered her things, and went outside. The sky above was ceaseless blue, and the sun almost warmed her face. Taking a long breath, Alina went down to the river's edge. She spotted a robin on her way there. Spring was at the door. "I'll set the fish trap out tomorrow," she murmured, though the water was most likely still too cold for them to be biting.

She scanned the trees across the water for any sign of the wolf, but didn't see anything. In the days following Crow's death, she had constructed traps for the wolf in her mind, but none of her ideas pleased her. If she was going to kill the wolf, she wanted to shoot it. She wanted to be there.

She left the river and went into the trees south of her cave. Maybe she could find a rabbit or some other small animal. In the months she'd hunted, Alina had explored these woods until she knew them well, but today she decided to go farther, just to see what was there. What had always stopped her was a high ridge that ran roughly east-west. This ridge, with its forbidding rocky face was where she normally turned back. Today she would climb over and see what lay on the other side. She started up the rocky slope, and didn't get far before she was panting with the effort. *I spent too much time sitting still this winter.*

But though the face looked steep and grim from the ground, there were plenty of ledges and handholds, and the rocks remained firm under her weight. When she reached the top, she sat down, panting and sweating, letting the cool wind wash over her. After only a short time, the wind chilled her, so she stood up and looked out to the south. Great swaths of forested hills stretched out below, rising to a purple line of rolling mountains that lay far on the western horizon.

She sighed and turned her eyes to the east, and she saw it – a thin column of smoke rising from the trees. *Not a forest fire,* she thought. *This is someone's cook fire.* It interested her that it was only the one column of smoke. Not a village, then, but one person, or maybe one family. It was still far away – most of a day's journey. Now she crouched down again, wary. No telling what kind of person or people were out there. She wondered again about Crow's bracelet. It might have come from that person. "That person over there."

She sat and watched the smoke rise into the blue sky and scanned the forest for more, and thought maybe there was more smoke farther out. Was that a thicker column, or a trick of the light? She couldn't be sure. If that was also smoke, it was probably a camp or a village. Alina sighed. This was a riddle she would not solve today. She gathered her things and began the long climb back down.

The sunlight and fresh air had done her good. She had a goose by the time she got back to the cave – the first fresh meat of the season. Alina's spirits rose as she plucked it, putting the feathers into the same basket with Crow's black ones, saving them to eventually make herself a pillow. While the bird was roasting on the fire, she went down to the river to collect some stones to use for the sides of the hob. She gathered as many as she could carry and brought them inside. She put three by the fire to heat up, and took her tightest woven basket down to the river. It was time for a bath.

CHAPTER NINE

Gunnar was nearly five years old when Bren came riding into the village with his fifth wife. There was not much of a turnout among the villagers to welcome her. They seemed to have grown weary of new wives. But Brega, Alina, Agnes and Kiah were there, children in tow, as Bren required. Brega said to Alina, "We will do what we can for her – just as we've done with the others."

Alina nodded. "I just hope she's more than nine years old." Brega winced, but did not reply. The miller and his wife had sent little Alina off south the year before, and Bren had chosen a fourteen-year-old slave as his new girl. She had gotten pregnant, and was now married to Herv, the horse master.

Bren rode first in the column. A party of armed men followed. More than a dozen were men Alina didn't recognize. *They must be the new wife's entourage*, she thought. Alina turned her attention back to Bren and noted that his hard frame had softened somewhat. He had a paunch, and was that a double chin lurking behind his beard? He was wearing a new tunic, blue with white fur trim, and as he drew near, she thought there was a strange light in his eyes. Behind him was something Alina had never seen before. It was a wagon drawn by two horses. That much she was used to, but this wagon had a little house built on it, with a door on one side and windows on both. Like Bren's tunic, it was painted blue with white trim. As Alina watched, a hand almost as white as the paint on the wagon emerged from the window on the near side and began to wave.

"Well, that's new," Alina remarked under her breath.

Brega laughed. "Keeps the rain off, I suppose." Despite the sound of mirth, there were little lines of tension at the corners of her eyes.

The riders came to a stop, and Bren sprang from his horse and hurried to the wagon. He pulled open the door with a flourish and offered a hand to the woman inside. When she stepped out, there was a gasp from the sparse crowd, and Kiah said, "That's a pretty dress."

The woman was clad all in white with a bright blue belt around her slender waist. Her hair, so blonde that it was nearly white as well, shone silver-gold in the sunlight. Her eyes were the color of cornflowers, her skin pale and perfect.

"I feel like a lump of mud on a log," Brega whispered.

Alina understood how she felt. Of all Bren's wives, Alina had always thought Brega the most beautiful, with her dark hair and blue eyes, but this woman's beauty was far beyond the everyday beauty of any of them. "I think," she said slowly, "that this one won't need any help from us."

Another figure began to emerge from the wagon, dressed in black. It was a man, bald and portly with a stern face, sagging jowls, and cold gray eyes. He looked around him, passing his gaze over the people as if they didn't matter, and scowled at the village's buildings. Bren turned toward the people and announced, "This is Maja, my wife. Please welcome her and give her the same respect that you give me."

He would have turned with her toward the great hall, but Maja stopped him. "Will you not introduce me to your women and their children?"

Alina bristled. *We are his wives, you cow.* She laid her hands protectively on her boys' shoulders. Bren began the introductions with Brega. "This is Brega, and her girls…." Here he hesitated.

"Ava and Inge," Brega finished for him.

"What lovely girls," Maja cooed, touching each of them under the chin.

Then it was Alina's turn, but rather than waiting on Bren, she took the bull by the horns. "I am Alina," she said, "And these are my boys, Gunnar and Dag."

Maja nodded and smiled. She shot a shrewd look at Alina before saying to Bren, "I would know these boys were yours if I met them across the sea."

Bren beamed with empty pride, and they moved on.

Alina's prediction turned out to be right. Maja needed no help from anyone. The fifth wife stepped into the role of first wife as if it were her due. She sat at Bren's right hand at meals, presiding over the servants as if they had always been hers to command. And Bren was clearly smitten. He could hardly take his eyes off her. In turn, Maja played the part of the love-struck bride with near perfection. But Alina knew it was an act.

She had walked into the hall just when they were at the end of what appeared to be a minor dispute. "You are my wife, and you will obey me," Bren said. With that he turned to walk away, and Alina saw Maja roll her eyes in contempt. This was just the beginning of a pattern with Maja. As far as Bren knew she was the perfect, favored wife, but in reality, Maja neither feared nor respected him.

Alina didn't bother to say anything to Bren. She had other things on her mind. She would never have guessed it, but the man Maja had brought with her was a priest. Maja claimed to follow the same God that Brother James had preached. She even convinced Bren to construct a church building so that this new priest – he called himself Father Otto – would have a proper place to tend his flock.

It was unfortunate, Alina decided, that Father Otto found out that she had been baptized, because he then took it upon himself to question her about what she believed. He cornered her in the great hall after a noon meal, saying, "I understand that you professed faith in Christ."

"I did," she admitted. "I was baptized about three years ago."

He launched into a series of questions. "Do you believe in the virgin birth?" Alina nodded. "Do you acknowledge the holy trinity?"

"I…I am not sure what that means."

Father Otto sighed and raised his gaze toward the roof as if asking Heaven why he had to endure her ignorance. "What about….?" Here he used a word she presumed was Latin.

"I have never heard that word."

Several more questions followed, most of which Alina shrugged at. His words sounded like nonsense to her. Finally he asked one she could answer. "What prayers do you know?"

"I know the Lord's prayer," she said, "And the prayer in John's gospel that He prayed over his disciples."

"And do you say the Lord's prayer every day?"

Alina answered, "Most days, but I also say my own words to the Lord. Brother James told me that's what prayer chiefly is."

Father Otto's face reddened as he cut her off. ""'Brother James isn't here, is he? You are in error about a great many things. It is my duty to teach you the true way of the church."

Alina sighed, seeing that she wasn't going to be released from his presence anytime soon. "Then why don't you instruct me?"

"Don't be impertinent!" he shouted.

The handful of people in the hall turned to look. Now Alina's back was up. She had had enough of his abuse of her and of Brother James's memory. She stepped closer to the priest and asked in a low voice, "Do you know what happened to Brother James?" His florid face paled. Evidently, he had heard something about it. Adopting the tone she used with her boys when they misbehaved, she added, "If I were you, I'd watch my step. You want to be very careful here."

"You are nothing but an ignorant woman," he growled. "By my word I can send you to hell."

Brother James had warned her about this moment, and had armed her for it. "Someday, other men will come after me," he had said, "and they will try to tell you that they hold your salvation in their hands. Do not believe their wickedness. Stand firm on your faith in Christ." Recalling this, she gave Father Otto a grim smile to show him his declaration did not frighten her as he clearly intended it to.

She held his cold gaze until he finally looked away. "You shall come to me when my church is built," he told her. "I will instruct you."

Alina had no intention of ever setting foot in his church, but she didn't say so. She just stood there, waiting, until he turned and left the hall. Behind her she heard scattered applause. Apparently, she was not the only one who disliked Father Otto.

Spring was in full bloom before Alina dared to climb the ridge again. She had taken down one small deer the week before, and the meat was dried and put away. On this day she decided to go back toward the ridge to forage for greens. There were plenty of greens that way, and she wanted to have another look from the top.

She started out at first light, still undecided whether to try to approach the place where she had spotted the smoke, but she wanted to give herself plenty of time to try. She went directly to the ridge first, reasoning that she could forage on the way home. But standing at the base of the ridge, she paused a moment, looking up at the steep slope. If she fell....

Never mind that, she scolded herself. *Just get up there.* She was surprised at first that the climb seemed so much easier this time, but of course, she had been out hunting and using her muscles and her lungs. Winter's weakness was fading. She reached the top and stood looking. She didn't see smoke anywhere this time. but that was not surprising. There was a stiff breeze coming up out of the south. Any small smoke would dissipate as soon as it left the fire.

Did she remember the direction where the smoke had been? Alina wasn't certain she could point to any part of the forest with certainty, though it had been to the east, to her left. Well, perhaps today was not the day to find it. She still wanted to go down and explore the southern side of the ridge. *I won't go far*, she told herself.

A dark line of clouds was approaching from the southwest, driven by the wind. She probably had a couple of hours before the clouds brought the storm with them. Alina started down the slope, half walking, half sliding on the new grass. Almost the second she reached the bottom, she heard snuffing noises and grunting. *Pigs*, she thought, and turned to climb at least part of the way back up the slope. About halfway up, she turned and sat down to watch and wait.

After a few minutes, she spotted them. She had been hunting often enough with her father and brother, and from the noises she expected wild pigs, but what she saw in the trees made her blood freeze. It was a bear — a female with a pair of cubs nosing around between the nearest trees. A shudder ran through her, and the scar on her leg sent up a flash of pain that seemed to run all the way to her back. *If I had stumbled upon them....* She had heard stories. She knew what a mother bear could do. She squatted down and curled her posture up as much as possible, trying to make herself look like one of the rocks on the slope. Now she had to wait.

But how long would it take for them to move on? She studied the slope of the ridge to her left. Even though it looked rockier, she thought she could get down all right from there. But did she dare move? All at once, the mother bear's head came up and swung around. She was sniffing at the air. Alina held her breath. *Does she smell me?* The bear raised up on two legs, scanning the area. Alina thought her heart might burst out of her chest. But after a few moments, the bear dropped to all fours again and began lumbering north and back into the deeper shadows of the trees. Seconds later, the cubs followed.

Alina sat still, trying to force breath into her lungs. Finally, a stone that was digging into the bottom of her left foot irritated her enough that she moved. She stood and shook her foot to dislodge the stone, and began to pick her way across the slope to her left. After putting some distance between herself and the bears, she started down again, and upon reaching the bottom, set out in the general direction where she had seen the smoke. But first she turned and studied the ridge so that she would know where to climb up again. There was a boulder sticking out of the earth near the top. Its shape suggested a pregnant woman lying on her side. *I can find that boulder again,* Alina told herself. With that, she turned and stepped into the trees.

As she went, she left marks on some of the trees so that she could find her way out again. After about an hour, she came to a clearing. A huge dead tree, twisted and hollow, stood sentry on the right edge. The clearing was so big her home village could have fit inside it. She wondered why she hadn't noticed it from the ridge. Keeping the tree to her right, Alina went straight through the open place, ferns and grass whickering against her legs.

A sudden gust of breeze lifted the stray ends of her hair when she reached the far end of the clearing. She looked up. The sky above was still clear, but she remembered the cloud bank. *Not much farther,* she told herself, *peering into the trees beyond. I can mark another ten trees, and then I should go back.*

She pushed on, but now every passing minute reminded her bad weather was coming. She was just about to turn back when another clearing opened up just ahead. *That will be the end of my exploring today,* she told herself, and stepped into the open space.

There he was, not five paces away, a little to her left. He had heard her coming, and was facing her as though he was waiting for her, his loaded bow in his hands, half-raised in her direction. His hair was black, and like hers, was braided in a single plait down his back. His eyes were black, too, and his skin was the color of willow bark tea. Or at least, most of his skin was that color. The skin around his mouth was pink, paler than hers, and there was a pink patch on his left temple. He was only a little taller than herself, lean and well-muscled. She knew this because he was bare to the waist. He wore a loin cloth and leggings, and leather shoes almost exactly like hers. As soon as he saw her, he lowered the bow.

Alina started to back up a step, but she knew running from him would do her no good. She was in his territory. So she stood frozen in indecision. The stranger was wearing a brace of rabbits tucked into his belt. He put the bow down and pulled the rabbits out as he raised one hand, palm outward, in a gesture of greeting and peace. After a moment's hesitation, Alina copied the gesture. Then he pointed to himself and said, "Otani."

Was that his name? She said, "Otani." Then she pointed to herself and said, "Alina."

"Alina," he answered with a nod.

He said something else, a short sentence, maybe. Alina shook her head. "I don't understand you."

He nodded again, as if he expected that she wouldn't. After a moment's thought, he separated the rabbits and held one out to her.

Alina put one hand on her heart, hoping he would understand that she was thanking him, then shook her head. Now she did take a step back.

He spoke again, his voice soft and low, but insistent. "Take it," he seemed to be saying. When she didn't move, he did something that astounded her. Still holding out the rabbit, he turned his head and most of his body away. It was the same thing she had done with Crow at the beginning. She had turned away so that the bird wouldn't be threatened. Now she was faced with a new dilemma. She didn't want to insult him. That seemed even more dangerous than taking his gift. So she took two steps closer, reached out and took the rabbit.

She stepped back again as he turned toward her. She laid her hand over her heart a second time and said, "Thank you."

Now he pointed at the sky toward the south and raised his eyebrows. Was she aware of the coming storm?

She nodded and took another step back. He said something, raised his hand again, and turning from her, picked up his bow and went his own way across the clearing and into the trees. Huffing with fear and excitement, Alina hurried back toward the ridge, pausing only to look for her mark on the trees she had passed. She could hardly believe it. She had found another person, and this one didn't seem inclined to rape and murder at first sight.

She stopped at the bottom of the ridge and sat a moment on the trunk of a fallen tree to catch her breath. *I have finally found another person.* She untied the bladder at her belt and took a swallow of water. Only then did she remember the bears, but it seemed they were gone. They probably had some sheltered spot to run to. And now she needed to get back to hers. She stood, gathered her things and started up the slope.

The wind gusted, whipping the tree branches around her as she climbed back down the other side of the ridge. She was nearly at the bottom when her foot slipped. She landed well, but banged and scraped her left elbow against the rocks. She made a cursory glance at the bloody spot, then hurried home. She had intended to gather some greens, but the storm was on top of her now. The sky rolled and boiled with clouds that were an odd shade of green. The strangeness of them made them more ominous, and now there was that heavy sweet scent in the air that spoke of storms. She began to run, crashing through the forest, heedless of anything but her need to get home. She was only a couple of minutes from safety when something small and hard struck the top of her head. Another hit her shoulder, and in moments there was a deafening rattle and clatter all around her.

She didn't stop to look, but round white things were pounding the floor of the forest. Pebbles? How was that possible? They hurt when they hit her. As she came pelting around the edge of her rock formation, one of the pebbles struck the back of her neck and went sliding down her spine. Ice! The sky was raining pebbles of ice! She had heard of ice falling this way, but she had never seen it. Just as she began to duck through the cave's opening, a clap of thunder slammed just above her head. She screamed and went to her knees for a second before scrambling to her feet and shoving the door into its place. She leaned against the door, panting and shaking. If the sky fell down and buried everything she would not have been surprised.

After a few minutes, despite the noise of thunder and hail, Alina decided that the sky was going to stay where it was. She let her gear drop and inspected the rabbit Otani had given her. The poor thing looked like rats had been at it. In her panicked race home, she had broken one of its legs, and its fur was gouged in places where it had smacked against the trees. *Oh well,* she thought, *it's still meat.* She skinned it and cut it up, dropping the meat into her pot for stew. No greens to go with it, but it would do.

The hail shower intensified, and the noise was so loud that Alina kept glancing dubiously at the ceiling of the cave. It didn't help that an occasional ice pellet rattled down inside from the crack. She wondered if Otani had made it to safety. But after about an hour, as suddenly as the storm started, it stopped. The abrupt silence rang in her ears. After a minute or two, Alina shakily got to her feet, went to the door and moved it aside. The wind was still blowing, and ice pellets lay in heaps on the ground, but the downpour had stopped. It wasn't even raining. Alina ventured out. That weird green sky was gone, and the clouds were breaking up, scuttling away on the wind. Overhead the sky shone a brilliant, blameless blue.

Maja seemed to know exactly what she was doing. Alina noted a few arguments between Bren and his new wife in the beginning, some of them heated, but as the next couple of years wore on, the arguments dwindled, and Maja came out on top. Now it was Bren who dwindled. Soon after he came home with her, he stood up at dinner and said, "Listen, all of you. Cotta needed a new ship. His old one was no longer seaworthy. So I told him to build another. He has finished it, and I will be there tomorrow morning to help him launch his boat for the first time."

This was typical of Bren. He liked to point out some improvement in village life, such as this new fishing boat, or a new kind of crop in the fields, and though he didn't build the boat or farm the land, he found a way to take credit. But for the past several months, he had made no such pronouncements. He sat silent most nights, speaking only to Maja. The former practice of men coming to Bren's table to speak to him also dropped away. If Bren was afraid of women in general, as Freda suggested, the rest of the men seemed to be afraid of Maja.

And then, Bren, who had shown nothing but contempt for Brother James's teachings, allowed himself to be baptized by Father Otto, and decreed that the whole village follow his example. Alina studied his face carefully as he came up out of the water. Whatever the expression was in his eyes, it wasn't joy.

Alina watched these developments with growing alarm. If Maja ruled Bren, what else might she convince him to do?

For her part, Alina watched Maja carefully, while avoiding Father Otto. She wanted nothing to do with the priest, though she was certain the day was coming when she would be ordered to attend Otto's church. So she made the most of the time she had. In the warm months, once Dag had turned four, she sneaked out to the forest with her sons to teach them wood skills, but now that it was cold, she kept them inside and taught them all the stories she could remember from Brother James.

The following summer, to her joy and relief, Ebbe paid another visit. "Father is not well," he told her after they embraced. "I don't think he will live much longer. I don't know whether Bren will let you go see him, but I am going to ask, and I want to take the boys, too."

Alina answered, "Whether I can go or not, I want the boys to meet him."

When Ebbe asked Bren, he started to refuse, but Maja broke in, her voice smooth as butter, "Her father is dying, Husband." She laid a hand lightly on Bren's arm. "I am sure she would be grateful if you allowed her to go." She then smiled and added, "I know I would be."

So Bren allowed it, and one week later, Alina left the village for the first time since she had come there. Ebbe had brought a horse for Gunnar to ride. The boy was nine years old, but from the way he sat in the saddle, Alina caught a glimpse of the man he would become. Dag rode in front with her most of the journey, though sometimes he rode with his uncle. Three of Ebbe's men traveled with them. Alina, who had hardly sat a horse during her marriage, was sore from unused muscles for the first couple of days, but she quickly adjusted, and wondered why she had denied herself the pleasure.

On the third day, Ebbe glanced over at her and grinned. "You look happy, Sister."

She smiled back. "Do I? I guess I am happy. I am with you and with my boys." She didn't need to add that she was not with Bren.

They arrived at her childhood village on the afternoon of the fourth day. "See that flat boat?" She said to the boys as she pointed to the ferry. "We are going to get off our horses now and ride the boat across the river." They dismounted, and Alina stepped onto the ferry with the children. Ebbe followed, leaving the horses with his men.

As Alina stepped on, the ferryman looked up and gave her a nearly toothless grin. "So you are back at last, Miss!"

"Peg!" Alina exclaimed. "You're still at it!"

He chuckled. "Oh, yes. My boy takes over for me in the mornings now, but this is my work and I will do it as long as I can." He eyed Gunnar and Dag. "Are these your sons?"

Alina laid a hand on Gunnar's head. "They are." She eyed Dag, who was standing at the edge of the ferry, peering into the water. Gunnar, on the other hand, had his arm wrapped around her waist, and regarded the old ferryman with solemn eyes.

A small crowd awaited them on the opposite side. Alina was hugged, kissed on the cheek, exclaimed and wept over. Looking around her again, she was reminded of the difference between this village and Bren's. This place was so much smaller, though it had grown. Several new houses had sprouted like dandelions in her absence.

Ebbe said, "Let's go see Father first. He has been waiting."

They climbed the steps into the main hall. Alina noted that the room was unchanged except for a pair of new hangings behind the head table. She followed her brother to the back of the room where a series of doors opened into the family's private quarters. Ebbe pulled open the door to their father's room.

During the journey, Alina had been anxious about seeing her father. Would he be very changed? Would he know her? Did he know what kind of life he had sent her to? Those worries fell away as she approached the bed. She knew him, and her father's eyes were on her with full recognition.

Alina didn't immediately go back across the ridge. Her encounter with Otani had been exciting, but it also unnerved her. She knew nothing about him, and she'd worked so hard to survive in this land, she didn't want to squander her efforts. He might be someone who would be at peace with her, or he might not. She was on edge for the first few days, wondering if he would track her here, but he didn't come, and she thought that maybe the hailstorm had erased most of the signs of her passing – except for the marks on the trees, of course.

After several more days, Alina decided that she would go there again, and this time she would bring him a gift. With that in mind, she waded across the river and went down the salt hole, where she collected enough salt to fill another small pot, brought it back and ground the chunks into powder between two rocks. When the pot was full, she tied the lid on and stowed it in her bag.

She planned to go the next day if the weather was good. But first, she went to her knees. "Holy Lord," she prayed, "I need wisdom in this matter. I have asked You to bring me to people of peace." She hesitated, thinking, then added, "If I should not go, will You please send rain and thunder?" She had no idea whether this was a legitimate request, but Brother James had told her that, when she was in doubt, to ask anyway. The next morning dawned fine and clear.

She climbed over the ridge and set out, looking for her marks on the trees. If Otani was not in the clearing, she didn't know where she would go from there. As it turned out, he wasn't in the second clearing. He was in the first, the one with the gnarled tree on one side. When he looked up and saw her standing there, he smiled and raised his hand in greeting before striding over to meet her. Alina returned the gesture. He halted a few paces away. She pulled the little salt pot from her bag, came forward a step and set it on the ground between them.

She backed up as he came and picked up the pot. He hefted it in one hand, testing its weight before he pulled off the cord that tied the lid on. He lifted the lid, peered inside, and said a few words in a questioning voice. He looked up at her.

She pantomimed touching the tip of a finger to her tongue, so he dipped a fingertip into the salt and tasted it. His eyes went wide and a grin lit up his face, showing white, even teeth. He was talking now, and he sounded excited. He laid a hand on his heart as Alina had done the first time, saying thank you. He put the lid back on the pot and carefully tied it with the cord.

Now what? Alina wondered.

He answered that question for her. He pointed to himself, then to the trees on the far side of the clearing. He pointed to her next, made a beckoning gesture and raised his eyebrows. Alina understood this to mean, *I am going that way. Will you come with me?*

Alina wrestled with herself for only a second before nodding and gesturing with one hand for him to lead the way. He smiled at her and led her out of the clearing, through the trees to the second clearing, and through that one. They had walked for about an hour when the trees ended abruptly at a rocky hill. He gestured to the left and went that way, circling the base of the hill until they came to a tumble of boulders. There he stopped and pointed up. Alina's eyes followed where he pointed and she saw a cave opening about halfway up the hill.

He started climbing up, and Alina could just make out the trail that led to the opening. It was not nearly as difficult a climb as her side of the ridge was. Before she knew it, she was standing at the entrance to his home. The cave Otani lived in was about half the size of hers, and there was no hole in the roof to let smoke out, so he had built his fire near the entrance. His bed, like hers, was a pallet of skins. This was at the very back of the cave. Along the side opposite the fire were his provisions and tools. It looked like he stored his food in boxes of stitched animal skins. Everything was neat and ordered.

Otani set her gift down gently on top of one of the skin boxes, then pointed to a duck he had shot and plucked. He pointed to her, then back to himself. He was inviting her to share a meal with him. Alina nodded and laid a hand on her heart. He grinned, picked up the duck and began to spit it. She looked around again. He apparently had only

hand…." Brega's smile was fond, and a little crooked. "I have to keep reminding her. We'll be all right," she finished.

"I will help you however I can," Alina said.

"I finally finished weaving the cloth for Bren's tunic," Brega said, changing the subject. "Now I just have to cut the pieces and sew them."

"It will be a beautiful tunic," Alina said, thinking that she had never loved her husband enough to put so much work into a gift for him. "When do you plan to give it to him?"

"I should have it finished in time for the harvest feast," Brega answered, and she smiled. "Thank you for your help with it. I wouldn't have been able to finish in time if I'd had to spin so much wool by myself."

Brega's worries for her oldest daughter were relieved the following month when Bren announced that Rolf had asked for Ava to be married to his son, and that Bren had consented. "We will celebrate their wedding at the harvest feast."

Alina reached out and squeezed Brega's hand. "I am happy for her – and for you." She knew that marriage might not keep Ava safe from the likes of Father Otto, but the girl would have the protection of her husband and his family. "This harvest feast will be unlike any we've celebrated before."

The next time Alina went to see Otani, she had one good sized fish that she had caught from the river and a couple of cattail stalks. Otani seemed happy to see the fish, and went to work preparing to roast it.

While the food was cooking, he reached out and touched Alina's braid, held the end of his own braid out next to hers, then raised his eyebrows in question. Was he asking why her hair was yellow?

How could she possibly answer that? She would have to tell him the story of how she came to be there. She took a straight stick from the edge of the fire. Its end was burned and blackened. She took another stick from his pile of kindling and put its end into the coals so she could replace the first when it was used up. She took the blackened stick to the cave entrance, beckoning him to follow. The rock that the cave sat on made a sort of shelf or porch just outside. It was fairly flat and smooth. Alina considered the size of the space she had to work with, and then she began.

She had always been able to draw things, but rarely had an opportunity. Now, on the left side of the shelf, she drew a depiction of the village – just a few houses and some figures of people. "My village," she said, though she knew he wouldn't understand her words. She pointed east, made the gesture emphatic. Far, far away east. He nodded, but looked puzzled.

The next thing she drew was the sea. She did her best to make the waves, but Otani frowned and shook his head, not understanding. So Alina went inside and got her water bladder. She poured a few drops into her hand, then pointed to the waves, spreading her hands to indicate something very big. Otani's eyes widened, and he nodded and pointed eastward. So he knew about the big water. Good.

On the right hand side, she drew what she remembered of the shore where they had landed. She pointed toward the east again, but ended with a downward point to try to help him understand that the shore was just over there. Not so far. He nodded. Her stick was no longer leaving black marks, so she retrieved the second stick and came back to her place in the entrance.

Now came the hard part. She drew the ship on the water. When he shook his head, she realized he'd maybe never seen a boat. Alina sighed. How to explain? But now the smell of cooked fish interrupted them, so they went inside together. While they ate, Alina had an idea. She took a small piece of wood and carved a tiny boat from it with her knife. When she was done, she poured water into a turtle shell that Otani used as a bowl, and set the little boat afloat.

He nodded and grinned, and told her a word she assumed was his word for boat. Alina repeated the word, then pointed outside toward her unfinished drawing. "Ah!" he exclaimed. He understood. When they finished eating and were back outside, he pointed to the boat and repeated the word. Alina smiled. She sat down, and with a newly-blackened stick, drew a figure of a man, and then one of a woman. She pointed to the man and counted on her fingers. "One, two, three, four, five," following this with hash marks in the dirt. Three sets of five, plus one extra. Sixteen men. She pointed to the boat again, to the man, to the hash marks. Sixteen men in the boat.

His eyes went wide, and he pointed to the boat and spread his hands apart. "Yes," she answered, nodding. "Big boat." She said all three words in his language, not hers. She was picking up words from him as quickly as she could. Now she pointed to the figure of the woman, made four hash marks, pointed to the ship again. Sixteen men, four women on the boat.

She sat back on her heels, considering. Otani pointed to the woman, held up one finger, and pointed to her. She nodded. Yes, she was one of the women. Over the boat she drew a circle in the sky and pointed toward the sun. He nodded. She drew an arching line from her village in the east to the shore in the west. She pointed up, tracing the path of the sun in the sky and held up one finger. One day. Otani repeated the gesture and said one day in his language. Alina repeated it back to him. Then she counted off the days by fives, making hash marks under the circle sun. Five days, ten days, fifteen, twenty. She stopped making the marks at thirty-three. She made a motion as if she was pushing the ship from east to west.

Otani's eyes widened, but he made the same motion toward the ship and pointed to her hash marks. Alina thought he probably understood that it had taken that long for the boat to go from her village to the western shore. So far, so good. She erased the ship with a swipe of her hand and drew it again at the shore. Now she drew, as well as she could remember, a picture of one of the men who had attacked her people. Otani's eyes went solemn as she did this. She made the figure's face angry, put a spear in its hand. Then she drew her finger across her throat in an unmistakable gesture.

She had seen five men get back into the ship, so she erased all but five of the hash marks under the figure of the man. With a final gesture, she erased three of the hash marks under the figure of the woman. Otani covered his mouth with one hand and made a sound that was somewhere between a grunt and a groan. Alina pointed to the man figure, to the five hash marks, to the ship, and she made the pushing motion again. Five men went back east on the ship.

Alina let out a long breath. There was much more that she would tell him if she knew how. But Otani figured out how to ask. He laid one hand on her shoulder gently, then took the stick from her. He drew figures of a man and a woman similar to hers, but side by side, and he joined their hands. He pointed to the woman and to her. *This is you.* He pointed to the man and raised his eyebrows. *Your husband?* In answer, she pointed to the ship. He shook his head as if in disbelief. Alina decided to tell him one more thing. She drew two smaller figures to represent her sons, the smaller holding the larger one's hand, and the larger holding the woman's. When he nodded, she pointed to the two figures and back to the village far off in the east.

Summer passed quickly. Alina busied herself helping Brega get things ready for Ava's wedding. The ceremony itself would be simple, the hall decorated with fall leaves and berries for the harvest feast. Brega, thinking ahead, had spun thread to make a new dress for the bride, and now she and Alina began weaving this thread into cloth. Bren had brought blue dye back from one of his trips, and Brega planned to use it on the dress.

When Alina wasn't helping with the dress, she was embroidering a small tapestry as her wedding gift. She wasn't as skilled with the needle as Brega was, and Kiah surpassed them both, but she could think of nothing else to give. So in her mind she drew a scene of two horses (Ava's favorite animal) in a meadow full of flowers, surrounded by forest. The challenge was to take what was in her mind and make it happen on the cloth. She stitched with greater care than she had ever given before, and to her relief, the tapestry slowly took shape. The horses looked like horses, and she even stitched a few birds perched in the trees and tucked a little white fox in one corner.

Between this project and taking the boys into the woods every day for training, Alina was busy. She would later think that maybe she had been too busy. Had she missed the signs?

The day of Ava's wedding dawned bright and clear, with the first hint of chill in the air. The whole village had been abuzz the past several days with preparations for the feast and the wedding. Trestle tables were set up outside the great hall. So many people were expected to come that they couldn't all fit inside. Gerda excused herself from waiting on Alina so that she could join the cooks with their preparations.

Alina and the boys ate their breakfast outside, but peeked in the door when they were finished. Dag gasped, "The forest is in there!"

Alina laughed. "It looks that way." Garlands of leaves and berries draped the fronts of the tables. *Someone spent a long time working on that,* she thought. And they had dug up a small tree, set it in a pot in the center of the hall, and garlanded it with strings of white wool. That's where Ava and her groom would be married. "So pretty," she murmured, turning away.

"All right," she told the boys. "We will go out into the woods this morning, but not for very long. When we come back, you will both have a bath…." When Gunnar groaned, she held up a finger. "No arguments. We will get cleaned up and dressed in our best things to honor Ava."

That evening, when they were in the great hall, scrubbed and seated, Alina looked around her with a smile. She was glad she had come back from Ebbe's. She would have been sorry to miss this. Instead of beginning with the meal, as was the custom, welcome cups were passed around, and the bride and groom took their places in front of the potted tree. Ava wore a delicate circlet of silver on her head. Her wedding dress, dyed the color of a summer sky, showed off her dark hair and blue eyes perfectly. The groom, grinning but nervous, was a blonde whose beard was just filling out. He was dressed in a russet tunic and new boots.

Father Otto performed the ceremony, but it was in Latin, so no one understood a word he said. The couple exchanged rings when he gestured to them. Otto raised his hands over the couple's heads, indicating that they were married. But no one cheered yet. The ceremony was incomplete. The groom said in a loud voice, "I give you, Ava this sword of my family for the protection of our future generations." His father stepped forward with the sword and put it in Ava's waiting hands. Now Brega stepped forward, also carrying a sword. Ava said, "I give you, Hurd this sword of my family for the protection of our future generations." Brega gave him the weapon. They both held their swords aloft, lowered them, and turned and kissed. Now the cheers broke out. Alina saw Father Otto shake his head and roll his eyes. Alina almost shook her own head. That man had no understanding. But hopefully Ava was now safe from him.

Then it was time for the feast. Alina had sat down to a harvest feast every year she could remember, but this one surpassed them all. There was a soup made from mushrooms foraged from the woods, dozens of game pies, roasted root vegetables, platters of fish, and at least six different kinds of bread. Bren had brought in wine from far to the south, and there were rivers of good mead. Then as if that were not enough, the servants brought in platters piled high with honey cakes, sweetened fruit, and other delicacies.

Bren's bard stood and sang a verse in honor of the couple. When he was finished, one after the other, men stood to drink to the health and prosperity of the new couple. Alina sat patiently though the toasts. Some were more dignified than others. Some were downright bawdy. These made Ava's and Hurd's faces turn crimson.

Then the toasts petered out, and it was time for the musicians and some dancing, but to Alina's surprise, Bren stood up, resplendent in the white tunic Brega had made for him, his silver torque polished and gleaming at his neck. He had been so quiet of late, and he hardly knew his own daughter. Alina hadn't expected him to say anything. Was he going to toast the bride and groom? He did not raise a cup. Instead, he called out, "Listen, all of you. As you know, the prosperity of this village has come from trade. I have taken my men to the south, to the east, and even over the sea to the west."

He paused. Here and there was a murmur of assent, but most were looking at Bren quizzically. Why was he bringing this up now? "Of course, I have men I trust to the east and south, men I can deal with. We treat each other fairly, and everyone prospers. I have no such advantage over the sea, and it is my intent to secure that opportunity for this village. With that in mind, I have decided to send some of our people there to build a colony so that we can trade back and forth."

Alina swallowed, and heard a dry click in her throat. She felt it coming, a doom she could not escape. Bren said, "My wives have proven to be trustworthy women." He turned toward them, smiling. "I will send you four, and pair you with four of our best men." There. He had said it.

A woman screamed. It was Ava. She jumped from her seat and shouted, "No! You will not send my mother away!" Her groom stood, put an arm around her and whispered to her. With a sob, she nodded and sat down again, weeping into his chest. Her sobbing was the only sound in the hall. No one else moved or spoke.

Alina, frozen where she sat, looked at Maja. She was wearing a smile that Alina recognized, and it made her blood run cold. She had seen such a smile before, years ago on a summer day in the woods with her brother. She had been about twelve years old. She and Ebbe had taken Geri, their father's best hunting dog, with them. As the day was rounding to noon, Geri had gone to sniff at a fallen log, the hairs on her neck bristling. In the blink of an eye, an adder shot out and bit Geri on the nose. Ebbe killed the adder, but there was nothing they could do for the dog. Her face swelled up, and the next day, Father slit her throat to end her suffering.

Maja's smile was like that snake's. Her mouth curved up at the corners, but her eyes were utterly cold. *She's behind this,* Alina told herself. *This has been her plan, probably from the beginning. She wanted to get rid of us, and at the same time allow Bren to make a grand gesture.* She glanced at Brega, who sat with her head high, and with tears streaming down her face. *She loved him once. I wonder if she still does.*

"I will meet with you four in my quarters after the feast," Bren was now saying to the women he had married. "I am sure you have questions."

Despite the best efforts of the musicians, the dancing was subdued. A few of the women moved about to the music, but hardly a man made it to the center of the room. Most of them were sitting or standing together in knots, talking, presumably arguing. Alina wondered if any of them would make an effort to stop this insanity, but she thought they would not. For better or worse, their fortunes were tied to Bren's. She looked over to her boys. Dag was chasing around the room with other children his age. He had not understood what the announcement meant to his little world. Gunnar, on the other hand, sat like a statue in his chair, his eyes pinned on Alina. She met his gaze, then got up and went to him.

"He's going to send you away," he said as she sat next to him. "Why does he hate us?"

Alina was not about to offer empty comfort to her son. "He doesn't hate us, Gunnar." She laid a hand on his and sighed, "He doesn't care about us at all."

"That's worse," Gunnar declared. "Well, I hate him." And Alina had nothing to say to that.

pair of cushioned chairs before a fireplace. Bren had turned one of the chairs around and was sitting in it. He didn't offer seats to his wives. They had to remain standing.

He held his hands up in a warding off gesture as they came filing in. "Let me say what I have to say," he told them. "When I have finished, you can ask your questions."

Alina glanced at the others. Brega was her usual calm self, though her eyes were swollen and red. Agnes was chewing the inside of her cheek, her arms crossed tight against her chest. Kiah looked bewildered, like she had no idea why she was there.

Bren said, "Now, I want you to understand that I am putting a lot of trust in you, sending you out like this. As I said in the hall, this will be an opportunity for prosperity for our village, and for you as well. I will pair each of you with someone to be your husband there, and you will make homes for yourselves. When you think about what you are to take with you, you only need pack your usual women's things—things to cook with, things to make clothes with. Don't worry about weapons or tools. The men will take care of those. We will set sail in the spring. And yes, I am going on the voyage with you." He paused and looked at each one in turn. "Do you have any questions?"

Kiah spoke up. "How can you expect us to take our children on a sea voyage? Won't that be hard for them?"

Alina closed her eyes, but kept her expression neutral. *Poor Kiah,* she thought, with uncharacteristic empathy for the younger woman. *This is going to be bad.*

Bren's jaw was set. He let out a little huff of breath before saying, "You won't be taking the children, Kiah. They will stay here."

Just as Alina expected, a cry erupted from Kiah that rose in pitch to an unearthly shriek. Brega tried to put her arms around the screaming woman, but Kiah beat her off with her fists. Bren shot up from his chair and grabbed both of her arms. "Be quiet," he told her, "or I will have my men take you away and lock you up until the day we leave. You'll never see your children again." Alina's jaw dropped open. This was harsh even for Bren. But it worked. Kiah's screams reduced almost at once to shaking sobs. She trembled all over.

"Do not worry about your children," came a silken voice as Maja stepped out from behind the curtain, her face a mask of compassion and concern. "I will take care of them. They will want for nothing."

Even Kiah, who seemed to understand so little, was shaking her head. "You do not love them."

Maja raised her perfect brows. "That is true. But your maids love them, don't they? Your children will still have their maids." She laid a protective hand on her belly, a gesture Alina knew well. *So, she is finally pregnant. She is pregnant, and he hasn't left her.*

Alina was so shocked that it took her a moment to register what Maja had said, that the children would be looked after by their maids. *Gerda. The boys will be all right with Gerda.* But Alina was not reassured. There was something else. Something evil lurked underneath. She almost expected to feel the floor writhe under her feet.

"Who do you plan to pair us with?" Brega asked, once Kiah was under control again.

"I have not decided yet," Bren told her, releasing his grip on Kiah and dropping back into his chair, as if exhausted. "I will let you know well ahead of time."

Brega nodded wanly, clearly expecting no good thing to come of these pairings. Alina said, "What is the land like on the other side?"

Bren gave her a look almost of gratitude. "It's a beautiful country, much like our own. Lots of trees, fertile soil, plenty of animals. You will be able to build a good life."

His answer was so enthusiastic that Alina wondered if he'd ever really been there.

Two mornings later when she woke, Alina realized that she had to do something to get her boys out of Maja's hands. "I will take care of them," Maja had said. That could mean so many things. She sent the boys to breakfast and paced the room. What could she do? She could run with them to Ebbe, but if Bren came after them – if he brought his fighters with him -- he would take them back. Ebbe didn't have nearly enough men to win a battle against Bren, and Alina didn't want to bring destruction down on her old village. But Ebbe had talked to Bren about having the boys over the summer, and Bren had consented. Could she convince him to let them go early? Somehow get a message to Ebbe warning him of the danger of sending them home again? Maybe Ebbe could hide them?

She went over the things she might say to Bren in her head, discarding a sentence here, a phrase there. She would have to take more care with these words than any she had ever spoken. *I can do this*, she told herself, remembering her success with the tapestry. *I can control my fear and say only true words he will hear.* Once she had her words lined up in her head, she went to breakfast.

She approached Bren later that morning. Ava's new father-in-law was talking to him, but when he saw Alina standing to one side, he excused himself and left. Bren nodded at her as she neared, his eyes wary. "I want to ask your favor with something," she began. She was a petitioner now, not his wife. Not anymore. Bren seemed to relax a little. She had come to him on his territory. He was comfortable with this. Good.

"What is it?" he asked. They were in the great hall, and no one was near them to hear. He leaned against one of the hall's pillars, his arms crossed loosely, to hear her out.

"You already understand that the parting from our children will be difficult," Alina began, careful to leave out any words referencing herself specifically.

"Of course it will," he answered, "but I trust that you will bear it bravely."

"You can help with that," she went on. "You graciously consented to allow the boys to visit my brother in the summer." She paused, and he nodded. "If they were to go early this year, perhaps a week or so before the ship sails, we can part with each other in private. That will allow me to board the ship calmly, and without tears." She wasn't sure this was true, but Bren hated displays of feminine emotion more than just about anything else.

"Ah, I see." He studied her for so long that she had to suppress the urge to squirm. His expression went from curiosity to amusement to calculation. Finally, he said, "Very well. Let us strike a deal. I will send the boys to your brother…." He stopped and stared at the ceiling a moment. "I think ten days will be enough. I will send them with my men ten days before we set sail. That will give the men time to get there and back again. Will that do?"

Alina nodded, but she knew better than to relax. He was going to demand more of her than a lack of hysterics. "And in return?" she asked.

His head went back, and he laughed. The sound filled the great hall. People turned to look at them, but Alina ignored them. "You know," he said, still chuckling, "of you four, Brega is the best, Kiah the most willing, and Agnes the most cunning, but you are the smartest." This did not comfort her one bit. She felt like she was dangling on the end of a string that he held – a string he had the power to cut. Finally he said, "In return, I am going to pair you with Huus."

If he had punched her in the gut, she would have not felt more pain. "No," she whispered, sinking onto a bench. How could he ask this of her? "Pair him with Agnes," she said. "She likes him." The words were out of her mouth before she thought about them. Now she closed her lips and clenched her teeth.

Bren's eyes went dark. "I am aware," he growled. "I have someone else in mind for her."

Alina studied him for several heartbeats. His mind was made up. She was not going to change it. This was the price she would have to pay for the lives of her boys. "But why me?" A worthless question, she knew.

To her surprise, Bren answered her. "Because you can handle him."

Then she surprised herself by blurting out, "You pair me with Huus, and one of us will not survive it." Bren's only reaction was a smile. He had already figured that much. She sat and thought for a minute, willing her brain to work, in spite of her shock. Finally she said. "It would be a bad idea to let Huus know that he is paired with me."

Bren raised his eyebrows. "How so?"

Carefully, carefully she put her words together, aware of the truth of them as she spoke. "You know what a braggart he is. If he finds out that he is paired with any one of us, he will begin to think he is your equal. You will have a hard time controlling him."

Bren nodded slowly. "You may have a point. Very well, I won't tell him until after we are aboard ship. Will that suit you?"

"None of this suits me," she answered, "but it certainly suits you." With that, she stood and walked out.

It was Otani who decided the question of whether he would go or stay. When they had finished eating, he pointed to the sun's position in the sky and said, "I must go now."

Alina wanted to ask him to stay, but she couldn't make herself say the words, so she just nodded and said, "It is dark soon."

He stood and went back to the cave to gather his things. She hesitated. If she didn't say anything to him now, was she missing her chance? After a minute's futile debate, she followed. By the time Alina got there, Otani was ready to leave. He smiled and placed a hand over his heart as she had done at first with him. "Thank you for the meal." She started to protest that he had brought the meat, but before she could speak, he added, "Thank you for showing me your cave." With that, he was off.

Deflated and still uncertain, Alina watched him go. When he was out of sight, she sighed, and her shoulders slumped. She had been praying, asking if it was right for her to be with this man, and maybe this was the answer. Maybe he wasn't thinking of her the way she thought of him. "Well, all right," she murmured, "At least I have a friend."

She decided that tonight she would do something she had been thinking about, but putting off. She had enjoyed making the drawings in the dirt to explain her story to Otani. In the past week she found several deposits of rusty colored rock. She had collected some of these and pounded them down to powder. She had also found chalk and gathered chunks of it. Now she took black coals from her fire. The smoothest walls were just inside the entrance. She paused to consider how much room she had to work with, and then she began to sketch.

It had been more than a year since she had seen them, but their faces were forever imprinted on her heart. It was far easier than she expected to capture Gunnar's solemnity and Dag's exuberance. She used the charcoal to fill in Gunnar's thick, dark hair – just like his father's. Dag had his mother's blonde curls. A mixture of chalk with just a hint of the rust powder made the color come alive. She put a long feather in Gunnar's hand, and drew Dag holding his favorite toy, a leather ball.

When she was nearly finished, she took a step back and surveyed her work. Or, that was what she meant to do. The images, so loved and familiar, were blurred by a sudden surge of tears. "I did everything for you that I could," she whispered to her boys. They stared silently back at her. "And I have kept my promise to you. I am alive."

But tonight, it no longer seemed like that was enough.

Gunnar surprised Alina a few days later. They were alone together in the house. Dag was outside playing. Gunnar laid a hand on Alina's arm and said, "I have a plan."

She frowned. "A plan for what, son?"

He dropped his voice to a whisper. "You don't have to go away on that boat."

Alina laid down her mending and gave him her full attention. "Tell me what you have in mind."

"We all have horses now," he told her. "Even Dag rides pretty well."

She nodded. "True."

"We could pack some food and water, and go." His face, still sporting summer freckles, scrunched up as he concentrated. "We could leave in the middle of the night and be far away before anyone knows we're gone. We could go to Uncle Ebbe…."

She interrupted him. "That's the first place they'll look."

His eyes slid away, and his shoulders slumped a little. "Yes, I guess that's right." He thought for a moment and said, "In the woods, then. We know how to live in the woods."

"Winter is coming," she reminded him.

"But if we go south," he countered, "it won't be so cold."

Alina nodded again. "That's correct, but we would have to go very far south, and we'd have to go across the sea there."

There wasn't much that made Gunnar cry, but now tears of frustration filled his eyes, and he slammed one fist on the table. "There has to be somewhere we can go!"

Alina reached out and pulled him to her. She could not tell him about the agreement she had made with Bren. And she wasn't ready to tell her son that she intended to sacrifice herself for his sake. "Let's both think about it some more." She stroked his hair. "Maybe between the two of us, we can come up with something." He nodded, wiped his eyes, and went outside. She watched him go with a mixture of pride and apprehension. She had to save them. Nothing else mattered.

That afternoon she went to see Holgur. He was sharpening a scythe. Relieved for her ears' sake that he wasn't hammering on something, she sat down on a water keg and watched him. He glanced up from his work and gave her a nod of greeting. "Lady Alina. How goes it with you?"

It was a courteous question only. She noted the way his face darkened when he saw who it was. She also knew that his anger was not directed at her. So she lifted a shoulder and said, "About as you would expect."

He grunted and laid the blade down. "I cannot believe…."

She held up a hand to forestall him. "Let's say nothing about that. I need something from you, Holgur. Well, two things really."

"Whatever you wish, Lady. Name it and it is done."

"First, I need a hatchet that I can take with me," she told him. "Do you happen to have one?"

He glared at her with his one good eye a moment. "I don't have one to spare, so I will make you one." He sat up straighter and laid one fist against his hip. "Do you mind telling me why you need a hatchet?"

"The second thing I need from you is your silence," she answered. "You cannot tell anyone about the hatchet, and you cannot repeat what I am about to tell you."

"You have my word. On my honor, I will keep silent."

Alina straightened her skirt and clasped her hands in her lap. "I will need a hatchet to defend myself because Bren is pairing me with Huus."

His mouth gaped open. "How? How could he do this to you?"

"I am no one special to him."

A low growl sounded from deep in his chest. A small shiver ran up Alina's spine. That growl, deep and feral, gave her a sense of Holgur's fearsome anger. She supposed that when he was younger, the blacksmith was a terror in battle. Even now, though she considered him a friend, she wouldn't want to cross him. He said, "I will make your hatchet nice and sharp."

A week later, he knocked on her door. When she opened it, he handed her a slim bundle wrapped in leather. "That's what you asked for," he said, eyeing Gerda, who stood behind her.

"It's all right, Holgur," Alina told him. "She knows."

"Ah. Well, in that case, I made these for you, too." He placed a small wooden box into her free hand. It was heavy.

"What's this?" Tucking her new hatchet under one arm, she untied the cord that held the lid on. Inside the box were at least a dozen iron arrow heads arranged in a layer of grease to protect them from rust.

He cleared his throat. "I understand you are good with a bow. These may come in handy."

"They may indeed. Thank you." She stood on tiptoe and kissed his grizzled cheek.

Alina slept badly that night. She turned over, and turned again, seeking comfort in the bed and finding none. Seeing the finished portrait of her boys rattled her. It was like they were in the cave with her, but as ghosts. She thought about washing them off the wall, but she knew expunging the images would not help. Their faces were inside her forever. Then there was the image of Otani's retreating back. She had hoped he would stay. She was so tired of being alone.

Brother James's words came to her then. "Your father in heaven is good, and he loves you. He gave up his own son for you. When things are hard, lean on your faith in him and pray. The Lord taught that if we have faith like a mustard seed, we can overcome our difficulties. We can do mighty things."

"What is a mustard seed?" she asked.

He laughed, and said, "All right, a dill seed then."

"But a dill seed is so tiny."

He nodded happily. "Yes, so tiny, and so full of life! The size is not important. The life is what matters."

With a sigh, she got up on her knees, then bent over until her forehead was on the pallet. "I don't even know what to say, or what to ask you for," she began, "but Brother James said you already know my thoughts. You have been with me all the way here, and to this very day you have kept me alive and made me strong, and for that I thank you. My boys…." What could she say? Tears flooded her eyes. Her chest heaved, and she sobbed, "They are in your hands. Take care of them."

After her tears subsided, she took a long, shuddering breath. "I thought Otani…I thought we might…." She stopped and fell silent.

The quiet voice came then, not one she heard with her ears, but very clear in her heart. *Can you be content if he is only your friend?*

"Can I?" she whispered into the dark. She paid lip service to friendship with Otani earlier, but now she needed to settle in her mind if she would be all right with that and nothing else. Marav had loved her, and she loved him. She wanted that kind of love again, but maybe Otani was not the one for her. She clenched her jaw and murmured, "And maybe there will never be anyone who loves me like that again." She considered her life ahead of her. She might have years yet to live. She imagined years of visits back and forth between his cave and hers. She forced herself to imagine him with another woman as his wife. She imagined him with children. And then she imagined a day when she still survived in this world and he did not.

She let out a long and painful breath. "If this is what you have for me, then I will learn to be content," she whispered. It was the best she could do. She lay there, quiet for several more minutes. Then, still curled up, she dropped over onto her side and fell asleep.

She woke the next morning, weary as if she had fought a battle. She got up and went out. She was nearly to the river's edge before she spotted Otani sitting on the tree trunk, waiting for her.

Winter passed far too quickly for Alina's liking. It would take years to teach her boys everything she thought they needed to know. She only had a few months. She continued to take them into the woods every day, stopping only when the snow reached Dag's waist. When winter drove them inside, she taught them the stories Brother James had told her, and every story of her people that she could remember. And she crafted a message that Gunnar would give to Ebbe, a message that would tell him what he needed to know without Gunnar understanding it.

They were past the winter solstice now. Time was drawing short. Alina decided it was time to talk to Gunnar about what was going to happen. She nodded to Gerda, who said, "Why don't you come with me, Dag? I think I saw some little cakes in the great hall this morning."

Dag sprang up. "Come on, Gunnar!"

"Your brother will be there in a few minutes," Alina said. "I need to talk to him first."

When they were gone, Alina turned to her firstborn. "You and your brother are going to visit your Uncle Ebbe early this year."

He was very still. "What about you?"

"I will be going across the sea."

"No," he whispered, his eyes filling with tears. "You can't go."

"I have to go, son." She raised a hand to forestall his protests. "Never mind why. Do you trust me?" He hesitated, then slowly nodded his head. "Good. Because this is important, more important than what happens to me. Do you understand?" Though Gunnar's eyes were rimmed with tears, he held them back. *He is learning,* she thought. "I have a message for you to give to your uncle. You must learn the whole thing exactly as I say it and tell it to him privately when you see him." She gently grasped his arm. "I can't trust anyone else with this."

Gunnar raised his chin a little. "I will carry your message."

Alina let out a long breath and chewed on her tongue a moment to keep the tears from her own eyes. "You are a brave young man. This is what I want you to tell your Uncle Ebbe. Say, 'Greetings from your loving sister. I am well. I am sending the boys to you early this year because I must soon make a long sea voyage. Do not be concerned for me, only be a father to the boys as you have always been. You may have heard that Bren has married again. She is as beautiful as the sea goddess, Ran. I am reminded of the time you and I went hunting with our father's best dog. This is what life is like. I pray that you keep in good health.'"

Gunnar wrinkled his nose. "The part about the dog doesn't make sense."

"It will make sense to your uncle," she replied. "Now I will say it again, and you repeat after me." They worked on Alina's message for the better part of an hour before she released him to go and find Gerda and Dag. When he was gone, Alina put another coat of oil on the inside of a leather bag. She had gotten the bag from a sailor. She traded with him – striking the deal with one good knife and a pot of mead. This bag was waterproofed, and best of all, it had straps that allowed her to carry it on her shoulders without having to use her hands.

She went over her mental list of things to take with her. She had the hatchet and the arrowheads. She had her knife. She had added three bowstrings to the arrowhead box. She needed a small cook pot, and some rope. Needle and thread. An awl. Each of these things would help her survive in the new land. She planned to take winter clothes and other personal items with her. Most of those things were already here in her house.

She had told Holgur that she needed the hatchet to defend herself, but her best plan was to not let Huus get close enough to make a fight necessary. It seemed to her, from Bren's reaction when she said one of them would not survive the pairing, that maybe he was counting on her to kill Huus, but she wasn't going to do Bren's dirty work if she didn't have to. She intended instead to escape the group and go alone into whatever wilderness was on the other side of the sea. Parts of her plan had already fallen into place. And now Gunnar knew her message. She would have him repeat it to her every day until the boys left.

Alina was counting on Ebbe to interpret the message. He had remarked once, after hearing stories about the goddess Ran, that he thought she could not be trusted. She hoped he would understand that Bren's new wife was beautiful like Ran, but dangerous as the tales said the goddess was, and that, given the opportunity, she would strike like an adder.

Chapter eleven

Otani sat on the trunk, facing the water. He gave no indication that he heard her coming, though Alina knew he must have. She hadn't taken any great pains to be quiet. She stopped and stared at his back for several heartbeats before stepping up to the trunk and sitting next to him. "You are here early." She wasn't quite fluent in his language yet. All she could do was to speak in the present, but she could at least make herself understood.

He glanced at her with a nod and a smile. "It is a fine day." It was, but that didn't explain why he was here. Alina smoothed a stray lock of hair behind her ear, watched the river, and waited. After several minutes, Otani showed her a stick that he held in his right hand. He bent a little and started sketching in the dirt at their feet. His hand shook slightly, and Alina frowned, wondering what had happened. She steeled herself for bad news.

Otani drew a figure of a man. Next to that he drew one of a woman. Despite her worry, Alina couldn't suppress a smile. He was going back to the way they had first understood each other. He pointed to the man and then to himself. Alina nodded. "That is you." He pointed to the woman and then to Alina. "And that is me." He nodded again. He looked at her for a long moment, then he erased the arms and drew them again, this time with hands joined between them. Otani looked at her again, his eyebrows raised.

Alina knew the words, but she was stunned, and she stammered, "You…you want me to be…your wife?"

He nodded, and his gaze toward her warmed. He had told her – weeks ago with pictures – that he was not married. She also understood that his village had cast him out because of his skin. Whether they thought he was bad luck, or that he might carry some disease, she didn't know, but when she was a child there had been a man in her father's village who had skin like Otani's. He had lived an otherwise healthy life. Still, she felt she needed confirmation from him. "You are not married to another woman?"

"No."

She believed him. So, it would be just the two of them. No one else to interfere. Also no one else to help, but that was a problem for another day. She answered him by putting her hand in his. Otani exclaimed, "Hah!" and with a broad and joyful grin, pulled her to him. Her head rested against his chest under his chin, and moments later she was startled to feel drops hitting the top of her head.

She pulled away. Tears ran down his face, but he was still smiling. "What is it?" she asked.

He wiped at his eyes. "Three summers ago, I lived with my people. I loved a girl, and I wanted her for my wife." He pointed to the pink skin around his mouth. "But this happened. The girl's mother was the first to notice it, and she told the elders. They said to wait to see if it would go away, but in a few months, there was more of this, not less. The girl would not talk to me, and then the elders told me I must leave. She married another, and I was sent to live alone in the forest." Alina took his hand again and held it tightly. She understood being cast away.

He took a long breath and went on. "I thought I would never have a wife, never have a family. I thought I would die out here alone." He gave her a long look. "And then one day, there you were." He raised their clasped hands and held them against his chest.

The yellow beads on his bracelet gleamed in the dappled sunlight. Alina saw it and said, "Tell me about your bracelet."

He nodded. "I had a sister. Nissi. She made this for me."

Alina's heart seemed to squeeze inside her. "She is dead?"

"No, but I had to leave her. She is twelve summers old now."

She sighed. There were so many ways to lose the ones you loved. Someday – she hoped it was far in the future – she would lose him, or he would lose her. She shook herself. The day was too fine to waste with sorrow, and this man was her husband. Or was he?

"With your people, what do you do to be married?" she asked. Trying to be clearer, she added, "Do you say special words or give…something?"

He smiled and bumped her shoulder gently with his. "I think, for you and me, it only matters what we want to do or say."

That's true. Ceremony doesn't have much point, she thought, *if there are no other people around.* So she said, "Then, I am your wife, and I am your wife as long as we live."

He laid his free hand over their linked ones and said, "I am your husband, and I will be your husband as long as we live."

She raised up and kissed him. He hesitated for a second before joining in. When she pulled away, he was grinning. "What is that?"

"That is a kiss," she told him. "Your people do not kiss?" When he shook his head, she said, "Well, I kiss."

His grin grew even bigger. "I like it. I will learn."

A few minutes later Alina was leading Otani up the rise to the cave. She slipped in, and he followed, but he stopped short just inside, where he stood, staring open mouthed at Alina's drawings of her sons. "You made this." His voice was barely above a whisper.

"I did," she answered. "Those are my boys." She pointed to the taller one. "This is Gunnar." And then to the smaller figure. "This is Dag."

"You have captured their spirits to live with you here?" He took a step back.

Alina didn't understand the word 'spirits'. It had never come up, but she guessed at his meaning. "I do not capture their spirits," she told him. "Only their – how they look." Now, with some unease, she remembered the laws as Brother James had told them to her. *You shall not make for yourself an image in the form of anything in heaven above or on the earth beneath, or in the waves below, nor shall you bow down to them.* She had excused herself the night before by saying that she had no intention of bowing down to these portraits, but now she thought maybe Otani had a point. How long before those staring eyes she had drawn *became* her children's eyes? How long before she could no longer remember them for who they were, but only saw them as she had depicted them? Her memories of them would set like cold wax into these pictures, and she would end up with less of her boys, not more, as she intended when she drew them.

With that thought, she went and snatched up the piece of skin she used as a rag, dunked it in the water pot, and began scrubbing the images from the wall. Otani exclaimed, "Wait, I didn't mean…."

She cut him off, but gently. "I understand, but you help me to see that this Is not right." She stopped and patted her chest with one hand. "My children live with me here, and that is all I need." She continued scrubbing until even the shadows of her drawings were gone.

"The pictures were very good," Otani remarked when she was finished.

"My boys are very good," she answered simply, dropping the rag.

He came to her, took her by the shoulders and drew her close. "You are very good," he told her. "I am glad you are mine." He bent down and kissed her.

In reply, she put her arms around his neck and pressed in to him. He must have picked her up, because the next thing she knew, they were on the pallet.

Alina and Otani didn't leave the cave for two days. Alina learned several new words. When they finally ventured out again it was because they needed to find food.

The ship that was being built for the voyage was the largest Alina had ever seen. It was supposed to hold ten men on the oars, Bren and the navigator, the four men who would stay behind in the other land, and the four women. That was twenty people. It also had to hold water casks, food stores, and the other gear they needed to bring with them. The biggest ship Alina had seen held a dozen men, and it didn't belong to the village. It was a trader that came and went from the south. This ship was easily twice the size of that one. She stood on the shore, arms crossed against the wind, watching the men hammer plank after plank onto the wooden ribs. *It's a skeleton*, she thought, and her heart thudded dully against her own ribs. She began to understand how small the ship was, compared to the vast water that stretched to the horizon. The likelihood that any of them would make it to the other side dwindled in her mind until she was fairly certain she would die at sea, but she didn't voice her misgivings to anyone, not even to Gerda.

When the spring thaw melted most of the ice from the lanes, Bren came to her in the great hall and said, "I am honoring my end of our deal in one week. Get the boys ready to go."

Alina's whole body seemed to have become heavy and cold as lead. *My plan won't work*, she told herself as she walked away. *Even if they go to Ebbe, even if Ebbe understands my message, Bren will come again for his sons, and then they will be in Maja's hands with no one to defend them.* She considered Gunnar's idea of running away. The very next day, however, she was glad she hadn't tried because Agnes did. She took her daughter, stole a horse, and rode south, intending to catch a ship on the southern coast that could take her somewhere else—anywhere else.

But Bren had anticipated the flight of one or more of his wives. Agnes was caught within the day. She hadn't ridden far enough or fast enough to escape Bren's men. She was bound and gagged when they rode back into the village with her. Her little girl wailed in the arms of one of the men. They took Agnes to the yard in front of the great hall, tied her to a post normally used for horses, and Bren himself whipped her.

Alina counted twenty lashes. Agnes screamed at the first dozen or so, then mercifully passed out. Her back was a lacerated, bloody mess, with ribbons of her tunic embedded in the open ribbons of her torn skin.

Alina held Brega's hand through the ordeal. Kiah was there, too. The three of them were required to witness Agnes's punishment. Maja was, of course, exempt. Kiah wept, and Alina laid a hand gently on her shoulder. To her surprise, Kiah permitted it. "Why did she do it?" Kiah sobbed. "Why did she try to run away?"

"She didn't want to go across the sea," Brega answered.

"She shouldn't have disobeyed," Kiah choked. "It's never good to disobey him." This was the most observant thing Alina had heard Kiah say.

When Bren was finished, he told his men to release her and take her to her house so that her maid could tend her. Then he raised his voice. "Let this be a lesson to you. I will not tolerate defiance." He turned toward the three women. "Which of you will take care of the little girl?"

Alina wanted to roar at him, *Do you still not know your child's name?* But she thought she might be the next one tied to the post. Brega said, "I will take her. Inge and I will look after her."

Bren nodded. "You will care for her until the day we depart. Agnes will be confined to her house. I do not permit her to see or talk to her child." Alina didn't know why it was this cruelty, rather than the whipping, rather than him throwing them all away like garbage, rather than him pairing her with Huus, but from that moment she despised him.

There would be no chance of her running away now. She closed her eyes. *Lord, will you help me? Will you show me a way to make my children safe?* She wanted to fall to her knees and scream her rage and frustration, but she kept herself upright, kept herself silent. She would not be a spectacle for anyone.

Brega hefted the screaming child into her arms and hurried off toward her house. Alina turned away. There was nothing she could do here, nothing she would be permitted to do. She was glad, so very glad, that her boys had not witnessed the lashing. They were out in the woods, so she got her bow from her house and headed out there herself. She knew their favorite places, and found them in less than an hour. They were crouched between a boulder and the massive trunk of a fallen tree. They looked up as she approached, and Gunnar signaled to her to get down. He pointed ahead and to the left, then silently moved back so she could get in there and see.

There was a man sitting in a clearing. His back was to them, and he was nursing a small campfire. He whistled softly as he laid another stick on the flame, but the moment Alina saw him, he stopped, and in a cheerful voice called, "You can come out now." He stood and turned around.

Alina choked back a shout of surprise. She got to her feet, and felt her knees trying to give way. "Marav?"

He laughed quietly. "Alina. I am happy to see you." He took both her hands in his and planted a kiss, chaste and discreet, on her cheek. It was the kiss of a kinsman.

She turned to her boys. "Gunnar, Dag, this is Marav. He is a cousin of your father's."

The boys stood up and came forward. "I remember you," Gunnar said. He shook Marav's hand. "You used to go hunting with us sometimes."

"Yes I did," Marav beamed. "You have a good memory, young man." He turned to Dag. "Now, you and I have never met."

"I'm Dag," the five year old pulled himself up to every bit of the height he had.

"Are you boys hungry?" Marav asked. "I have some bread and cheese here. More than enough to share." They sat and accepted the food. Marav told them, "If it's all right with you two, I would like to talk to your mother for a bit." Gunnar looked up, studied Marav for a moment, then nodded.

Alina went a stone's throw away. "I cannot tell you how happy I am to see you, but why are you here?"

"I heard what Bren is planning to do with you, and I had to come. I am here to help in any way I can."

She shook her head, bemused. "How did you hear about this?"

He lifted his shoulders. "I am family, remember? Word gets around."

She considered this before saying, "I don't think you can help me, but you can help my boys."

He put his head to one side. "You underestimate me, Beloved. I can get the three of you out of here."

She studied him. He was thinner, and there were silver threads in his beard, but his sea-green eyes were the same. He had done what he could to protect her once. She thought she should protect him now. "One of the other wives tried to run away last night. They caught her, and Bren lashed her."

"She didn't have help," he answered. "I know how to evade men like his."

She clenched her teeth until her jaw hurt. "And if you fail? I will be punished. My children will be forced to watch, and Bren will kill you." She backed up a step. "To tell you the truth, I thought he already had."

His smile was grim. "He meant to, but I got away from him. I am telling you, I can take all of you to a safe place."

Alina thought about it for a moment, and said, "But if I go back, I can buy time for you to get them away."

Now it was his turn to study her. "You are the mother bird leading the fox from her nest." After a moment, he dropped his head in resignation and added, "I shouldn't be surprised. I came for you, and I knew your children would be coming, if I could convince you." He heaved a great sigh, and his voice broke when he said, "Are you sure you won't come? The voyage your husband is planning is almost certain death."

"That may be, but for the boys to stay here with the new wife will be certain death for them." She crossed her arms and paced a few steps. "I was going to send them to my brother, but Bren would bring them back sooner or later. Having them stay with my brother is only a reprieve. If you're sure you can get them away, then I beg you to take them."

"You don't have to beg." His voice was gentle, but the set of his face was grim. He reached out and laid his hands on her shoulders. "Give me one day, and I will be ready to go with them." He glanced at the boys. "They will be sons to me. And when they are grown, I will send word to your brother that they are safe."

Tears filled Alina's eyes. She wiped them away with shaking hands. "You once said you would always love me. Now I believe you." She embraced him with all her strength, and kissed him lightly. Then, staring into his sea-green eyes, she stepped back. It was the hardest step she had ever taken. She called, "Let's go now, Gunnar, Dag."

Alina and Otani found a herd of deer on their first day of hunting together. Otani took down a young stag. They tied its hooves to a pole Alina made from cutting a sapling, and they carried the stag between them on their shoulders. Alina was walking behind Otani, so she had plenty of opportunities to admire the swing of his hips and shoulders. She found she couldn't help grinning for the joy of being with him.

When they got back to the cave, Alina built up the fire while Otani went to work skinning the deer. *This is wonderful,* she thought. *I don't have to do it all myself now. I have someone to share everything with.* She set the drying rack up next to the fire, and went out to help her husband.

That evening they had a hearty meal of meat and greens and roasted cattail roots. Otani took a drink from his cup and smiled at her. "This is good."

"The food is good?" she asked.

The smile turned to a grin. "This life with you is good."

She returned the smile. "Life together with you is good, Otani. I am happy with you."

He lightly touched the scar on her calf. "What happened here?"

She didn't know the word, so she drew a picture of a bear in the dirt. "He almost kills me, but I kill him."

Otani's eyes widened. "You killed a bear? By yourself?"

She pointed to the cave entrance. "I shoot him through there."

He looked at the scar again. "This was a bad wound. What did you do for it?" When she told him, he covered his mouth in shock. He pulled her to him and laid his cheek against the top of her head. "And you were alone."

She nodded. "I think I am going to die, but after a few days, I start getting better."

She pulled back to find him smiling. He held the smile for a moment before his expression grew thoughtful. "Maybe you have the words now. Can you tell me why your people left you here alone?"

So now she had to talk about this. She took a deep breath and began. "My husband has five wives."

An exclamation of surprise erupted from him. "Five? Why so many?"

Alina shook her head. "I do not know. I do not understand it myself. He likes women in his bed, but he does not like them much – anywhere else." She paused, thinking, a little frustrated that she couldn't talk about the past in the past. That part of Otani's language had not come to her yet. "I am his second. I do not know, when we marry, that he has another wife. I try to please him, but he grows tired of me."

Otani frowned. "How could any man not be pleased with you?"

"Thank you, husband. She managed a smile. "He marries two more women, and gets tired of both of them. Then he marries the fifth. This one is different."

"Different how?"

Alina shrugged. "I am not sure. She knows how to control him."

Otani's lips were a tight line. "I do not know this woman, but I do not like her."

"I don't like her also. I think she is bad. I think she tells him to send us away." Otani said nothing, but stirred the fire. "I don't understand why he doesn't just kill us. Easier, quicker. But he decides to bring us here. He tells the story that he wants families of his people here so he can trade back and forth." She watched the flames leap and fall back.

"We make the trip in the big boat, and on the way, we only lose one man in a storm. Then we are here, but after the sun sets, people fight us. They kill one of the other women first." She saw Brega fall to the ground again, and shuddered. "She is a sister to me. Then they start killing the men, who fight back. I am already hiding in the trees." *Never mind why for now,* she thought.

She picked up a stick and drew a quick sketch of the beach and the ship in the dirt. "Here is the ship. The men are here, low on the beach and then in the water as they fight. Here are the trees. We have a fire about here, and that is where the first woman falls. The other two women are here, and the men who attack us are…." Here she stopped. She didn't have the word for what they were doing. "They are hurting the women." She looked at Otani. "You know what I mean."

"Rape," he answered. "They raped the women."

Alina repeated the word, which felt oily in her mouth.

"How is it that you were already hiding?" he asked.

Alina wanted to tell him everything, but still she hesitated. Would he understand her limited words? Would he think she had done the wrong thing? However his knowing all her story fell out, she didn't want to keep secrets from this good man. Taking another deep breath, she plunged in. "Bren – that is my old husband's name – he tells his wives that he is matching us with men to be our new husbands here. The man he chooses for me is a bad man. He is a man who rapes, and he murders a girl. I do not want that man to touch me, and so before we leave my home, I make a plan to run away as soon as I get here. I wait until dark. The woman – the one who dies first — helps me, and when the bad man walks down to the water, I go into the trees. It is only a little time later that my people are attacked."

Otani nodded slowly. "So your men who survived the fight left you. They had no idea whether you were alive or dead."

"It does not matter if I am alive or dead," she corrected him. "If I swim out to the ship and get on it, they are throwing me into the sea." She pauses, then confesses the thing that bothers her to this day. "I want to help the other women. There are two men – one with each – but I don't help. I run away. I think I am wrong."

Otani considered this, then slowly shook his head. "You could not have saved them. Even if you had killed both men and freed the other women, you would not have gotten away with them. The people who attacked you would have caught you, and you and I would not be talking about this." He paused and added. "It may be that those women are alive."

She had not considered this possibility. Now she did. They were alive when she left them. Maybe the men took them and – what? Made slaves of them? "Yes," she finally said. "You are right. Maybe they are alive." The thought didn't comfort her. There were lives that were worse than death. "There is not much hope for them," she concluded. "I think there is never much hope from the time Bren decides to send us away."

"Your old husband was a bad man," Otani said, and he pulled her into his arms. "You are a strong woman, and you escaped his evil plans."

'Evil' was another new word for her. She tucked it into her mind. "I also steal a bow and arrows," she said into his chest. "They belong to one of my men, but my men can't get to them."

"That was a good idea." His voice above her, low and soothing, calmed her fears. "Those things helped you to survive."

She let out a long breath. He understood. He understood that she had to get away, that she couldn't help the other women, that stealing the weapon was right and necessary. Her anxiety about what he might think of her melted away. "I think that is all I have to tell you. I walk west for nine days until I find this cave."

"Nine days," he repeated thoughtfully. He was silent for a long time before he said, "And you made this your home."

"Now it is your home, too," she replied.

"Yes," he said. "This place is better than my place. If it's all right with you, I want to go back to my cave and get my things and bring them here."

It was pouring rain the next morning, so they had to stay inside, but neither of them complained.

Alina sat down with Gunnar that night after Dag passed out on his cot. "I am going to send you away tomorrow with Marav," she said. "I have known him a long time, and I trust him. He will take you boys somewhere far from here. I want you to do as he says, and watch after your brother."

"What are you going to do?" Gunnar asked, his eyes already full of the misery he knew her answer would bring.

"I am going to buy you time to get away," she answered. "It's all I can do. Your father's new wife is…." She hesitated, then decided that he was old enough to hear it. "She is a wicked woman, and I think your life will be in danger if you stay here."

"She wants us out of the way of her own children."

Alina's mouth dropped open. "Did someone tell you that?"

Gunnar shook his head. "It just makes sense when you watch her. It's like she's playing that game Father brought back from the east last year. If she clears the other player's pieces off the board, nothing can stop her winning."

Alina touched her forehead to Gunnar's. "I want you to promise me to do your best to get out of here and grow up, yes? Do whatever it takes. I promise I will do my best to survive where I am going, and at least we can think of each other alive in the world."

"I promise," he said, and added, "I have something for you." Turning away, he pulled a leather roll from under his cot. "I made this, but don't open it until you come home."

Tears stung her eyes, but she was confused. "Until I come home?"

His cheeks reddened. "Till you come to your new home…" he waved one arm vaguely, "…over there."

She took his face in her hands and kissed both his cheeks. "You will take Dag first thing in the morning into the woods to the same place you were today. Marav will meet you there. Don't say anything to Dag before you go, understand?"

Gunnar nodded. "Because he'll blab."

"I put his old blanket into his pack. That's how he will know that I have this planned for him. As for you…." She ducked her head, took the amber pendant from around her neck, now hanging on a new green ribbon, and slipped it over Gunnar's head. "This belonged to my mother. I want you to have it. When you grow up and marry, give it to your wife. Go to bed now. Try to sleep."

The look he gave her was so forlorn, she pulled him into her arms and held him with all her strength, feeling his sobs against her, and muffling her own into his shoulder. After a time, he pushed himself away, and without another word or look, ran out the door. He didn't stay long in the dark. After a few minutes, he was back again, his eyes red and swollen, but dry. He climbed into his bed, and Alina tucked him in. "Sleep well, my son."

He did sleep. She heard it in his breathing, and she couldn't help but envy his oblivion. Alina thought that maybe children's bodies understood what was best for them, that some kind of primitive knowing allowed them to eat and sleep even in stressful times. If that was true, adult bodies lost that knowledge somewhere along the way. She tossed and turned and prayed through the night. In the morning, bleary-eyed and wrung out, she sent the boys off. She squeezed Dag until he squealed, then kissed him. She turned to Gunnar and murmured, "Remember your promise."

He nodded once. "And you remember yours." He gave her a quick kiss before saying to Dag, "Ready?" And they were gone.

Alina didn't step out her door to watch them go. She paced the room for a while, forcing herself to think about the things that had to come next. Finally, she gathered her determination and went to breakfast. This day was going to be a long day of play-acting, and she had to get it right. She sat down next to Brega and Inge, and Agnes's little girl, Tena.

""Where are your boys?" Brega asked.

"They wanted to be in the woods today," she told her. Looking around, she asked, "Are our esteemed husband and his darling wife not with us this morning?"

Inge snorted, and Brega shot her a warning look. "Let's not invite trouble, shall we?" To Alina, she said, "I haven't seen them. I suppose they'll come in eventually." She smiled and covered her daughter's hand. "Why don't you tell Alina your news?"

Inge smiled wanly at Alina. "Ava and Hurd have invited me to come live with them – after you leave on the ship."

"Oh!" Alina picked up her cup and stared into the mead. She kept her voice light. "That is great news. You'll enjoy living with Hurd's family." She glanced at Brega, and an understanding look passed between them. Hurd's family would protect the girl far better than her maid could have done. *Maja's probably not interested in Bren's daughters,* Alina thought. *She's after the sons. They're the ones who could inherit.* Still, it was a better layer of protection for Inge.

Bren and Maja never did come in by the time Alina was ready to leave. She wanted to make absolutely sure that plenty of people saw her at breakfast, so when she got up, she hit a clay bowl with her elbow, sending it crashing to the floor.

"Oh, what a mess!" she exclaimed, as the conversations in the room faltered. When a serving girl came over to clean up, she said, "Here, let me help you with that," and she stooped to pick up the shards. That would have to be good enough. She walked out, and went to sit with Holgur for a while. He would also be a witness that she had been in the village that morning.

She spent the rest of the day visiting with various people. This served three purposes. First, she needed every witness she could get. She needed people to say that she was in the village the entire day. Second, she couldn't stand the thought of going back to her empty house. And finally, most of the people she saw were those she was saying a final goodbye to, though they couldn't know it.

Just before dinner, she looked in on Agnes. Agnes was lying on her bed on her stomach. The maid, sitting in one corner, raised a finger to her lips as Alina came in. "I just got her to sleep," she whispered. Alina nodded and silently moved closer. Agnes's back was bare except for a cloth that covered the wounds. There were a few spots of blood seeping onto the cloth. Some of those lash marks had gone deep.

She went to the maid and whispered. "Can I get you – or her – anything?"

The woman's eyes filled with tears. "Nothing will help her now. And thank you, Lady, but I don't need anything."

Alina frowned. "Do you think her wounds will kill her?"

"Oh yes," the maid said, "But not the wounds on her back. Some hurts go too deep to mend."

Alina thought about this as she left. Why couldn't Bren just let her go? She wasn't harming anyone by running away, and the point of sending the wives across the sea was to get rid of them. She let out a long breath and wondered, not for the first time, why he didn't just kill them and get it over with.

She started toward the great hall for dinner. Before she went in, she caught Holgur by the arm as he passed her. "Have you seen my boys?" She felt a sting of regret for the question.

His brow bunched into a frown as he considered her question. "No, Lady. Don't think I've seen them all day."

"They went into the woods this morning, but they're usually back by now." He followed her inside, and they stood scanning the room before she sighed. "I don't see them, and they're not at my house."

Bren came in moments later with several of his men. She went to him. "Have you seen our boys?"

Bren shrugged. "There's a whole herd of them outside playing. Aren't they there?"

Alina shook her head. "I looked. Gunnar and Dag aren't with them."

At that moment, Gerda came in, nearly bumping into Alina and asking, "Are the boys with you?"

Gerda was in the dark about what was going on, but her timing could not have been better. Alina looked at her with alarm, saying, "No, they aren't."

Bren put his hands on his hips. "When did you see them last?"

Alina swallowed. Only the truth, she thought. "This morning. They went into the woods. But they are usually back by now."

He gestured to the men around him. "Let's go." They filed out.

Alina started after them. "Let me come with you," she said. "I know their favorite places."

Bren paused. She was surprised that he was actually considering bringing her. "No," he finally said. "We'll find them. You stay here." And they were gone.

Alina did what she thought she would normally do in such a situation. She paced up and down just outside the hall. Gerda brought her a mug of hot mead. "Drink this, child."

Alina took the cup from her and drained it, hardly tasting the drink. Gerda watched her pace for a while before saying, "If anyone can find them, Bren's men will."

She nodded, but wondered if there was more in Gerda's words than she was letting on. Did she suspect? She hadn't told Gerda what was really going on because she wanted to protect her. Gerda had already taken on enough risk for her sake. Alina was going to spare her this one.

"The boys know the woods," she murmured as she paced. "It's almost a playground to them, though I have taught them to take care. They know the woods are wild. Gunnar is really good out there. If he can keep himself and his brother safe, he will."

The men came back hours later, empty-handed. Alina ran to meet them, but Bren shook his head. "We found one trail heading north, but it disappeared, and it's dark now. We will go out again in the morning."

North, Alina thought. So that was Marav's secret. No one escaping here would choose to go north. *There is nothing but ice and snow that way. I hope they don't find the trail tomorrow.* She thought of never seeing her children again, and her eyes filled with tears. She covered her mouth and turned away from Bren to hide them. A heavy hand was laid on her shoulder. She looked up. It wasn't Bren. It was Holgur. He had gone with the men into the woods to search.

"We will find them, Lady," he said, his voice hoarse.

She nodded and laid her hand briefly atop his. "Thank you, Holgur. And she thought, *Thank you for everything.*

CHAPTER TWELVE

It took Alina and Otani three days to move his things from his cave to hers. The problem wasn't that he had a lot of possessions. The problem was getting everything over the ridge and back down again. They quickly realized that they could only take as much as they could carry in one trip, and they had to hand things up as they climbed and down as they descended. On the second day, Alina brought her rope, and they were able to lower bundles from the top of the ridge to the bottom. So Otani sat at the top, tied bundles with the rope and fed them down to Alina who waited below. She had to climb up a few times to free something that was stuck on the rocks, but using the rope made the whole venture safer and quicker.

When they were gathering the last few things – a couple of rolled-up hides and some empty leather boxes, Otani paused and looked around the cave he had called home for nearly three years. "This was a good place," he said. Then he grinned at her. "But your place is better."

Once his possessions were in her cave, Alina decided that they needed one more shelf for the food stores. "I want to get them off the floor," she explained. "When I am – when I was sick after the bear, I woke up?" She glanced at him. Had she said it right? He nodded and gestured for her to go on. "I woke up and there were animals here in the cave with me. Or maybe they were spirits. I don't know. I never saw animals like them."

She described them to him, and Otani chuckled. "Racoons. They like to steal."

"They steal a lot of my meat," Alina said, not seeing the humor in it. "That is why I am building these, and that is why I made the door."

"What is your word for this?" Otani asked, laying his hand on the lower shelf. She told him and he repeated it, saying, "I have never seen one before. You should show me how to make a shelf. I want to know this." He paused and thought for a minute before lifting a shoulder. "My people do not need shelves because they do not live in caves. When they have extra meat, they tie it high in trees with ropes, or they bury it with large rocks on top to keep the animals out."

"Do you ever see or speak to any of your people?" she asked.

He nodded, looking a little sheepish. "There is a thing I should tell you."

Alina crossed her arms. "Tell me."

"Every year when the leaves fall, I go to my village. I stand outside, away from the people, and they come and speak to me." He went and stood at the entrance to the cave. "They stand about this far away. They tell me their news and bring me things I need – clothing, some food, maybe a tool. Last year they gave me a new spear. I always bring something for my family. I usually bring meat and skins." He stopped and looked at her hopefully.

"You want me to come with you?" she asked. He nodded. "And you want me to bring them something? Salt, maybe?"

"I know your salt place is a secret…." he began.

She interrupted him. "You are my husband. How big a pot of salt do you want to give them?"

He gestured with his hands. A pot about twice the size of the one she gave him. "We can do that. Let me make a pot first, and then we will go and gather the salt." She spoke with more confidence than she felt. The salt hole was vital for her, but she hated going down into the dark. *This time I won't be by myself,* she thought, and went out to dig clay for the pot.

Bren's men never found the boys. Maja expressed her concern by sending some of her own men out. Huus went with them, leaving Alina with no doubt about his loyalties, but they had no success. Bren never accused Alina of staging their disappearance. Her deception, alongside his arrogance made it impossible for him to imagine that any wife of his would dare defy him the day after he punished Agnes.

The boys were gone, and Alina breathed easier, and though she still had to appear to be distraught, she no longer troubled much about her own departure. She had a plan. After that, whatever happened, happened.

She decided to continue visiting Agnes, though she couldn't explain to herself why, and she sat next to the bed and told her as much of the village gossip she could remember. Agnes never responded, leaving Alina to wonder if she even heard her. One afternoon when she had run out of things to say, she got up to leave when she heard Agnes murmur, "No one wants me."

Alina sank back down on the chair. Agnes was still lying on her stomach, but she faced Alina as well as she could. "My father and mother were only ever interested in my brothers. They gave me to

Bren as soon as it was decent." She sniffed. "I thought I could make Bren want me. I did everything he wanted, everything I could think of to keep him." She sighed. "You and Brega tried to tell me. I should have listened to you." She seemed to study Alina for a moment before adding, "At least you two are friends. You have each other."

Alina laid a hand on Agnes'. "I can't make you any promises, but as long as we are together, we can help each other, yes?"

When she went to dinner that evening, Bren stood up and announced, "We will set sail in three days. Those of you who are leaving need to have everything ready by that time." He rubbed his hands together as if he was announcing a coming feast. "We will meet this opportunity with strength and courage." There was a general cheer around the room, though Alina noted that most of it came from men who were not going.

The day before they embarked, Alina said her final goodbye to Holgur. He embraced her, and though she was tall for a woman, she felt like a kitten being hugged by a bear. When he released her and stepped back, he wiped the tears from his good eye with the heel of his hand. "I wish I could go with you…." he began. Alina knew this. Holgur had gone to Bren demanding that Bren put him on the ship. Bren refused, saying that he couldn't risk his best blacksmith on the voyage.

"I need one more favor from you, Holgur." Alina was fighting back her own tears.

"Name it."

"Don't come down to the ship to see us off." She reached out and took his callus-thickened hand in hers. "Let this be my goodbye to you."

He raised his head and stared off toward the shore a moment before nodding. "That is well thought of, Lady." He expelled a breath and said, "If anyone can make a life over there, you can."

She gave his hand a final squeeze. "I will do my best."

That evening, she asked Gerda for the same favor. "It will be hard enough to leave," she said. "And I want to turn my face forward, if you understand me."

Gerda's jaw was set, but she inhaled and said, "I do understand you – except in the matter of your sons. How can you leave when you don't know what's happened to them?" It was unfair, and Alina gave her a long look without replying. After a moment, Gerda's eyes widened. "You do know what happened. You arranged something for them."

Alina sank down on the edge of the bed. "You have always known me best." Her eyes filled. "I have been praying to be spared this journey, but it looks like the Lord would have me go."

Gerda sat beside her. "I am thinking he supplied a way for your boys, though, didn't he?"

Marav. Her answer came in a hoarse whisper. "Yes."

Gerda reached out and took her hand. "You believe what you believe. You act as you must. If anyone can survive over there, it's you."

Alina sighed. Her survival seemed to be almost a given among the people who knew her best, but since her boys had gone, and despite her promise to Gunnar, simply surviving wasn't going to be enough. She didn't answer, but she put her arm around Gerda. "I don't know what I would have done here without you. You have been a mother to me, and I will never forget you."

Gerda turned to embrace her, and she clung to her for a long time before she tore herself away. "Fare you well, Lady Alina." Her voice broke, and she cleared her throat. "May your God watch over you and bring you safely to a new life." With that, she stood and went out, closing the door behind her. Alina put her face in her hands and cried.

Sometime later, bleary-eyed and tired beyond words, she gazed around the little room that had been her home. *Home.* She sniffed and sighed. Gunnar had told her to wait to open his gift when she found home. But what was that going to be, assuming she survived to get there? A roof over her head? Shelter would be necessary, but it was only a bare beginning. This place had not felt like home to her until…. She cast her mind back. When did she start thinking this was home? After the boys were born. *Of course*, she thought. *Home is family.* Her hands balled into impotent fists on their own. *I may never have another home. But maybe my boys will.* With that thought, she shucked off her shoes, laid down and pulled up the covers, hoping sleep would smudge away her dark thoughts for a little while.

She was surprised the next morning that she had slept through the night. She woke, refreshed and determined. She went to breakfast, then back to the house to get her bag and cloak. She walked down to the shore, watching her feet make their steps, not allowing herself to think about much of anything. When she got there, most of the village was turned out to see them off, but thankfully, Holgur and Gerda had kept their word and stayed away.

People surrounded her, holding out their hands for a final goodbye. She shouldered her bag and began clasping the offered hands. The women wept. The men spoke encouragement, but their expressions were grim. It was clear that none of them thought there was much possibility of anyone surviving such a long voyage.

She spotted Maja standing almost at the water's edge with Father Otto at her elbow. Alina stepped up alongside her. Without looking her way, Maja remarked, "The tide has turned. You'll be on your way very soon."

The tide turned when you showed up, Alina thought bitterly. She had given some thought about what she might or might not say to this woman. She had prayed about it, and now she gave her the words she had. "May the Lord bless your child with wisdom and a long life."

Now Maja did look at her, her blue eyes wide with surprise. "That is kind. Thank you."

Beside her, Father Otto grumbled, "An empty blessing from a woman who will not come to the church."

Maja turned on him. "Hush. That is enough from you." A purple flush crawled up his face from his neck, but he didn't reply.

At that moment, Bren announced, "All is ready. It is time."

Alina lifted her chin, squared her shoulders, and stepped to the rope ladder that hung down the boat's side. Bren gave her a nod of approval – she was fulfilling the first part of their deal after all – and steadied the ladder for her as she began to climb, while gulls wheeled and cried overhead. Brega came up after her, then Kiah. Agnes came last, refusing to speak to Bren or to the other women. Alina didn't blame her.

The men, most of them rowers, followed, four of whom would stay in the new land. The navigator came up next, a whip of a man with a bald head covered in a black wool cap. Finally, it was Bren's turn. He climbed onto the deck and hauled the ladder up after him. That done, he turned to the people watching on the beach. "My friends," he called out, "today we embark on a new venture that will bring even greater prosperity to our village. My wife, Maja knows my mind concerning you, and she will govern in my absence." A grumble of discontent followed this. The people clearly didn't trust her. If Bren heard, he made no sign of it. He simply said, "The tide has turned. It is time to go. Look for us at mid-summer."

With that pronouncement, the anchors were heaved up and secured, the sail unfurled, and the rowers began the long task of moving the ship westward. Agnes and Alina sat on the bench at the stern of the ship, facing forward, but Brega and Kiah stood, looking back and waving and calling out goodbyes. Alina was glad she had said her goodbyes before now. She stared down at her hands folded in her lap, trying not to think, but it was impossible to keep the memories of her boys at bay.

She glanced up and realized to her dismay that she was facing the rowers, that she would be facing them for the entire trip. A few of them glanced at her as her eyes swept their faces. Huus, thankfully, was on the oars farthest from her, at least for now. As far as she knew, he was still unaware that she was supposed to be paired with him.

The ship slipped out of the harbor into the waves of the sea. Alina felt the rocking of the deck, and for the first of many times, she pulled the hood of her cloak down to conceal her face.

Three days later Alina took Otani across the river and showed him the salt hole. He peered down into the darkness and touched the ladder. "What is this? Did you make this?"

"It's a ladder," she answered. "Yes, I made it so that I could get in and out of the hole. Let me have a look at it. I want to make sure it's still in good condition." She laid down on her stomach and grasped the top of the ladder, moving it this way and that. It felt sturdy in her hands. "I think it's all right," she finally said. "I will go down first so you can see how I do it." He agreed, but seemed reluctant. "When I am about halfway down, hand me that torch." She swung around and planted her feet on the second rung and started working her way down. When she had taken a couple of steps she looked up and held out her hand for the torch.

Otani had made the torch from rushes tied together, and they had brought a pot with a couple of live embers. When Alina reached the bottom, she called, "Toss some kindling down." He nodded, and a few seconds later, she stepped out of the way as small sticks clattered to the floor, followed by a handful of dry leaves and grass fluttering down.

Alina looked up. Otani was at the rim of the hole, looking dubiously at the ladder. "It's all right," she told him. "It will hold you. Turn backward like I did and let your feet find the steps."

He did as she directed, and after a minute, was down in the hole with her, saying, "Let's get the fire going and light the torch."

Alina was happy to agree. She didn't like the dark of the hole any more than he did. When they lit the torch, Otani held it aloft and they peered into the gloom. The underground cave's walls were streaked and spotted with white deposits that sparkled in the light. Otani let out a wordless exclamation, and Alina said, "That's a lot of salt."

She held the torch for him while he hammered at a white streak with a stone he had brought for the purpose. It took them less than an hour to flake enough salt from the wall to fill the pot she had made, and to refill her own jar.

"This cave goes back farther than we can see," Otani murmured. "I would like to come again and explore it to see how big it is."

"We will need more than one torch to do that," Alina said. Staring into the blackness suddenly made her eager to get out. "I am ready to go.""Yes. This torch won't last much longer," he said, and they started back toward the ladder.

As Alina put her foot on the bottom rung, she paused and looked up, half expecting that old nightmare to come true, but neither Bren nor Maja were at the top of the hole, nor was Huus or even the bear. She drew in a long breath and started up. She stopped to look around when her head cleared the top. Only when she was satisfied that no threats awaited them did she come out. Otani followed.

Alina sat down in the grass and turned her face to the sun. Otani flopped down beside her. "I see now why you don't like going in there."

"I feel like I am trapped," she answered. "Even though I have the ladder, and I know I can get out, it feels like I never will." She described the nightmare to him. She glanced over as she talked, loving the way he listened. He gazed up at the clouds as though making pictures in his head of everything she was saying. "And then it was Maja, my husband's fifth wife who was staring down at me." Otani put a hand over his mouth, his eyes wide. "And she said, 'I'll take care of this.' I was sure she was going to pull the ladder up and leave me in the hole."

Otani's voice sunk to a near-whisper. "What did she do?"

Alina shrugged. "I woke up."

He was silent for what seemed a long time. Finally he said, "I do not understand how you are still alive. You were surrounded by people who wished you ill, people who wanted to be rid of you. You have said that you don't know why your husband didn't just kill you. I wonder that, too."

Alina sighed. "First of all, if we ever speak of him again, please call him Bren. He is not my husband." She turned her head and met his eyes. "You are." When his gaze softened, she added, "He wasn't quite right in the head, and because of that, I am alive." Now she smiled. "I haven't had a nightmare since we agreed to be married."

He pulled her to him and kissed her. She put her arms around him, but suddenly the hairs on the back of her neck stood up. She felt eyes watching from somewhere. She pushed herself away and looked around. Off to her left where the tall grass gave way to trees she spotted a shadow she knew. "Wolf," she murmured, and reached for her bow.

Otani reached for his at the same time. He shifted his body into a crouch. "I don't see it," he whispered.

Alina answered, "It's behind that big oak. I don't think you can see it from there." She also worked her body into a crouch, and waited. The shadow didn't move.

"You have seen this animal before."

She nodded. "Several times, but this is the first time since spring." She nocked an arrow to the string. "I don't have a good shot."

"If you shoot and miss, it will run away." He pulled an arrow from his quiver. "Is that what you want? Or do you want the meat and the pelt?"

That was the question. She had taken shots at the wolf before, and had missed each time. Was it because the wolf was cunning, or because she was reluctant to kill it? "I don't know what I want. I should kill it. It's a nuisance, and it killed the crow who was my friend."

"Alina, let's try to kill it. If we don't, it will keep coming back and coming back." He was right, of course. She nodded wordlessly. "You stay here and keep its attention on you," he whispered. "I will see if I can circle around and get a line to shoot."

She didn't like it. She didn't want to be separated from him, but she saw sense in his plan. He crouched lower and crawled on his hands and knees through the grass, looking for a vantage point. Alina raised one arm above her head and lowered it again. Then, after a pause, she raised her head so that the wolf could see her face. She kept doing things to let the wolf see her. In the meantime, Otani had gone off to her right, and was moving steadily toward the trees.

Alina chewed the inside of her cheeks. She did everything she could think of to keep the wolf's attention on her without startling it and scaring it away. At the same time, she kept one eye on Otani until he disappeared into the grass. She thought she might be able to hear him, but he was like a ghost on the ground, invisible and silent. At one point, she saw the wolf look away from her and start, the muscles in its haunches ready for flight. A moment of indecision, and then a yelp of pain, and the wolf took off running. Alina realized much later that this moment was the last time she would ever see the animal.

She stood up. Otani did, too. He raised his hands and let them fall in a gesture of frustration. Alina asked, "Did you miss?"

"I hit it," he answered, "But only a grazing shot." He marched toward the trees, rooted around for a minute, and plucked his arrow from the ground. "I wounded it in the flank. I'm sure it will recover."

Alina didn't understand why she felt relieved. She tugged on his arm. "We have what we came for. Let's go back."

He nodded, looking in the direction where the wolf had fled. "Maybe that was enough to make it wary of us."

"Odd that it's alone," Alina remarked as she started toward the hill.

Suddenly Otani stumbled, gave a small grunt of pain and began to limp. "I turned my ankle on that rock."

When they reached the river, he said, "We should go and collect more willow bark, since we're on this side of the water already."

Something in his voice made her stop and study him. "You really hurt yourself, didn't you?"

"Only a little," he answered. "A cup of willow bark tea will help."

They stopped and stripped bark from one of the trees. Alina stuffed it into her bag, and they went back downstream to wade through the shallow patch. By the time they got there, Otani was limping noticeably. They stopped to take off their shoes, and she saw a growing bloom of bruise on the outside of his left ankle. Alina set her jaw and started into the water. The sooner they got back to the cave the better.

"Ooooh," he remarked with a sigh when he stepped in. "That feels good." He stopped for a moment, letting the cold water rush against his ankle.

"We need to keep moving," she told him. "When we get to the other side, you can sit on the bank and soak your foot there."

She had him put his arm around her shoulder so that she could support him on the way across. They were a couple of steps away from the opposite bank when one of the straps on Alina's bag slipped from her shoulder. Thinking of the two pots of salt she carried, Alina pulled the bag off and tossed it onto the bank. The motion made her slip on a mossy stone, and she and Otani both tumbled into the stream. She came up spluttering and shouting, "Are you all right?"

He must have been sitting on the river bottom, because he was up to his neck in the water, grinning. "If you wanted to play you could have just said so." He splashed her.

"You infuriating man!" she exclaimed in her own language, but she laughed and splashed him back. He ducked under the water, and the next second, strong hands were around her ankles, pulling her under. She squealed in surprise, but then a pair of warm lips caught hers. She felt his laughter against her chest, and a moment later they surfaced. He kissed her again, and the contrast of his warmth against the cold water felt new and delicious. She gave herself up to the sensations, gave herself up to him.

When it was over, she held him for a long time, feeling his heart beat against her, praying that she would have him for years to come. At last, she was aware that the sun was going down and the air was chilly. She pulled away and stood up. "I am going in. I'll brew tea for you." Then she grinned and put her hands on her hips. "Does your ankle feel better now?"

He threw back his head and laughed. "Much better!"

Little of the voyage stuck in Alina's mind after it was over. First came seasickness. She wasn't bothered much by the pitching of the boat, but the other women were thoroughly miserable. Several of the men were sick, too. After a few days the sickness let up, though Agnes was ill off and on for most of the trip. On the twelfth day, a storm bore down on them, and it seemed that the ship would tumble end over end and shatter to splinters. Up one towering wave they went, only to plunge, crying and screaming into an abyss on the other side. Alina was certain they would all meet their end, but in an eternal afternoon, the storm blew over, and the sea began to calm. Bren assured them afterward that this storm was a mild one. Nevertheless, one of the rowers was pitched overboard. The sound of his scream as he went flying into the sea would stay with Alina the rest of her life.

It was mid-morning on the thirty-second day that the navigator pointed and called out, "Land! Land!"

Alina wasn't sure what he was seeing. The sea still appeared to stretch, relentless, to the horizon. A few hours later she saw it, a smudge of purple far in the distance. That evening Bren announced, "We will most likely land late tomorrow afternoon, if the tide is with us. If not, we will stand out and wait for it to turn."

It had become customary, when the sea was not too rough, for the women to take turns walking the deck. Brega was currently walking, sometimes stopping at the bow to stare at the purple line that seemed to become less hazy with every passing hour. That left Alina alone – as much as she could be alone on a pitching ship – with Agnes and

Kiah. Kiah's head was forward, swaying with sleep. Agnes glanced at her, then to Alina before she said, "Brega sneaked my girl in to see me the night before we left."

Now it was Alina's turn to glance Kiah's way. This was information that was too juicy for Kiah not to share, and she wasn't bright enough to understand that it could land Brega in real trouble. *Or,* Alina thought bitterly, *she would understand perfectly and tell Bren to spite Brega.* "I am happy to hear she did that," she murmured.

"I really hoped he would just let me go when I tried to get away. He doesn't care for me, and he certainly has no interest in our daughter."

"Nor in my sons," Alina replied, and immediately realized her mistake in mentioning them.

Agnes leaned close. "You sent them away, didn't you?" When Alina didn't reply, she added, "I thought so. You played the grief-stricken mother pretty well for a few days, but then it was like you forgot about them." Agnes lifted one shoulder. "I don't care. You did the right thing. I won't tell Bren."

Brega approached the bench then and said, "I think it's your turn, Agnes."

She got up and strolled off like she was walking down the lane at home. Brega took her place on the bench and watched her go for a moment. Alina said, "She told me what you did for her."

Now Brega glanced over her shoulder at Kiah. Finally, she nodded. "I couldn't let Bren have his way in that matter. It was little enough that I could do."

Alina threaded her arm through Brega's and they sat together in comfortable silence. After a moment, though, Alina groaned and pulled the hood of her cloak down to cover her eyes. "What is it?" Brega asked. "Huus again?"

Alina nodded. "He must have traded places with the other rower on his seat. He will not stop staring. I think he knows it bothers me, and so it amuses him."

"Want to trade places with me?" Brega asked. Alina said she did, and they changed seats, which left Alina sitting next to Kiah.

The younger woman looked up as Alina sat, a strange light in her eyes, and said, "I heard you and Agnes. I know what you both did."

"So you're going to tattle to Bren?" Alina asked.

"You make it sound like I am a child," she answered petulantly. "I will tell him because he is my husband, and it's the right thing to do."

"Your husband is throwing you away like yesterday's chicken bones," Alina answered with some heat. "Do you not understand that?"

Kiah's bright blue eyes filled, and she said, "He is doing what he thinks is best for us."

Alina hadn't had many chances to laugh in the past few weeks, but she burst out laughing now.

Leaning forward, Brega said, "You can tell him what I did, Kiah. I don't care."

"Not just what you did." Kiah's lips drew up into a pout. "I heard what she did." She pointed to Alina.

Brega let out an uncharacteristic sigh. Kiah had pushed her to the end of her patience. "What is it you think she did?"

"She sent her boys away," she spat. "Sent them away from their father."

Brega met Alina's eyes. There was a look of understanding and surprised appreciation. "You clever girl. Good for you. Are you sure they're safe?"

Alina shook her head. "I can't possibly know."

Brega nodded, "Well, I won't ask how you did it. Or maybe I'll ask after our husband has left us behind in the wilderness." She shot a pointed look at Kiah.

"I am still telling," Kiah insisted.

"And what do you hope to achieve?" Alina asked. "Nothing will happen to Brega. The men on this ship love her." It was true. Brega had made a point of learning all their names and giving a few words of encouragement to each of the men as she handed out the daily rations. She had even led them in a short memorial, singing an old sea song she had learned from her father for the sailor who was lost. Those who didn't know her already had quickly responded with words and smiles of their own.

"As for me," Alina continued, "All I care about is that my boys are away from that monster who is now is wife. His one and only wife, Kiah. Once we set foot there," she pointed to the shore on the horizon, "we won't belong to him anymore. He could toss me overboard, and I wouldn't care."

This wasn't exactly true. She hoped to survive, but she thought maybe it was all right to let Kiah think so. A gentle voice spoke in her heart, *Don't lie to her, my child. This is a hard time for each of you.*

Bowing her head, Alina said, "I am sorry, Kiah. That wasn't true. I don't want to be thrown overboard. I want to live."

Kiah crossed her arms, but said nothing more. Brega looked at Alina, shook her head and shrugged. After a while, it was Kiah's turn to walk. She went up and back again once, arms folded tightly, head down in contemplation. She turned and went back toward the bow. This time she stopped there. Bren was talking to the navigator, and Kiah at least knew enough not to interrupt, but when the navigator took a seat, Bren glanced at her. Now she was talking to him.

"She's telling him," Alina murmured. "You and I are both in trouble."

"I am not sure I care, at least not for myself," Brega answered. "I loved him once. Really loved him, I mean, but he has broken my heart again and again. There's nothing left."

Bren stepped back from Kiah, looked at the women on the other end of the ship, pointed to Alina, and gestured for her to come. She stood and made her way forward. As she passed her coming back the other way, Kiah said, "You are in so much trouble."

"And what benefit is that to you?" Alina answered. Alina noted her expression of confusion, as if the question had come in another language, but her bewilderment wasn't enough to make Alina feel sorry for her – at least not sorrier than she felt for all of them.

Bren stood at the bow, his hands on his hips, waiting. Alina stopped in front of him. "You wanted to talk to me?"

"What is this I hear from Kiah?" he asked.

Alina shook her head. "Kiah thinks she knows many things. Which thing are we talking about?"

Bren's brow lowered. "She tells me that you sent our sons away, that they didn't go missing. Is that true?"

Help me, Lord. "I never said anything of the kind." That much, at least, was true. It was Agnes who said it. Alina had had the good sense to keep her mouth shut.

"She said she heard you say so."

Alina sighed. "Well, I didn't." She meant she didn't say so, but apparently Bren interpreted this to mean she didn't send the boys away.

He shot an exasperated look toward the women's bench. Alina hoped he would do as he always did and simply deal with the problem that was on the surface, in this case, who said what. Never mind that the boys were gone, that he would likely never see them again. He said, "And what about Brega?"

"What about her?"

Kiah says that, against my orders, she brought Agnes' daughter to see her before we left. Is that true?"

Alina shook her head. It was not her truth to tell. "You will have to ask Brega about that."

He ran his hands through his hair and turned back toward the approaching land. "If I had known how difficult you women would be on this voyage, I would never have brought you."

Alina had to bite her tongue to keep from laughing for the second time that day. The women were the whole reason for this trip. Had he forgotten? She took advantage of the pause to change the subject. "Do you still think we will land tomorrow?"

He nodded and let out a long sigh. "We still don't know whether the tide will be with us, but yes, we are making good speed. In fact, we've made better speed on this trip than I expected."

She turned with him to look forward. After a minute, she noticed that he was studying her. He said, "You know, I had forgotten how beautiful you are."

He misses Maja, she thought. Aloud she said, "That's because you never loved me."

"What?" he exclaimed. "Of course I did."

She gave him a wry smile and shook her head. "No. You love the wife you have now. It's all right," she added. "I have known it for a long time."

He was silent, and seemed to be searching for something to say. Finally, he spoke. "I know you would never put the boys in danger. I told the men to keep searching for them. I am confident they will find them. And someday, when the boys are grown, I will bring them with me to visit you."

Alina let this absurdity fly away over her head. Something in her was coming, something important, though she didn't know exactly what. But suddenly, she did know. She felt words building in her, but she had control of them. She could choose to say them or not. It only took a heartbeat to decide. She stepped in closer, reached out, touched his silver torque with the tips of her fingers. He started to smile — perhaps he thought she was flirting — but the smile faded as the words tumbled out. "Through peril and hardship will you return home, but your hearth will be cold and quiet, for your children are gone, from the oldest princess to the newest baby boy. She has ordered them slaughtered. This will be a sign to you – your wife will bear you a daughter. In time she will bear a son, but you will know the child is not yours. In this way, your authority will pass to a stranger's child."

Alina stepped back. Tears streamed down her face, and her fingertips felt burned. She looked toward the nearest rowers. No one gave any indication that they had heard. So she came close again, noted how Bren's face had gone pale, and added on her own, "Their blood is on her hands, but it's on your head. You took the serpent to your bosom."

She made to step back again, but Bren caught her wrist. "You don't know this. You cannot possibly know this."

Alina swallowed. "I didn't know, but the Lord does."

"Maja wouldn't dare," he muttered.

Had she not been weeping she might have laughed again. "She gave the order before our ship's mast disappeared over the horizon."

Bren glanced toward the other women and said, "You will say nothing of this to any of them, do you hear?"

She wrenched her wrist from his grasp and wiped her eyes. All she could see now were Ava and Inge. They were dead. "I am neither stupid nor cruel." With that, she left him and started toward the bench. Her legs felt unsteady beneath her. Images of what the slaughter must have been like filled her mind. Had they killed Hurd's family to get at the girls? She thought they must have. And there was Agnes' Tena, who was the same age as Dag, and Kiah's little twins. *Innocent! Innocent!* She staggered once, just as she reached the bench.

Brega caught her arm. "Are you all right?"

Alina glanced at Bren. He was watching her, and there was death in his eyes. No, she didn't want to be thrown overboard. She smiled at Brega. "I missed my footing." She turned to Agnes. "You can go and walk again if you wish."

Agnes shrugged. "I think I'll wait a little while. It looks like you used up the goodwill there."

Alina nodded. No doubt she had.

CHAPTER THIRTEEN

It took more than a week for Otani's ankle to heal. In the meantime, Alina did the hunting by herself, and Otani kept busy with tasks close to home. He gathered wood, kept the fish trap baited, and even gathered greens, once Alina had shown him what they were and where to find them. When he was ready to go out again, they hunted together and brought down another deer.

"Maybe we could also hunt when we come back from visiting your village," Alina suggested, the thought of preparing for winter was never far from her thoughts. "That way, we will already be in the area. We can sleep outside one night, or in your old cave, and hunt the next day."

He had cut off a piece of cord to tie his own basket. Now his hands paused. "We should go at the full moon, I think, not the one that's coming, but the next one. They will expect me about that time."

Alina nodded and stood, stretching her back before she picked up the basket. When she stooped, Otani grasped her arm. "What is this?"

He was staring at her belly. She hadn't told him yet, and she wasn't sure why she waited. But now she said, "It is what it looks like."

His face lit up, and his smile was like the sun coming up on a fine morning. "When?" he asked, pulling her down into his crossed legs. "When will the baby come?"

"I think late in the winter," she answered, snuggling against his shoulder. "I should have told you sooner, but...."

"I am your husband now," he murmured. "I am not the man you had before. You are my own, and I am yours. This child – our child – is precious to me."

Alina nodded wordlessly. He saw into her more deeply than anyone ever had. Not even Marav had known her like Otani knew her. She pulled in a deep breath and let it out again. "Is the rest of your family like you?"

One of his hands had been lightly stroking her belly. Now it went still. "The rest of my family?"

She nodded. "You've told me about your mother and your sister. Are there any others? What are they like?"

He grunted. "Well, I have only a grandfather and two cousins. Everyone else is gone a long time ago."

And that is probably part of the reason why the village rejected him, she thought. No one much to speak for him. She sighed and settled into him. He tilted her face up to his and kissed her. Their lovemaking that afternoon was deliberate and gentle, a slow fire. When it was over, he rolled her on her back and put his mouth close to the swelling in her belly. "You in there," he called softly. "I am your father, so you must listen to me. We are waiting for you, but we are patient. Grow big and strong. We will see you soon." For no reason she could name, Alina began to laugh quietly. After a moment, Otani was laughing with her.

The rest of the voyage went quickly. The tide was going in as they approached the shore, so there was no need to sit in the boat and wait.

Everyone was eager to disembark and be on land again – even if the land was strange to them.

Dirk, the man who was paired with Brega asked, "Bren, have you been to this place already?"

Shaking his head, Bren said, "It is nearly impossible to put a ship in at the exact spot where you landed years ago, so no. This is a different place. I believe we were farther north than this at that time, but just look at it!" He swept an arm toward the forested shore as if he was responsible for creating it. Alina saw the muscles working in Dirk's jaw, but he said nothing else. He must have been thinking the same thing she was – Bren's talk about sailing back and forth was nothing but empty words. Once the ship left them, how would they ever find them again? Alina wondered why Dirk had agreed to the trip. Surely he could have gone somewhere else. After all, he wasn't married to Bren.

They pulled the ship in as close as they dared, taking frequent soundings before they lowered anchor. Once that was done, the afternoon was quickly dropping toward evening. Bren said, "I want us off the ship in a quick and orderly fashion." He pointed to the navigator. "Olaf and I will go first. The men from this bench..." he marched toward the stern until he was halfway. "…to this bench will follow us and form a line in the water from the ship to the shallows to assist the women. The women will go next, and the rest of the men will go after them." He grinned. "We don't want you girls to get lost." A few of the men laughed at this. None of the women did.

The rope ladder was dropped over the side, and Bren descended first. When he was gone, Huus stood up and looked directly at Alina. He grinned – his teeth had gone ragged and brown in the years she had known him – and stabbed a finger in her direction. The message was clear. He had been told that Bren was giving Alina to him. He would claim her the moment Bren gave the word, and there would be nothing she could do about it.

We'll see, she thought, and averted her eyes. Brega took her hand, leaned in close and whispered, "Whatever I can do to help you, I will."

After only a few minutes, it was the women's turn to go. Brega had decided that she would go first, so they climbed down the ladder in the order in which they had been married to Bren. Alina's boots were stowed in her bag. All she wore as she went in the water was her tunic, and she gasped as the cold sea found her bare feet. The first man caught her arm as she went in, and she was glad. She was a fair swimmer, but the iron pot in her bag was heavy. About halfway to the shore, her feet touched the bottom and she could stand. And, of course, the next man in line was Huus. Alina took as big a step as she dared to her right to avoid him, and he bared his awful teeth at her. But then she was past him and wading into shore. Even then it was hard going with the waves crashing at her back, threatening to push her face-first into the surf.

Behind her she heard Kiah squeal, "I can't do this!" But Alina knew she would. Someone would figure out a way to bring her ashore.

Finally, she waded onto the beach. She glanced back and saw that one of the men had slung Kiah over his shoulder and was carrying her toward the beach. All Alina could see of her were her legs and her rump. The rest of her dangled behind him, where she lay immobile like a slaughtered animal. Shaking her head and facing forward again, Alina followed Brega until she found the spot near the trees where they would bed down.

She decided then that, if she could get away, she would go far away from the sea so she'd never have to look at it or hear it again. She'd had enough.

And that was how it started, except really, that was how many things ended.

Late summer was a busy time for Alina and Otani. They hunted and trapped, saving as much meat as they could for the coming winter. They dried berries and greens, packing them in with the meat, and they gathered a couple of large baskets full of nuts.

Otani had just finished telling her a story, one of his people's legends, about a wolf that got itself in trouble with a god. Alina was grinning and nodding at the end of the story. It sounded so much like the stories she'd heard as a child. When he finished his tale, Otani cocked his head at her and asked, "What do you believe?" When she looked over at him, he clarified, "About the gods, about spirits?"

"Well, most of my life I believed one thing, but now I believe something else," she began. "When I was growing up, I heard many stories like yours, stories about gods and goddesses, about talking animals, ghosts and spirits." She paused to think, and he nodded at her to go on. "When I grew up, a holy man came to our village. This was about six years ago, just after I'd had my second son. This holy man — his stories were quite different."

Her hands paused at her task, and she gazed, unseeing, into the fire. "He told us about one God, and he said this God was the only one." Now she thought about the Father and the Son, and wondered if that meant there were two gods. Or three, if you counted the Holy Spirit? She wished Brother James was still alive, and that he was here so she could ask him. "Anyway, this God had a son, who he sent to be born on the earth. The son was called Jesus, and he lived down here as a man for thirty-three years."

She glanced over at Otani. "He taught people about his father, and he did things – he healed the sick and made food appear where there was almost no food, and he even calmed a storm."

"That sounds good," Otani ventured with a smile.

"Everything he did was good." Alina tied the lid on the basket she had just filled. "But you know how people are."

Otani's smile faded. "You said he lived thirty-three years. Did someone kill him?"

Alina swallowed hard. The image of Brother James nailed to the tree swam before her eyes. She blinked back tears. "He let them kill him. His friends buried his body, and after three days, he came out of the grave, alive again." She sat still, her hands atop the basket as if she was afraid it would fly apart. "I don't understand all the whys, but he died and came back to life so that we could be free of the wrong things we do, and so that we don't have to be afraid of death."

"That would be something, to not be afraid." Otani stood and carried his basket to the shelf. There he stopped, eyes wide, his mouth slightly open, as if transfixed.

"Otani?"

"I have just realized how…." He pushed the basket onto the shelf and turned toward her. "Do you see how perfect that is? That a god would come as a man, that he would live and die? That means he understands us, really understands what it's like to be here. And from the other side, from our side, we can understand what he is like." He sat down again. "You should tell me everything you learned. I want to know if this god of yours is the same as the Creator that we believe in."

Alina lifted one shoulder. She felt inadequate. "I will tell you what I remember, but Brother James wasn't with us long. Also, I wouldn't say that I'm not afraid of death yet. Sometimes I still am – afraid for myself and for others."

He stared into the fire for a long moment before holding up one finger. "There is another thing." She didn't answer, but when he met her eyes he asked, "This son of your god… was it his own people who killed him?"

Now Alina had to search her memory. "Well, yes" she finally said. "Some of his people killed him."

Otani nodded. "Then he understands you and me."

Alina frowned. "How do you mean?"

"His people didn't want him. Our people didn't want us."

"Oh." Alina had never thought of it that way. "But some of his people loved him." She sighed and added, "I guess the same is also true for us."

"Tell me this -- I have heard you praying," Otani said. "What kinds of things do you say to him?"

"I thank him for providing for me, for the day, for my life, for my food, everything. I ask him to care for the people I love, for my boys, for the people I had to leave behind…" she glanced at him and added, "…for you."

"Maybe I should talk to your God." Otani paused and leaned over to kiss her cheek. "I should tell him thank you. Do you think he would understand me if I speak to him in my own language?"

Alina laughed at that. "I hope he would, because I don't speak the same language his son spoke." They continued to work for a while before she changed the subject. "Do you still want to go see your people this full moon?"

"I think so," he answered. "It will be a little early, but they won't be surprised to see me."

"I want to show you something," she said, and from one of the shelves she took a length of woven grass and cord. She held it out to him. "This is a belt. I made it for Nissi, your sister."

He took it and studied it. "I wondered what you were doing with this." Alina had woven long grasses into an intricate pattern of plait. Some of the grass she had left its natural gold color, and the rest she had dyed either green or rust, staining the blades with a pulverized red rock paste, or with green grasses. She had woven cord into the edges and one cord down the center to make the belt stronger. The ends dangled, three on each side. They were the ties for the belt. At the end of each cord she had threaded a seed like the seeds on Otani's bracelet.

"What do you think?" she asked.

"I think she will treasure it," he answered. "You did beautiful work on this."

In spite of his assurances, Alina was anxious about meeting his people, but she tried for his sake to keep her worries to herself. She busied herself putting her pack together for the journey. She was bringing the salt pot, the belt, and one basket of dried meat. Otani was taking nuts they had gathered for his mother. The nuts were in a basket

Alina made for the purpose, with a handle and a lid that could be latched. And Otani had made a new stone knife for his grandfather.

"Is this enough for them?" Alina asked, surveying the gifts one last time.

"It is more than I usually take," he smiled. "But I have you to help me now. My people won't be surprised to see me, but they will be surprised to see you."

Alina didn't reply. The surprise was the part that worried her. "Full moon tomorrow," she finally said.

"Yes, but I think it might rain. We may have to wait a day or two."

It rained that night, but the next day dawned clear and sunny. *Well,* Alina thought as she left the bed, *let's get this over with.* After they had eaten, they gathered their things, lodged the door into place and set out. In about an hour they reached the ridge, where Otani stopped and looked pointedly at Alina's gently protruding belly.

Alina shook her head. "I am not helpless. I am only pregnant. I can climb this ridge as well as I ever did."

"Then start up," he said. "I will follow."

He wanted to be behind her in case she slipped. *All right*, she thought. *That is sensible.* And she began the climb. They made it to the top without incident and surveyed the other side from there. After a moment, Otani gestured toward the shadows under some trees to their left. A herd of deer moved silently through the patches of sunlight and shadow. Or, Alina thought they were deer. As she studied them, they looked wrong to her. They were far larger and taller than deer, their heads heavier and broader. *Horses?* she wondered, and then she caught sight of the buck. His antlers were like nothing she had ever seen, flattened paddles with the pointed ends sticking out from the flat parts like fingers sticking out of a palm.

"What are they?" she asked, mystified.

"Moose," he answered. "We should not move from here until they are gone."

Her voice sunk to a whisper. "Dangerous?"

"Very." He was silent for a moment, then added, "Even a bear will run from a moose. My people send groups out to hunt them."

When the herd had gone, they climbed down from the ridge. They passed through the two clearings, and the cave Otani had made his home. After that, he turned a little east and followed a course through the forest that he knew, though Alina could see no path. They stopped at midday and ate a quick meal. "It will be about another hour's walk," he told her when they set out again.

A breeze was in their faces, and it wasn't long before Alina smelled wood smoke. They skirted the base of a hill, and there was Otani's village. Alina saw maybe three dozen dwellings made of hide and tree branches. These formed most of a circle around an open area in the middle where people were working, talking, going about their business. One man looked up and saw them standing there. He called out, "Otani and a stranger!" All activity ceased as each person turned to look. Then they were moving toward them.

Otani reached out and touched Alina's hand. "It is all right. Do not be afraid."

The crowd of villagers stopped about a dozen paces from them, and silence fell. Alina's heart thudded hard in her chest. The looks Otani's people were giving her were not especially friendly. Women talked behind their hands to their neighbors, a gesture that she instantly recognized. These people were like her own, probably in many ways. She guessed more than fifty people stood there. They ranged in age from toddlers to one or two with white hair. A man with a spear stepped out and stood between them and the crowd.

At that moment, Alina heard a girl cry, "Otani!" She pushed her way through the people and made straight for him. The man with the spear grabbed at her, but she eluded him and launched herself into her brother's arms. "Nissi," Alina heard him murmur.

She watched the man with the spear. He clearly wanted to pull the girl from Otani's embrace, but he also didn't want to catch whatever disease or curse he thought Otani had, so he just held his spear and scowled. A tiny boy, naked as the day he was born, pushed his way through the legs of the adults and stared at Alina while he picked his nose. Alina grinned at him. After a moment, he grinned back, then turned and ran away.

"Otani." A man's voice interrupted the reunion, and Nissi slipped back to the ground and turned. The speaker was an older man, barrel-chested and tall. His eyes darted to Alina and back to Otani. "You come with a stranger."

Otani replied, "Yes. This is Alina. She has come from…." He hesitated, then to Alina said, "I think it will be better if you tell him your story yourself."

Alina nodded and asked, "This is your head man?" Otani said he was, so she turned to him. "Sir, I came here just over a year ago. My home land is across the big water. It took many days in a boat to come here. The night we arrived, people attacked us. I was able to hide myself, and I believe I may be the only one of us left alive in this land. The others who lived went back on the boat and are gone."

"You speak our language well," the head man observed.

"Otani taught me," she answered.

He appeared to be thinking for a moment before he said, "Then maybe you can help us with something. We have another stranger among us, probably one of your people, who has not learned to speak with us." He turned to someone in the crowd and said, "Bring out the *something*." It was a word Alina didn't know.

She asked Otani, "What is that word?"

"It is someone who has no standing among our people. Someone who works and is fed, but is not one of us."

A slave, Alina thought. *I wonder who it is. One of the women, maybe? But how would she have gotten here?* Her heart thudded painfully in her chest, and then the air blew out of her lungs when a lanky figure appeared from the back of the crowd. His hair fell around his shoulders in dirty tangles, and his unkempt beard had grown halfway to his waist. He looked confused until his eyes met hers.

She saw Huus gather a breath and he shouted in his own language. "That is my wife!"

That night Alina lay staring into the darkness, wondering if she could have done or said something different. *I told only the truth, Lord,* she thought. *I did what I had to do. This is in your hands now.* She turned her head and was just able to make out the sleeping forms of Nissi and of Sidua, Otani's mother. She was lying on a pallet of skins in their lodge. Otani was out in the woods somewhere close by, waiting for her, waiting to see what would happen.

When Huus shouted, Alina felt the world start to go black. She grasped Otani's arm and bit on her tongue until it bled, until the ringing in her ears dissipated. Huus was the last person she expected to see. She had figured that all the men would be dead or gone home. How had he survived the attack? And what was he doing here?

The head man turned to her. "What is he saying?"

With a shock she realized she had a powerful advantage over Huus. She knew the language, and he did not. He had not bothered to learn it. She swallowed hard and tried to calm herself by breathing deeply, but her voice still trembled when she told the head man, "He is saying that I am his wife, but I am not, and never have been."

The head man crossed his arms. "Then why does he say so?"

I was supposed to be given to him when we got here. But we were attacked almost immediately. I want to be completely honest with you, sir. I had hidden myself because I wanted to get away from him. He is not a good man."

People who had been staring at her began eyeing Huus. Some even backed away from him. "What do you mean by that?"

"In my home village, he raped at least two women. One woman was really just a girl, no older than Otani's sister," she replied. "This girl he murdered. There were three other girls, slaves, who disappeared in the following years. I don't know that he killed them, but he did kill the one. I am certain of it."

An angry murmur ran through the crowd. The head man held up his hand for silence. "How can we know you speak the truth?"

Alina shook her head. "You cannot. Even if he could speak your language, it would be his word against mine. Have any women gone missing from your village?"

"No…." he began, but someone in the crowd shouted, "Sina is gone."

"Well, yes," he admitted, "but she was only six years old."

"Did you find her body?" Alina asked.

He shook his head. "We do not know what happened to her." He frowned thoughtfully before asking, "If he did these things, why did your people not punish him?"

She almost said, *Well, they sent him here, didn't they?* But that would come back on her, since she had also been sent. Instead she answered, "The man who was my husband didn't want to believe Huus did those things. I don't understand it myself. He refused to see what was in front of his eyes."

Now Huus shouted, "What are you saying to them?"

Alina said to the head man, "He wants to know what I am telling you."

He nodded. "That is fair enough. Tell him."

So she did, and before she had finished, he tried to come at her, shouting that she was a liar. It took three men to tackle him to the ground and subdue him. To the head man, Alina said, "He is saying I am a liar. I am not. I have told you the truth. And I should warn you, if this man remains with you, you need to keep close watch on your girls and your women. None of them should ever go anywhere alone."

So now she lay awake in the dark, chewing her thoughts. The head man had called for a council of the village's elders. They would meet the next day and discuss what she had told them. A weight of responsibility settled on Alina as she pondered possible outcomes. This was no longer just about her and Otani, not even about her, Otani, and their child. Whatever happened next could have mortal consequences for lives in the village. She wondered about the little girl who had gone missing. It was possible, of course, that a wild animal had dragged her off. Or Huus.... She grunted and turned on her side. She couldn't stand to imagine what he might have done.

She finally fell into troubled sleep, full of nightmares she could not remember when she woke. She felt as weary upon waking as she would have been if she hadn't slept. She got up and tried to make herself useful to Otani's mother, Sidua. The one bright spark that morning was Nissi. She was wearing the belt Alina made for her, and when Alina saw it, she smiled and patted it. "I am glad you like it," she said.

Nissi's smile widened. "You are Otani's woman, aren't you?"

"I am his wife," Alina nodded and smiled as she said it, so it didn't feel like she was correcting the girl.

"And you are having a baby."

"I am. Sometime this winter."

"So I will have a niece or a nephew!" Nissi exclaimed in a sing-song voice. "I love babies."

Alina didn't bother to point out that, unless Nissi came to the cave, she wouldn't get to see the baby much. And who knew what the elders would decide? Surely they wouldn't insist that she become Huus' wife. She went to the door of the lodge and peered out. A group of men and women ringed a fire in the center of the village. She counted at least a dozen of them, some of whom were elderly with gray hair. She thought it odd that no man was bald, and no one had a beard or mustache. She had noticed early on that Otani had almost no facial hair. It seemed that the men here were all like that.

She accepted breakfast – a bowl of stew – from Sidua and was sipping at it when Sidua asked, “What is my son’s life like?” Alina considered the question, then answered, “We have a cave on the other side of a ridge over there,” she pointed in the cave’s general direction. “The cave is near a river, so we have plenty of fish and game. We hunt, and fish, and gather. We store food for the winter – the same things you do here.”

“We call that ridge the Old Man’s Spine. How did you find each other?”

“I was hunting in the spring, and I was curious to find out what was on this side of the ridge – the spine,” Alina told her. She related her journey through the woods, and how she met Otani in the clearing. “I came again after a few days, and we began to visit each other. We agreed to be married at the beginning of summer."

"He is a good provider,” Sidua remarked.

“He is,” Alina agreed, and it occurred to her that Otani had been their provider before he was driven from the village. “Is Otani’s grandfather still living?”

Sidua nodded. “He is out there with the elders talking things over.”

Alina let the bowl rest in her lap. “The last three years were hard for you.”

Sidua had just taken a sip. She hesitated, swallowed, and looked over at Nissi, who had gone still where she sat. “Yes, very hard,” she finally said.

Alina calculated in her head. Could she and Otani support his family on their own? With the two women to fish and gather, they might manage it. The cave was big enough to shelter them, but Otani had to have a say in any offer to take his family with them, so instead she said, "He misses you both. He speaks of you often." Then, not knowing if it would help anything, she added, "What he has in his skin, well, I knew a man of my people who also had that. No one caught it from him. He lived a normal life, although he had to be careful in the sun. It burned the light patches."

Sidua let out a long sigh. "Our people were too quick to judge him. They said he was bad luck, that he was cursed. And now they hardly speak to us."

Alina glanced toward the lodge door. "How long do you think it will take them to make a decision?"

Sidua shrugged. "A few hours, a few days. Who can say?"

"Alina," Nissi spoke her name as if testing it. "Can I comb your hair?"

Alina nodded. "If you have a comb. I didn't bring mine."

With what sounded like a chirp of happiness, Nissi produced a wooden comb and sat down behind Alina. She untied the leather strip that held her braid and began unworking it. "Your hair is different from ours," she remarked. "Not only because it is yellow, but it also curls like the ends of vines."

"Many of my people have yellow hair," Alina told her, closing her eyes as Nissi began to comb. "No one where I come from has hair as dark as yours. I think it's beautiful."

"And I think yours is beautiful. With your blue eyes and yellow hair, you are like the summer."

They asked Alina about her people, and she told them about Brega and her girls, about Gerda and Holgur, about living near the sea. Nissi in turn chattered about her own doings and the people of her village. "There," she finally said as she tied the cord onto the end of Alina's braid. "I am finished." She gave the braid a little shake and laughed. The sound of Nissi's laughter, light and untroubled, reminded her, uncomfortably, of Leda.

Sometime in the middle of that night, Alina started awake. A shadow lurked in the open doorway of the lodge. She sat up ready to call out, but the shadow melted away. She frowned and rose to her feet. Without sticking her head out, she peered into the darkness, but saw nothing except the embers of a few dying fires. Finally, she did come partway out of the door and stared until her eyes watered, but nothing was moving in the night. *Maybe I dreamed it,* she told herself.

The sky was still cloaked in gray the next morning when Alina's eyes flew open again. Nissi had just come into the lodge carrying something big. Its weight swung from her hands, and she gingerly laid it down. Sidua was still asleep, snoring gently on her pallet. Alina sat up and whispered, "What is that?"

Nissi's grin seemed to light up the dim room. "I went out to relieve myself, and Otani was there. He brought us this." She pointed to the carcass at her feet.

Alina rubbed her eyes. "Is it a deer?""Yes, a small one." Nissi's eyes shone in the dark. "We will eat well for the next few days."

Now Sidua snorted and sat up. "What is going on?"

"I met Otani at the edge of the woods, and he gave me this to bring home."

The girl's words finally penetrated Alina's sleep-addled brain. The shadow in the door. She stood up. "Are you saying you went out to the woods alone?"

Nissi nodded, but her carefree expression sobered. "Why? Is that wrong?"

Alina took her by the shoulders. "Did you not hear what I said to the head man about Huus?" There was a note of panic in her voice, but she didn't try to control it. The girl needed to hear how serious she was. "You must never go out alone. Not ever."

Now Sidua was standing, too, and Alina thought she might object to her correcting her child, but she made no move to intervene. Alina turned and pulled the skirt of her tunic up to give Nissi a good view of her leg. "You see these scars? I got these from a bear. It nearly killed me. But I would rather meet a bear with no weapons in my hand than meet Huus." She took a step back. "As long as that man is among you, never, *never* go anywhere by yourself."

Sidua stepped over to have a look at the deer. "Your sister is right, girl," she said to Nissi. "Wake one of us, or find one of your friends."

Nissi bowed her head. "I am sorry, mother. I won't do it again."

Your sister. Alina felt tears well up. She grabbed Nissi and pulled her into her arms. "I just want you safe."

After a moment, Sidua cleared her throat. "Let's see what we can do with this deer."

Alina was glad to have a task to attend to. She skinned the animal and helped Sidua butcher it. Nissi took the hide outside, staked it to the ground, and began scraping. It was nearly midday when a boy came to the lodge saying that the elders had more questions for Alina. She had been expecting it, and had a good idea what the questions might be. She sent up a prayer as she walked across to the ring of people gathered at the fire.

The head man, Tunye was his name, stood to speak. "Alina, we have a few more questions for you. Will you answer them faithfully?"

She bowed her head. "I will be truthful, sir.

"Why did your people come here?"

She took a deep breath and began, "My husband had five wives." She waited for the exclamations of surprise to die down before she went on. She described Bren's marriages and his fathering children on unmarried women, and then she told them about Maja. "She is very beautiful. And she understands how to…." Here she paused, searching for the word she wanted. "She understands how to persuade him."

One of the old women let out a cackle. "Just like my daughter-in-law."

Alina told them about Bren's decision to bring them across the sea, ending with, "I have never understood why he went to so much trouble. It would have been far easier to kill us, or to sell us as slaves. Maybe it was because he wanted to make himself look bigger in everyone's eyes." She glanced at Tunye. "Are you answered?"

He scowled. "This husband of yours, will he be coming here again?"

"I do not believe so," Alina said, remembering what she told Bren before they landed. "The outcome of our voyage was so poor, his people will not support him in another venture like it."

The woman who had laughed earlier now stood. Her expression had gone solemn. "You say he was your husband. Did you have children?"

Alina briefly shut her eyes. "Two boys," she answered. "And yes, I was forced to leave them behind."

The woman grimaced and sat down. A man waved an arm, and without standing said, "Surely you must have done something to make your husband want to be rid of you."

"I bore him children," she answered flatly. "He only likes women when they are in his bed, and he is not interested in his children when they come."

Another exclamation of surprise followed this. "What kind of man is that?" someone piped up.

Alina sighed. "That is a question I cannot answer."

Otani's grandfather stood. Nissi had pointed him out to Alina earlier. "You said that you were certain the slave murdered a woman. What made you certain?"

"It is an ugly story," she answered, "but if you must hear it, I will tell you." She described Agnes's rape, the bruising, the bite marks, and Agnes saying Huus had done it. Then she told them about Leda, about Holgur seeing him following her, about how they found her body. "The bite marks were the same," she concluded. "But Agnes changed her story and said Huus hadn't raped her in the first place."

"Why would she do that?"

"I have no idea," Alina admitted. "Maybe he threatened her." Otani's grandfather sat down, looking puzzled and disgusted.

After more questions – it seemed that many of them were about the ship – Tunye said, "Enough. Bring the slave."

Alina's stomach turned over. Had they decided? Huus was marched in between two sturdy men carrying heavy wooden clubs. Tunye regarded him for a long moment, then said to Alina, "We will ask him questions, and you will tell him what we want to know. You will tell us what he answers. Will you speak his answers faithfully?"

"I will speak his answers faithfully," she replied, and wondered, *But can you discern a lie in another language?*"

"We want him to tell us why he thinks you belong to him as his wife."

Facing him, Alina said, "Huus, they want you to explain why you think I am supposed to be your wife."

Huus hawked and spat at the dirt near her feet. "Bren promised you to me as payment for making the voyage."

Bile rose in her throat. Payment. So Bren did sell her as a slave. She translated. Then she said, "I have a question for him, if you will permit it." The head man nodded and she asked, "When did Bren tell you he was giving me to you?"

"The day before we landed," he answered with a leer. "Before that I didn't even know that I was chosen to stay here." Alina bowed her head, inwardly nodding. So all those times she had caught him staring at her on the ship — he'd been staring out of spite.

Alina turned back to the head man and translated the exchange. Tunye pointed out, "Your master is gone, and she is now married to another. Why should we give her to you now?"

When he heard the question from Alina, he bared his ragged teeth. "She is mine."

She translated this and a murmur ran around the circle. Some were shaking their heads. Tunye said, "Alina, go back to your lodge. We will call you when we have decided." He nodded to the two men flanking Huus, and they led him away, but as he passed her she heard him hiss, "I will have you, you whore!"

Late that afternoon, she was summoned again. To her relief, Huus wasn't there. Tunye stood. "We have deliberated, and we are in agreement." She braced herself for bad news, but he said, "We have decided that the slave has no claim on you as wife. You say you are married to Otani. We advise against that union, and we urge you to stay in the village with us, but we will not force you to do so."

Alina felt her knees go weak with relief, but she managed to hold herself upright. "Thank you…all of you." She pulled in a breath – now that she could breathe again -- and added, "Otani is my husband, and I will stay with him." She looked at each of them. "But I urge you to remember the words I spoke to you yesterday. If you cherish your daughters, you must not let them go anywhere alone as long as Huus lives among you."

"They will chafe if we restrain them," one man muttered.

"Let them chafe," Alina answered, not bothering to hide the anger in her voice. "At least they will be alive to do so."

Otani's grandfather stood. "We must be truthful with you as we believe you have been with us. None of our women will have anything to do with the slave, and so we were reluctant to make you take up with him. His habits are filthy. He does not bother to learn to speak to us, except for a few words here and there. He does what we direct him to do, but never anything more. Was he like this when he was in your land?"

"I was only focused on his crimes," Alina admitted, "so I didn't notice much else about him. He wasn't so dirty then, but I don't know about how he worked. I did hear that he wasn't much good in the woods as a hunter or tracker, but that Bren – the man who was my husband – valued him because he could fight. That's about all I know." She considered, then said, "I have a question for you, if I may." Tunye nodded. "How did he come to you? It was surely not your people who attacked mine."

"No, that was not us," Tunye said. "We had heard of stirrings among the *something* (another word Alina didn't recognize). They have waged war on us in the past, so we sent scouts to spy them out. Our men found a large party of them on the move, and they trailed them to the sea and saw the fight against your people as you described it. When it was over and the enemy departed, our men counted the dead. The slave, though, was breathing. He had been wounded, but still lived. Our men nursed him until he could walk and brought him here to us." He grimaced. "It might have been better if they had left him."

"Did your scouts say anything about the women?" Alina asked. "One was killed immediately, but there were two others. Did they survive?"

Tunye shook his head. "They did not. You did the right thing to hide yourself." His eyebrows raised, "And you hid yourself well. Our men did not spot you."

It was a good thing they didn't, she thought. *If they made me come with them when they revived Huus, the council would have probably given me to him.* A shudder ran up her spine. "With your permission, then," she said, "I will go back to Otani." This seemed to be the signal for the council to break up. Everyone stood.

Otani's grandfather, a stocky man with white hair bound in a single braid, and lines like canyons on either side of his mouth, laid a hand on her shoulder. She felt a tremor in that hand. "I believed you from the start," he said softly, "because my grandson believes you."

She covered his hand with one of her own. "I am honored to be part of your family." *Would they come live with us,* she wondered, *if we invited them?*

She returned to the lodge. To Sidua she said, "I am allowed to go." She took her mother-in-law's hand in hers. "Thank you. It is my hope that we can come more often." She started gathering her things, and that was when she noticed it. "My bow," she said, turning in a circle and surveying the lodge.

"Your bow? It was right by the door," Sidua answered, coming over. They stared at each other for a long moment, then began picking up everything that was on the ground to see if the weapon was under something. But it was gone.

"I saw someone in the doorway last night," Alina said. Her voice sounded small in her own ears. "I almost shouted, but then whoever it was had gone." Her stomach sank. "Huus. It had to be him."

"Go and tell Tunye," Sidua said. "Maybe he can start a search for it and find it."

So Alina did, and Tunye sent men to search the entire village, beginning with Huus' lodge. But she knew Huus well enough to know he wouldn't keep something like a bow and arrows close at hand. He would hide them. The men found nothing, but when they brought Huus out, he looked at Alina and one corner of his mouth twisted up.

When she was alone with Tunye, she said, "Your slave is armed now. You and your people will have to be doubly vigilant."

He nodded once. "I saw his face. I will have the men keep a close eye on him. If he has your bow, he will go to it eventually, and we will be there when he does."

Finally, she went back to the lodge. "Will you and Nissi come with us?" We can provide for you. You are not safe here."

Sidua shook her head. "We have our friends and our family around us. We will be safe enough."

Nissi said, "I wish you would stay here."

"Not without your brother." She swallowed, reached out and tucked a stray lock of Nissi's hair behind the girl's ear. "Well, if you're sure you won't come, I must go." She shrugged into her bag.

Sidua said nothing, but nodded. She and Nissi accompanied Alina to the edge of the woods, where they stood just inside the tree line and waited. It was only a few minutes before Otani slipped out from behind the trees to their right. He and Alina embraced Sidua and Nissi in turn before leaving. When they were out of earshot, Otani asked, "Are you all right?"

"I am not" she answered. "Huus came in the night and took my bow and arrows."

Otani stopped in his tracks and stared at her. "Are you sure it was him?"

"Sure enough." She described what little she had seen, and then told him about Huus' near-smile when he looked at her. Finally, she concluded, "The bow was probably his to begin with. Maybe he thinks he's just taking back his own."

"If he hates you as much as you say, why didn't he shoot you while you slept?"

She had asked herself the same thing, and she knew why. "That kind of death would be too quick and too clean. He makes the women he kills suffer first. And he wants me to suffer."

CHAPTER FOURTEEN

The morning after they got back to the cave, Otani felled a small tree and started carving a bow for Alina. This task took him three days, but when he was finished, Alina thought that this bow fitted her better than any she'd had before. She gathered straight branches and pieces of flint, and together they made a batch of arrows. Otani had killed another deer on their way home. Alina used its skin to fashion a new quiver.

Through these days they were alert and cautious every time they went out into the open, even if they were only a few steps from the cave. Alina realized that, over time, she had become too relaxed when she was near home. In the back of her mind, her familiar places seemed safe. She wasn't thinking that anymore.

"You said Huus is not a good tracker?" It was not the first time Otani asked.

"I remember hearing a couple of Bren's men talking about him. They had just come back from hunting, and were complaining about how useless Huus was in the forest. One said he couldn't track *a wagon on a rutted road.*" These words were in her language, and she knew Otani wouldn't know what it was, but he seemed to get the gist of what she was saying, and didn't ask.

Otani grunted. "Then he will have a hard time finding us."

Alina wanted to think so, but she thought Huus might find a way. She had accused him to Bren – more than once – had escaped him when they landed, had stolen his bow and arrows, and then showed up at the village telling the people what kind of man he was. She had piled humiliations on him. *I am far too tempting as prey for him to ever give up hunting me.*

They agreed that they needed to keep a closer watch on his village, so they made the journey at the full moon two times after that. They took game with them, giving it to his mother. After the second trip, Alina realized that her time to give birth was coming soon, that she needed to stay close to the cave. "I don't think I can climb that ridge now, and I will only slow you down."

"If you aren't going, I am not going," Otani answered. But he did go out one afternoon to hunt, saying, "I won't go far, and I won't be long. You stay inside, and if that *something* shows up, shoot him like you shot the bear." Alina didn't know the word he used, and she didn't bother to ask, but she repeated it to herself.

She stayed inside, working on a cradleboard for the baby. Otani had cut the wooden back for it, and now Alina was stitching rabbit skins to line the board. When that was done, she would make the bindings and the straps. She had just started stitching the final inside seam when she heard a soft noise – the lightest pattering, like a scattering of sand — outside and looked up from her work. The first snow had begun to fall. Alina put the cradleboard down and went to the opening. It wasn't just snow. It was snow mixed with sleet. Everything would soon be covered in ice.

She began to pace back and forth in the cave, hoping the storm would not somehow trap Otani outside, but knowing it could. The wind picked up, and she sank down on the bed, listening to it howl at the door. "Lord," she prayed, "Otani is out in this storm of yours. Guide him to safety, and bring him home to me."

About an hour later, scuffling at the door had her on her feet and running to the opening. It was Otani, and Alina swiftly moved the door aside to let him in. "It is good you didn't come with me." He panted and blew as he set his gear down. "Everything out there is slick with ice, and it's blowing so hard, I could barely see where I was going." He was empty-handed. "I had no luck hunting."

"It's all right." Alina put water on the hob to heat. "I am just happy you are back." She took the bear skin from the bed, still warm from her body, and laid it across his shoulders. "Sit," she told him. "Get warm." She ladled a bowl of stew for him from the pot.

He blew on it and took a sip. "Ah, that is good. He gripped the hot bowl, turning it round and round in his cold fingers. He took another sip, then looked her up and down. "You are all right? I suppose nothing is happening yet?"

She shook her head, passing a hand over her belly. "It will soon, though."

He swallowed. "The last time I was at the village I tried to talk my mother into coming with me – for you."

She nodded. "You were very persuasive."

"Not persuasive enough." He hung his head. "She was unwilling to leave Nissi, and unwilling to bring her. I think she still believes I could give her my disease."

She laid a hand on his cheek, and with her thumb she traced the pink flesh at his mouth. "Thank you for trying. You and I will be able to manage on our own."

They were brave words. She offered Otani encouragement she didn't feel herself. From the moment she realized she was pregnant, she prayed for a delivery like Dak's – normal, relatively easy. She didn't allow herself to think about the problems she'd had with Gunnar. And there was no woman to help this time. No Gerda. No midwife. She and Otani were on their own.

Midwinter came and went with more ice and snow than Alina had seen the previous winter. "Is this a normal winter for you?" she asked one frigid morning as they picked their way up the icy path from the river back to the cave. "Or was last winter more like what you are used to?"

"This is a cold one," Otani replied, tightening his grasp on her wrist as one of her feet skewed on a frozen patch. "Careful."

Alina gritted her teeth and took another cautious step. She could hardly see her feet for her swollen belly. "It's like this every winter where I came from. Lots of snow and ice. And the summers there were not as warm or as long as yours." She paused and added, "Your summer nights here are shorter than at home. We had daylight, or near daylight almost all night in the summer. And here the winter days are longer. I wonder why that is."

"That is strange," he commented as she took the last couple of steps and ducked into the cave's opening. When they were both inside, he said, "I am glad for the cold, though. I think it will make Huus think twice about looking for you."

Alina nodded. This winter might buy them a few weeks' time. "Tunye said his men would be keeping an eye on him."

"They will," Otani answered, "but a wily man might find a way around them."

Alina sighed. She didn't know if 'wily' was a word she would associate with Huus. For all she knew he might be. *But he won't come today*, she thought. The skies were the color of lead, threatening another snowfall. If Huus was as useless in the woods as Bren's men said, he wouldn't survive long in this weather.

She went to take some meat from the shelf to add to the stew when she felt a rush of wet down her legs. Otani heard it and looked up. "It's time," she told him.

At her direction, he pulled the bearskin off their bed and laid an old deerskin atop the pile of skins beneath it. He looked at Alina. "Will you want to lie down now?"

She pulled the basket of meat down and shook her head. "Not yet."

He came and took the basket from her hands. "You shouldn't be doing this. Let me see to it."

She bit back a smile. "Are you the one who knows what I should and shouldn't be doing?"

He sighed and shook his head. "No, but I am not comfortable watching you lift things like this."

"Then put it down by the fire and let me do my job." She leaned in and kissed his cheek. "I need to keep busy for a while."

"I can understand that," he murmured, setting the basket down.

"Don't worry," she told him as she knelt by the stew pot, "I will be ordering you around before you know it."

"You already are," he muttered under his breath, but there was teasing in his voice and Alina laughed. She cut up a chunk of dried meat and dropped the pieces into the stew, tasted and adjusted the broth, adding salt and wild onion. When she was satisfied with that, she continued working on a screen she had begun a few weeks before.

She'd had the idea back in the summer. She wanted some way to let the air pass through the cave while keeping most of the insects out. She had woven cloth often enough to know that there were gaps between the threads. This knowledge allowed her to imagine what would result if she wove cord and intentionally left little gaps. Otani had built her a frame, saying he wanted to see this new thing, and she had filled about a quarter of the frame with woven cord.

This task was easy on her body, but as the pains came – and came closer together, her hands faltered and she was pausing to breathe. From the corner of her eye she saw Otani watching her. After a couple of hours, the pains were one on top of the next, and she said, "I think I am done with this for today."

Otani helped her up and over to the pallet. Alina sighed as she lay down, and then moaned. Or was that the wind outside? She wasn't sure anymore. *Ice on the walls,* she thought, though the walls of the cave were dry. *Lord, let this baby be all right. Let us both be all right....*

She had no notion of how much time was passing. She was only aware of the tidal pull of pain. But before long she felt the urge to bear down. Her body knew what to do. She heard Otani ask, "Do you want me to have a look?" She nodded and gasped, "The baby's head...." He examined her, then with bright eyes said, "It has lots of hair."

So the baby was turned right. Alina drew strength from that and began to push with each pain. She had heard somewhere that the first birth was usually the hardest, that the births that followed were easier. After a time, though she hardly knew what she was doing, she threw off the bearskin cover, rolled over and got up on her hands and knees.

Otani stationed himself behind her, and with only a handful more pushes, he caught the baby as it slipped out.

Alina's head drooped, her breathing slowed, and she sniffed when she heard her child's first cry. "We have a beautiful daughter," Otani said. He tied off the cord and cut it with his knife the way Alina had told him he should. Then he washed the child with a piece of wet skin and wrapped her in a rabbit fur blanket that Alina had stitched together. Alina slipped back under the bearskin, and Otani handed the baby to her, saying, "Ten fingers and ten toes. She is perfect."

He pulled the old deerskin from under her when the afterbirth came out, used the same wet rag to wash her, then covered them both. He went to the fire and poured hot water into two cups into which he had earlier crushed mint leaves. He added a few drops of the sweet stuff that Alina now knew was a kind of tree sap to each cup and brought them both to the pallet. He handed Alina's cup to her.

She breathed in the steaming freshness of the mint and took a cautious sip. "Here, you hold her for a little while." He set his cup down on the floor beside the pallet and took the baby from her arms. The ordeal was over. Everyone was all right. Alina smiled at Otani. "We do have a beautiful daughter."

He had been staring at the baby's face. Now he raised his eyes to meet hers. They were rimmed with tears. "I lived for nearly three years with the thought that I would never be a father. Now I have you and I have her. My own family." He gazed down again at the sleeping child and said, "I am still amazed that we found each other." He raised his free arm and made a sweeping gesture. "In the whole of this great forest, you found me. If you had come the day before, I would not have been there, and not the day after."

Alina nodded, thinking, *And I could have found someone else. I could have found someone like those people who attacked us on the beach.*

"Do you have a name in mind for her?" He stroked the baby's feathery black hair with the tip of a finger.

She had thought about naming her Brega, but Otani's people didn't have the sound of the 'r' in their language. "I was thinking Ava would be a good name." Her best friend's oldest child.

"Ava," he repeated. "I like the sound of it. Someone you knew?"

Alina nodded, choosing for this day to believe that everything would be all right, that she and Otani would grow old together, that they would see this child, Baby Ava, grow up, that Otani's people would someday accept him back into their circle. She chose to believe that Huus' threats would come to nothing. They slept peacefully that night, face to face, with the baby between them.

After those first bitter storms, winter dissipated quickly, and spring began to poke its green head out from under the ice sooner than either of them expected. "We should go back to the village," Alina said one morning when the baby was about two months old. "I want to know what's going on there, and I am sure your mother and sister would like to see the baby."

Otani frowned. "Do you think you can climb the ridge with her?"

Alina lifted a shoulder. "I don't see why not. She's no heavier in her cradleboard than my bag. Besides, I feel like I need to get out and walk. I've been stuck in this cave long enough."

Otani stared off toward the cave's opening. Alina knew he was weighing the merits of the journey against its risks. Finally he said, "Let's do a shorter walk first. We can go downriver, maybe find a good fishing spot, see if there's anything to gather and come back. If we manage that, we can try for the ridge."

Alina felt strong enough in her body, but she understood Otani's caution. "All right," she agreed, "Let's go downriver tomorrow morning."

But it rained the next day, a heavy, soaking deluge that left the ground awash with mud and standing water. They waited three more days to let things dry out. By that time, Alina was itching to make the journey to the village, and she finally convinced Otani they should go. So they packed up what they needed and set out.

This day was chilly, but the sun shone in a clear sky, and there was little wind. They made it to the base of the ridge without incident. Alina settled her bow on her back, sliding its length beneath the straps of the cradleboard.

Otani said, "Are you sure you don't want me to carry her?"

Alina smiled. "She is light. I can take her."

Otani glanced up at the climb, and Alina saw what worried him. "I will be able to climb this. And I will be careful. You come after me and keep watch." Otani gave a reluctant nod, and Alina started up. Her muscles, long unused in the cave over winter, took a while to warm to their task, but by the time she was halfway up, she was comfortable with the climb. She reached the top, panting a little, and moments later, Otani joined her. By silent agreement, they sat down to rest and look out over the forest below.

A few moments later, she heard Otani draw in a breath, and wordlessly, he pointed down the slope to their right. It was the exact color of the rocks around it, but when she finally spotted it she whispered, "Is that a wild cat?" It was hardly more than fifty paces away. Its eyes, golden and huge in the tawny face, stared up at them, its haunches bunched and ready to spring. It was the most beautiful animal she had ever seen, and maybe the most dangerous.

He nodded. "Stand up. Slowly, now."

In unison, they rose to their feet. A breath or two later, the cat blinked, turned and ran down the slope and into the trees. "Will it follow us?" Alina wasn't afraid for herself. Mercifully, Ava was asleep. But what might such a predator do if it heard her child cry?

"It won't. It knows we can overpower it," Otani answered. "Do you still want to go down there?"

She gathered in a breath, though it didn't quite reach the bottom of her lungs. "I think so. Between the two of us, we will be safe enough." He gave her a look. Alina sighed. "All right. Let's go back. You know the dangers of this part of these woods, and I don't."

Now it was his turn to let out a long breath. He laid a hand on her shoulder and looked to their left. A trail of smoke far off marked the village. "Well, we've come this far. Let's go."

He led her down, though the two clearings, to his old cave. There he stopped. "I want to have a look." She climbed up with him. Some animal had used the cave in Otani's absence. There was a litter of small animal bones and a wad of skin with fur still attached. But what caught Alina's attention was the neat stack of firewood at the back of the cave. "Did you do that?" she asked.

"Yes, while I was waiting on the elders to talk to you. I thought we might need to camp here overnight."

They went back down and continued through the forest. When they reached the village, they both stopped and waited. A young boy spotted them and shouted, "Otani and the pale woman!" Alina almost laughed, but Otani rolled his eyes and shook his head. Out of the corner of his mouth he said, "My cousin's son."

"Well," Alina chuckled, "if your family can't disrespect you, who can?"

He spread his arms wide. "Everyone can. Let them come!"

They did come, wrapped in extra skins against the chilly day. Nissi came running, and this time no one tried to stop her, though a few people shook their heads. She embraced Otani first, then turned to Alina. "I am so happy you are here again!"

Alina smiled. "Would you like to meet your niece?" She turned so that her back was to the crowd. "Oh!" She heard Nissi exclaim. "Oh, she's so beautiful! Can I hold her?"

"Yes, let me get her out of this cradleboard." Alina shrugged it from her shoulders, and laying it on the ground, undid the laces. She pulled the baby out and passed her over to Nissi, to a general murmur of satisfaction among the watching people. Alina looked up. Sidua was coming from her right, a huge smile on her face.

And in the back of the crowd stood Huus. She felt her stomach drop. The happy moment was over. He narrowed his eyes at her, looked from her to Otani, to Nissi, to Sidua, and then to the baby. The corner of his mouth twisted up.

Neither of them was willing to stay in the village overnight. They returned to Otani's cave that evening and set out for home the following morning. Once they were there, Alina paced back and forth from the far inner corner to the opening while she nursed the baby. Huus would come for her. It was only a matter of time. He had a weapon, and he held a grudge. Her only hope was that he might lose himself in the forest and never figure out where she and Otani lived. *But no,* she told herself, *he will figure out a way.*

Otani busied himself setting snares close by. He brought in several pieces of flint that first evening and began work on a new spear. "You will have to come with me when I go hunting," he remarked as he started flaking a stone.

Alina nodded. She had been thinking the same. "Ava will cry sometimes and scare off game."

He lifted a shoulder. "Better that than leaving you both here by yourselves."

She stopped her pacing. "We should go." When he looked up at her with a questioning frown, she repeated, "We should go from here, go farther west, find a new place where he will never think to look, or go across the river." She heard the panic in her own voice, and hated it.

He chipped away a flake of stone and said, "I think it would be a mistake to leave here. We can defend the cave pretty well, and he's only one man. If we went away, we might run into somebody worse, or many somebodies."

She took a deep breath, considering, and said, "Actually, we would probably be safer in your village than we are here."

"Yes. If I was allowed to live among my people, I could keep my eyes on him, and others would, too." A long pause followed and he said, "I could go back to my old cave and you could take the baby and go to the village. I would come every day and watch over you."

The baby had fallen asleep. Alina laid her down on the pallet. "I don't want to do that unless we can think of nothing else." A moment later, a thought occurred to her, and she said, "We could put out snares for him."

Now Otani put his tool and his stone down and gave her his full attention. "You mean pit snares?"

She squatted down beside him. "My people use them sometimes to trap wolves."

"Well, that is dangerous for us, too." He paused, considering. "But of course, we will know where the snares are, and avoid them. No one else ever comes this way. The only problem is digging that kind of snare. The ground is full of stones, and in the forest, it is full of tree roots." He picked up his stone and turned it over in his hands. "But I am more than willing to do the work if it will keep you safe from him."

"He has a reputation for not being much good in the woods," Alina said slowly. "So he would probably tend to follow anything that looks like a trail."

They talked about different kinds of snares, how they could construct them, how effective they were, how deadly each one would be, and finally Otani said, "All right, let me think on this."

His hesitation – if that was what it was – chafed Alina. She wanted to do something, and she wanted to start on it right now. But, she thought on further reflection, *we might have been better off waiting to go to the village, and I pushed Otani to go. But when would have been better? Huus would have been there, regardless of when we went.* These thoughts circled like buzzards over some dead thing until she shook them off and put more wood on the fire.

When she woke the next morning, Otani told her he was going out to pick a place to dig a pit. "You're not going alone," she told him. They packed food for the day, and looked over the trail they used to go from the ridge to the cave. There was a spot where the trail twisted around the bole of a huge pine tree.

"Here," Otani pointed. "I can dig a pit between the tree and that berry bush."

It was easier said than done. Otani had sharpened a stone and attached it to a thick handle of wood. It dug into the earth well enough, but there were many roots to get through. Otani used Alina's hatchet on these, but even so, when the day was done, the hole was only waist deep. They would have to come back the next day.

On the way back to the cave, Alina came up with the idea of making a net to snare Huus. Otani's people didn't use nets, so she had to explain them to him, using their old pictures-in-the-dirt way to talk about them.

"So it would be something like your screen?" he asked, his brow furrowed.

"Yes and no. We would tie knots here where the cords cross," she answered. "The knots will hold everything together. This is something my people use often. We catch fish with them."

"Do we have enough cord to do this?"

"No, but there's plenty of vine out there. It's woody, but I used it for the drying rack, and it held up. It would work."

So as they walked, Otani gathered vines. By the time they returned home, he had a good armload of them. "Some of these have thorns," he cautioned, dumping them on the floor.

She nodded. "The thorns are easy enough to cut off." She sighed, thinking of the enormity of making a net big enough to snare a man.

They had shot and hung up a pair of geese the evening before, and now Otani set to plucking and cleaning them while Alina took care of the baby and started working on the net. She had to turn the ends of the vine into cord in order to join them together, and the most efficient way of doing this was to chew on the ends to separate the fibers. The vine was bitter, though, and so while the geese cooked, Otani took them from her and pounded the ends between two rocks. By the time they went to bed that night, the vines were stripped of their thorns, and Alina had three lengths fitted together that she thought would be long enough for one end of the big net.

The next day was cold and raining, and that was fine with Alina. Maybe the weather would keep Huus away. But it also kept them from finishing the pit. The following morning, they heard noises outside – voices. One man calling softly to another. Alina's heart skipped and thudded in her chest. They hadn't finished the pit, and who was out there? Otani picked up his spear and peered out the top of the opening. With a grunt, he moved the door aside and went out. Alina followed. The morning was so foggy she couldn't see the river from the cave. In the mist stood two of the men from Otani's village. One of them Alina recognized. He was Otani's cousin Mato. The other was called

Elu. Otani had been smiling when he stepped outside, but his smile faded when he saw the other men's solemn and wary expressions.

"What is going on?" he asked.

Elu looked at Mato who said, "We came to warn you, Brother. The slave escaped the village, and we think he's out here somewhere." He cleared his throat, glanced at Alina and added, "Your wife was right about him. He is a murderer."

Otani's eyes went wide, and he paled. "Who did he kill?"

Mato shuffled his feet. He drew in a breath and said, "The slave set fire to your family's lodge last night. Your mother and your grandfather are dead. Nissi is burned. She lives, but she may not survive."

Otani dropped to a squat and with a groan, buried his face in his hands. He began rocking back and forth, sobbing. Alina swallowed hard against a sudden thickness in her throat. Everything in her wanted to be down on the ground weeping with her husband. Instead she drew in a long, shuddering breath and steeled herself to be strong for him. With an impatient hand, she wiped sudden tears from her eyes and asked the two men, "What makes you think the slave is in this area?"

"We tracked him to the Spine," Elu answered. "and we think he must have gone over it." His gaze met Alina's. "Surely he is on the hunt for you."

She was almost relieved. These men, at least, believed her and recognized what Huus was after. "We have seen no sign of him yet."

"I will help you hunt him," Otani said in a strangled voice. "It is my duty to my family."

She felt her stomach drop in horror. *Are we not your family?* she wanted to say. How could he think of leaving her?

He stood and met her eyes. "Shut yourself up inside. He can't do anything to you if you're in there. Use those extra rocks I brought in against the door." He laid a hand on her shoulder. "I promise I won't go far and I won't be gone long. if we can find him and kill him…" he laid a hand on her shoulder and let his breath out in a huff, "…it will be over."

He ducked inside, retrieved his bow and arrows, and the three men took off in the direction of the ridge. Alina heard Mato say, "We last picked up a sign of him on the way down the Spine, so we will start there."

She watched them go until they disappeared into the mist. She started back toward the cave, but thought, *Oh, no! The water pots are empty. I need to get water before I shut myself in.* She picked up a pot and started out, but the baby was fussing in her cradleboard, so Alina swung the board onto her back and trotted down to the water, hoping the movement would soothe the baby.

She filled the pot, noting that the fog was thickest near the water, and was on her way back to the cave when she heard a soft step behind her. Too late, she started to turn when something slammed into the side of her head. She cried out and hit the ground face down. The next thing she knew, her arms were snatched behind her, and the cradleboard was stripped from her back. In horror, she flipped over just in time to see Huus dancing out of reach with her baby. He grinned his monstrous grin, and without a word, took off running upriver.

Alina shot to her feet, swaying a little. She sucked in all the air her lungs would hold and let it out in a shattering scream. Then, sobbing, she ran into the cave, grabbed her bow and arrows, and took off after Huus. She was only dimly aware of the pain above her left temple and of the blood dripping onto her tunic. With hardly a pause to track him, Alina chased after her enemy. She had to catch up with him before he brutalized her child.

She came to the rock barrier that separated her part of the forest from the burned part, and in seconds she scrambled up and over. She could hardly see ten paces ahead, so running blind, she kept the sound of the river on her right. She was now farther upstream than she had ever been, and this place was unfamiliar. She searched the vegetation for signs of his passing, fully aware that he meant for her to follow. The cold mist sent a shiver through her, and for a moment she thought she'd lost his trail, but bending over she found newly broken twigs and set off running at full speed again. The river made a bend to the left, and she followed it, and then up a short bluff, and there he was, standing in a clear space at the top. His feet were planted, his left foot at the edge, and the cradleboard swung from his left hand out over the water.

Alina skidded to a halt and brought up her bow. The mist was thinner here, but in spite of it, in spite of the tears standing in her eyes and the throbbing in her skull, she could see him well enough.

"If you shoot me," Huus called out in a gleeful tone, "I will drop it into the water." She didn't answer. She just stared him down along the length of the arrow. He pulled something from inside the neck of his tunic, and passing it over his head, tossed it in her direction. Whatever it was landed at her feet. "Recognize this?"

Alina allowed herself a fraction of a breath to look. Her amber pendant, strung on a loop of dirty leather, gleamed up at her in the misty light. And now she knew. She had suspected from the time she told Bren about the fate of his children that hers might yet be caught up in the slaughter. So her boys were dead. Her sorrow would come, but it made no difference in this moment. There had to be some way to be rid of Huus and save her daughter.

She hoped to delay him a little and said, "What a brave man you are, killing women and children."

He lifted a shoulder. "Just following orders." Little Ava was fussing, working up to a full cry. Huus made a face. "Maybe I should just drop it now to shut it up."

"Who ordered you to kill Leda?" she asked. "Who ordered you to rape Agnes? Did you kill that little girl here who went missing?"

"Agnes was a whore, and so was Leda. Nothing but a little whore."

"And the children?"

He grinned. "You mean your sons? I killed them myself," he boasted with a smile. "I was doing as I was told, but I enjoyed it. That was a fine, fine day."

The tension in her arms and shoulders was almost unbearable, but still she hesitated.

"Shoot him!"

The shout came from just over her right shoulder. It startled her, and she released the arrow, which impaled Huus through the throat. She heard a splash as her husband dove into the river, and then a smaller splash as the cradleboard dropped. Elu trotted past her and went to stand over Huus' body, but Alina ran to the edge of the bluff. Otani surfaced just in time for the cradleboard to slam into the side of his head. He cried out in pain, but grabbed the board and held it aloft while he swam back to shore. Mato waited there for him, his arm outstretched, and he hauled Otani and the now-silent baby onto the riverbank.

Alina raced down the bluff to where Otani was trying to undo the cradle board's laces. Ava's lips were blue. "Here, let me." Mato pushed Otani's hands aside. In an eternal moment, he had the baby out, had draped her over his forearm and was pounding her on the back. And in another moment, the baby spat out a gush of water, drew in a breath and let out a screaming wail.

Mato passed the baby to Alina. Then he frowned. "You're bleeding."

"I am all right," she answered as she stripped the remaining sodden rabbit skin from around her daughter and shoved her up under her tunic, gasping at the icy cold of her child's skin against hers. Otani came over and helped her get the screaming, squirming child into position against her chest, and then he said, "Run!"

And so she ran.

The run back to the cave seemed much longer than it had taken to get here in the first place. She even halted a couple of times, panic-stricken, wondering if she was lost in the fog. But the sound of the river at her left told her she was still on course, and she soon discovered she wasn't alone. Elu ran behind her, protecting her back. Getting over the pile of rocks was far more difficult. She only had one hand to climb with, but her child's screams spurred her on, and she made it. Once she was down, she put fresh speed to her feet. Moments later, it seemed, the baby quieted, and Alina's heart fell. Was she still alive? She had no time to find out. She had to get her inside.

At last, she ran up the path and ducked into the cave. Falling to her knees near the fire, she pulled Ava out. The child was awake, crying again, her eyes scrunched tight, little fists waving in the air. Elu watched for only a moment, apparently to make sure they were all right, then stationed himself just outside the entrance to wait on Mato and Otani.

There was an abrasion on one side of Ava's face, but otherwise, she seemed unhurt. The cradleboard had probably saved her life. Alina offered her breast, and at first the baby turned away with an angry wail, but then changed her mind and began to suckle furiously. Alina let out a long sigh, and only then realized how horribly her head ached.

When the baby finished feeding Alina laid her down in the bed, and suddenly her breath caught in her throat, caught her unprepared, and forced its way out as a sob. She covered her mouth with both hands and bent over as hot tears and heaving sobs shook her. *My boys.... My boys....* She was vaguely aware of Elu coming in and standing over her, and she heard him mutter, "The child lives," before he retreated outside.

Now the voice came, soft but clear and insistent. *Will you trust Me now?*

As if in a dream, she saw herself standing at the edge of a black place. It might have been a precipice, but there was no way to know. There was no bottom to the darkness, no other side. She knew what this darkness was. It was her faith without trust. Brother James' God was her God. Her faith, though she couldn't explain it, was more a part of who she was than her arms and legs. She couldn't abandon it, couldn't abandon Him. Alina trembled, envisioning what her life would be, burdened with a faith devoid of trust, of love. "No," she whispered through a shuddering breath. "I will trust You. I have to."

Now she saw something else, a memory. She was looking along the shaft of her arrow at Huus' face as he jeered at her. *I killed them myself,* he'd said. *It was a fine, fine day.* All at once, she knew Huus had been lying. She thought a while, trying to recall, and everything she remembered coming from his mouth was a lie, an evasion, or a threat. Of course, there was the matter of the pendant. How had he gotten it? But she was convinced that, whether her boys were alive or dead, Huus had not killed them. And as far as Gunnar and Dag were concerned, Alina was right back where she was the morning she sent her sons into the forest to meet Marav. She did not know if they lived. It was up to her to trust and pray. Alina heaved in a long breath and let it out.

Otani came in with Elu and Mato at his heels, and when he saw her tear-streaked face, he cried, "The baby! Is she…?" He sank down beside her with a groan.

Alina shook her head and handed the baby to him. "She is all right." She laid a hand on his arm and repeated, "She is all right."

Mato and Elu went hunting that afternoon and brought in a deer. They butchered it and scraped the hide, saying they didn't want Alina to do anything except tend to the baby and rest. And she did let her body rest, but her thoughts would not. When he first came in, Mato said, "I found this lying on the ground. Is it yours?" He laid the pendant in her hand.

"It is mine." She drew out her knife and cut away the leather cord, which she threw into the fire. She stared into the amber's familiar depths, and for a moment, thought she might cast it into the fire, too, but it was all she had left of her mother and father. *I should give it to my daughter someday,* she thought, closing her fist around it. She would tell Ava the stories that the pendant represented. She would tell her about her grandparents, about her uncle Ebbe, about her half-brothers, Gunnar and Dag. She reached out and handed the pendant back to Mato. "See that little shelf with the shell and pebbles on it? Put it there with those."

She let out a long sigh. It was over, wasn't it? Alina struggled to think so. Otani had said that if they killed Huus, it would be over – the threat of Huus and his murderous rage, the fear of what he might do. And the fear of him was gone, but he had left a trail of destruction and death that would haunt them the rest of their lives.

She glanced over her shoulder at Otani, and saw that he had risen, that he was standing near the opening with the two men. They were whispering. Alina called out, "What is going on?" Otani gazed at her. He seemed to be measuring her. "Tell me," she insisted.

Elu, at a nod from Otani, held out a bow and quiver of arrows. She recognized them at once.

Otani said, "Elu found these down near the river."

A deep shiver shook Alina. Huus had been down there, watching and waiting. Alina knew then what he had planned. She saw it as clearly as if he had told her himself. He would shoot the men first. Alina swallowed, thinking, *and that would have left me to fight him alone.* No doubt he thought he could overpower her, and he intended to then kill the baby – probably making Alina watch. After that, he figured Alina would be easy prey. "The fog," she murmured. "He couldn't see you from the river. The fog may have saved all of us." Fresh tears streamed down her face as she bowed her head and whispered, "Thank you."

Later that evening, Alina sat down beside Otani, who sat hunched by the fire, staring into the flames. She said, "We have to go to Nissi tomorrow. She needs us."

Without meeting her gaze, he answered, "I will go. I want you to stay here. You will be safe enough now."

Mato said to Alina, "One of us can stay behind with you while Otani sees to his sister."

"She is my sister, too," Alina said. Her voice was much milder than the churning anger and grief inside. "I will not be left behind."

Otani looked toward her, but not at her. He lifted a shoulder as if to say that it didn't matter whether she came or not. It stung, but she reminded herself that he had just lost his mother and grandfather. She stood and picked up the cradleboard, which Mato had placed near the fire so that it could dry out. She turned it around to give the other side a chance to dry, then went to the pallet and sat next to her sleeping child. Before long, the day caught up with her, and she lay down and fell asleep.

When she woke the next morning, Otani was gone, and Elu was there with her. "He went to Nissi," she said dully as she sat up.

"Yes, but you don't have to worry," Elu reassured her. "I will stay with you until he gets back."

Alina shook her head. "No you won't. You will come with me. I am going." She picked up her bag and began packing things into it.

"I'm not supposed to…." he began.

"Will you really try to stop me?" she interrupted. When his shoulders fell, she added, "You know I am doing the right thing. If Nissi dies, and I had the chance to see her again and didn't take it…." She shook her head. "I can't stay here."

"You are right, of course," Elu answered. "I will go with you. Otani will be glad that you came." He spoke like a man who was trying to convince himself.

They packed up the meat that was left from the hunt, gathered the things they needed, and set out. They reached the village by mid-afternoon. Nothing was left of Sidua's lodge but a pile of burned rubble and ash. "Nissi is in Mato's lodge," Elu told her, pointing it out. "His wife has been tending to her."

"I wonder where Otani is?" Alina stopped and turned a slow circle.

"I think he will be with his sister. The elders will not make him stay outside now."

Alina grunted. It was cold comfort. They shouldn't have kicked him out in the first place. But then, she might never have met him. Elu led her to Mato's lodge, and after coughing politely to announce herself, she ducked inside.

Otani was not there. Mato's wife, Nila, looked up, and relief flooded her face. Alina didn't know her, but judging by the dark circles under her eyes, she had been tending to Nissi the whole time. "She is asleep," she murmured as she stood. "Are you here to help with her?"

Alina nodded. "For as long as you need me to."

"Then if you don't mind, I will go to my mother. She is looking after my children." With a nod, she left Alina and Elu.

"I will go find Otani and tell him you are here," he said.

And just like that, Alina found herself alone with Nissi. The baby started to fuss, so she cleaned and fed her before turning her attention to her sister-in-law. Nissi's face wasn't burned on her right side, and the left was red, but not blistered. Alina could almost believe the girl was merely sleeping, except that her legs and her left arm were covered with poultices. Alina eased herself down beside her and watched her chest rise and fall.

There was a new hollowness inside she had never known before. She felt empty, and she had nothing in her hands, nothing to give Nissi to help her, nothing to ease her pain or make her better. But now she remembered something Brother James had helped her memorize. It hardly seemed to matter whether Nissi could hear her. She needed this for herself as much as she needed to share it. So she began to recite, translating it as best she could into her new language. "The Creator is my…provider. He gives me all I need. He makes me lie down in green meadows. He leads me beside quiet water."

A shadow appeared in the doorway, and she was surprised to see it was Tunye. The head man came and stood just inside the door. When she stopped speaking, he motioned for her to go on. She murmured, "He makes my spirit new. He leads me in the right paths for the honor of his name. When I walk in the valley of death's shadow, I won't be afraid…." Her throat went thick, and she had to stop and clear it. She covered her mouth briefly and blinked back tears. After hauling in a long breath, she continued, "I won't be afraid because you are with me. Your… protection comforts me. You make a feast for me where my enemies have to watch. You pour oil on my head. My cup is full and running over. I am certain your goodness and your…kindness will follow me every day of my life, and I will live in God's home always and always."

When she had finished, Tunye sat down beside her. "Where do such beautiful words come from?"

"They are in the sacred…." she began, and realized that she knew no words in Otani's language for books or writing. As far as she knew, his people did not have either. “It is a song, I believe,” she finally said, “Though I do not know how to sing it.”

He nodded. “I came to apologize to you. We…that is…I let you down, and the cost has been two honorable lives. I understand that it could have been much worse. My own words fail me, but not as badly as I failed you.” He ran a hand over his mouth and added, “Noya, Otani’s grandfather, was my oldest friend. He was like a brother to me from my childhood.”

Alina didn’t trust herself to speak, so she only nodded.

“I have already talked with Otani,” he continued. "We were wrong about him. The bad luck that some feared was in him was actually in us. You helped us to see that, and you brought us to a new place of peace. You are both welcome to live among us, if you choose.” He paused and sighed, “And if you choose not to, we will accept that and understand.”

When she didn’t answer, he stood and laid one hand lightly on her shoulder. “You are both very brave.” She heard tears in his voice, but she didn’t look up. And then he was gone.

Nissi didn’t wake up for the next hour while Alina sat there, now humming songs, now murmuring prayers. When Mato’s wife returned with her ten-year-old daughter in tow, Alina asked, “Do you know where Otani is?”

Nila answered, “I think he is at the *something*.” It was another word Alina didn’t know. But Nila caught her blank look and said, “Where his grandfather and mother are buried.” She pointed. “There is a clearing in the woods that way.”

Graves.

The daughter was cooing at the baby. She looked up at Alina and smiled. "She is so cute!"

"We can watch her while you go to your husband," Nila said. "But don't be gone long."

"Oh," Alina was taken aback by the woman's kindness. "Thank you. I just fed her a little while ago. I will be back as soon as I have found him and spoken to him." She glanced at the baby, reassuring herself that she was in a safe place. "Her name is Ava."

She hurried out in the direction Nila had shown her, ignoring the stares of the people she passed. The clearing wasn't hard to find. There was a fairly well-used track leading to it. When the trees opened up, she saw Mato standing a few paces to her right. He didn't look surprised to see her. Otani was stretched out, face down on the ground between two mounds covered with stones.

Alina went and sat cross-legged near his head. He was quiet, but his breathing sounded ragged. She didn't speak, and she didn't touch him. The sun was warm in the sky – a blessing after days of misty cold, and she lifted her face to its light. She had hardly known Sidua or Noya, but she remembered them now. Noya had been so kind after the elders' meeting, telling her that he believed her, in his own way welcoming her. Sidua had also accepted her, calling her Nissi's sister, feeding and housing her. She drew up her knees and rested her forehead on them, letting tears fall for them, for Nissi, for Otani, for her sons.

Presently, Otani stirred. He sat up, his arms draped loosely around his knees. "I should have been here. I should have been here for them. Maybe I could have stopped him. You warned me what Huus was. I just never imagined…." His eyes filled with fresh tears.

“I didn’t imagine it either,” Alina answered. “Who in his right mind could?" She swallowed hard. "You had to choose, Otani. If I had stayed here, and you had been in the woods, the baby and I might be dead, too.” She put her face down again, miserable with grief and regret. “I hope Nissi lives.”

A moment later, Alina felt his hand on her back. “I am sorry about yesterday,” he said, his voice husky with tears. “I should never have told you to stay away.”

“I had to come,” she whispered.

“I know.” He scooted toward her and put his arms around her. “You belong here.”

She leaned into him. “Tunye says we can come and live in the village.”

He bent his head and kissed the top of hers. “Yes.”

“I think we should at least give it a try, don’t you? For Nissi’s sake?”

“Mato and Nila said that they can care for her,” he answered, “but my heart tells me that she needs us.”

“Then we should go back to the cave and bring our things.”

“Let me build a lodge for us first,” he said, then, “I will miss the cave.”

“So will I,” she answered, thinking of the life she and Otani had spent there. “But my hope was always that I would find people who would accept me.”

The men of the village came together to erect a lodge for Alina and Otani. They used willow saplings for the frame. Alina learned that there was a small, spring-fed lake less than an hour's walk away. She went with the builders and dug up cattail reeds to weave mats to cover the frame. When they were finished, the lodge was roughly the same size as her cave, with a hole in the center of the roof to let smoke out. Otani had insisted on a large lodge for them because it looked like Nissi might recover from her burns. He also insisted on making bed frames so that they would not be sleeping on the ground.

When the lodge was finished, Mato and Elu and two other men went back to the cave with them to help them carry their things. "It's too bad we can't bring that," Elu said, pointing to the hob.

Alina smiled. "It was easier to build than it looks. I can make another." She was laying out Gunnar's feather hanging on the piece of leather he had originally wrapped it in. *I have finally found a home, my son,* she thought. *I wish you and Dag were here to see it.*

She let out a long, shaky breath, rolled the bit of hide, and tied it. When they were ready to leave, and everything they could carry was outside, Alina asked for a minute alone. She went back in, trailed her fingers along the walls and the shelves, and gazed up at the beam of sunlight pouring golden through the crack. She thought of the work she'd done in that place, the narrow escapes, the hopes and the prayers. One final prayer here, then. "You brought me to this place," she whispered. "You kept me alive. You brought me to people of peace. Not everything turned out as I hoped, but I thank you for the things that did. If my boys are with you, please let them know that I love them, that I do not forget."

CHAPTER FIFTEEN

Epilogue

TEN YEARS LATER:

The young man sits astride his horse on a bluff overlooking the sea. He is watching the blaze of sunset over the water. The bank of clouds nearest the horizon is on fire – yellow and orange and scarlet, while those further up in the sky have turned muted shades of purple and blue, fading to gray. The wind stirs in the young man's dark hair and ruffles the fur of his cloak. His eyes are the pale blue of winter ice.

From this place he could board a ship and in two days' time be in his father's village, but he will never go there. His reluctance is not from fear, though riding into that place would put his life – and possibly his brother's – in peril. His father's wife still rules that village. The reason he never goes is that he is uninterested. With his adopted father's help, he has built his own life. He has no need or desire for whatever his first father built. And he has heard rumors that the village is declining. Many sailors and merchants avoid the place saying its former prosperity was gotten with innocent blood, and is cursed.

One year ago, almost to this day, he went for the first time in more than ten years to see his Uncle Ebbe. Ebbe, shocked to see him alive, welcomed him with a warm embrace. "And your brother?" he asked, "Does he also live?"

"He does. The man who rescued us and sheltered us – our father now – insisted that we remain in hiding until we were grown. This year he thought it was good to send me to you to let you know we are alive and safe."

Ebbe covered his eyes with one hand for a moment and drew in a long breath. "I lost your mother," he finally said, "and I was sure, when word reached us of the slaughter, that you boys were gone, too."

"Mother provided a way out for us," Gunnar told him. "But I think she would say that the Lord had a hand in it, for Marav, our father, showed up just at the right time."

"How did you get away? That wife of Bren's had men scouring the country. My only hope for you was that, when they came looking for you here, they hadn't caught you yet." He gestured to a table. "Come and sit. Have something to eat and tell me your story."

"Marav took us north," Gunnar explained while a servant set dishes on the table. "He said my father's men would expect us to go south or east. Once we were two days' ride away, he made a false trail going even further north. He intended to take us west from there to the coast, where he had arranged to have a ship waiting for us. We finished making the trail we wanted his men to see, and Marav had found a way for us to get off that trail. It was over stony ground, and very little snow was left there to mark our passing. He told me later that he had begun planning the whole thing the moment he learned of Bren's intention to send his wives over the sea."

He picked up his cup and tasted. The mead was hot and sweet, and there was a spice in it he couldn't identify. "As we were about to leave the false trail and head west, Marav said he wished we had some token we could leave behind to convince them to continue north." He raised his eyes and met Ebbe's. "I had Mother's amber pendant. She gave it to me the night before we escaped, and made me promise to do whatever it took to get myself and Dag to safety. So I took off the pendant, untied the ribbon – so that it would look as if it had come undone by accident – and threw it as far as I could up the trail. By that time, we could hear them coming. They weren't following silently as they should have been. I think they were counting on speed and numbers to overtake and overwhelm us."

"The noise they made – shouting and calling out to each other – warned us in time to take the side way west. There was a fold in the hills there, and we just managed to get into it when they came galloping over the rise behind us. We watched them from our hiding place, and finally one man stopped his horse and got off. He was a tall man, very thin, and I remember that his hair was long and stringy. He bent down and picked up the pendant, and he called out to the others and pointed to the north. In moments, they were all going that way, unaware that there wasn't much more trail to follow. We waited until they were gone, and then went down the hillside. It was about an hour's walk to the coast."

"You said you rode. Marav could not have gotten you as far ahead of them as he did without horses," Ebbe remarked.

"We did have horses the first day and most of the second," Gunnar answered. "No one realized we were missing until late afternoon of that first day (this was my mother's plan) so we had a good start on them. The next day he gave the horses to a farmer in exchange for his silence. I asked him later if he was worried that the farmer might betray us, but he said the people in the area surrounding Bren's village were angry at him for taking so many women and then sending them on a death voyage. They were willing to assist in anything that would fly up his nose."

Ebbe grinned. "He has quit sending his men through here to trade. I ordered my people to make them unwelcome." He chuckled. "My ferryman doubled his fees for them. Peg was a happy man for a short while."

Gunnar nodded, but he didn't smile. "I only wish Mother had come with us, though I know our chances of escape would have been far less." His eyes filled. "I hate that she had to die to save us."

Ebbe sat back in his chair, his eyes fixed on Gunnar's. "Ah. I have a friend you should talk to." He turned to the servant. "Send someone to find Dirk and bring him here."

The servant left, and Gunnar said, "Mother's first plan was to send us to you with a message. I think, though, she finally understood that us being here would not keep us out of that woman's hands."

Ebbe frowned. "She had a message for me?"

Gunnar nodded. "You want to hear it?" When Ebbe said he did, Gunnar recited the words he had carried with him for all those years. "'Greetings from your loving sister. I am well. I am sending the boys to you early this year because I must soon make a long sea voyage. Do not be concerned for me, only be a father to the boys as you have always been. You may have heard that Bren has married again. She is as beautiful as the sea goddess, Ran. I am reminded of the time you and I went hunting with our father's best dog. This is what life is like. I pray that you keep in good health.'" When he finished, he asked. "What was that business about the dog?"

Ebbe ran one hand over his face, his eyes red-rimmed and glistening with unshed tears. "My father's hunting dog." And he told Gunnar how the dog had been bitten and how their father had killed her out of mercy. "So Alina meant to tell me that this wife of Bren's was beautiful, and utterly deadly." He sat back in his chair and blew out a breath. "And she was right. That woman proved your mother right. She didn't just kill the children born of Bren's wives, you know. She also killed the ones born of the women Bren used and married off."

Both men fell silent, each lost in grim thought. Moments later, another man came into the hall. He was tall and lean, with gray at the sides of his blonde beard, and sharp blue eyes. "You sent for me?"

Ebbe gestured to an empty chair. "Dirk, I want you to meet Gunnar. Gunnar is Alina's oldest son."

Dirk gaped, and then grinned as he shook Gunnar's hand and sat down. "So you did get away! I am pleased."

Ebbe said, "Dirk was on the ship with your mother. He was one of the few who returned."

Gunnar grimaced. "Then maybe you can answer a question I've had for a long time." Dirk gestured for him to continue. "Why did you and the other men go on that voyage? Surely you could have stayed here and prospered. Why risk your neck on such a venture?"

Dirk stared into his cup for a moment, then said, "I still ask myself that same question. Bren had promised me his first wife, Brega. She was a worthy woman. And he had said I would be master of the new village." He sighed. "I suppose I thought I could make it work, and I was tired of being under Bren's thumb." He raised his eyes. "We are distantly related. Our family had… expectations. And I was young and thought I was invincible."

"And the other men?"

"One owed Bren more money than he could ever repay. I believe Bren threatened to sell him as a slave if he didn't go." He shrugged. "I don't know about the others."

Ebbe said to Dirk. "Tell him what you told me about Alina."

Dirk appraised Gunnar for a moment before saying, "I assume you heard what happened with your father's venture to the other side of the sea."

Gunnar answered with a dismissive wave of his hand, "He was never a father to me. He is only Bren. Marav is my father. And yes, the news of that disaster traveled a long way."

Dirk nodded. "Good enough. You may know then that we were attacked shortly after we arrived. Brega was killed almost immediately." He toyed with the cup the servant had brought him, but did not drink. "Anyway, I was going to be on first watch that night, so I made it my business to know exactly where everyone was." He sketched the shape of the beach on the table with the tip of a finger. "Here's the sea. Here's the tree line at the upper end of the beach. Campfire was here. The strangers attacked from over here." He sat back. "The women had bedded down near the tree line. Two of them, your mother and the third wife, Agnes, were on one side of a big pine. The other woman, Kiah, was lying a little apart from them. After the attack began, I tried to fight my way back up the beach, but there were too many against me. I saw them throw Agnes down. I saw where they were on Kiah…." Here he trailed off and shook his head.

"I understand," Gunnar said grimly.

"I couldn't see your mother," Dirk concluded. "She wasn't where she had been, and she wasn't either of the women being raped. After that, I had no more chances to look. The fighting was fierce. But I believe that she hid herself, and if she was half the woman I was told she was – wise in the ways of the forest, I mean – there is a good chance that she got away with her life."

Gunnar blinked. Ever since Marav had broken the news to him about the fate of the voyage, he had assumed the worst. "We promised each other," he murmured. "We promised we would do whatever we must do to live."

And now here Gunnar sits astride his horse, looking to the west, looking out toward a land far beyond the horizon where maybe, just maybe, his mother still walks. He misses her. And not for the first time, he feels the loss of the pendant. He has so few tokens of her. But he has his life. "Thank you, Mother," he murmurs. With that, he turns his horse and rides down the hill to where his father and brother wait.

Made in United States
Cleveland, OH
21 December 2025

29087178R10174